The Bald Giants

Thirty-Nine French Scientific Romances

The Bald Giants

Thirty-Nine French Scientific Romances

translated, annotated and introduced by
Brian Stableford

A Black Coat Press Book

ISBN 978-1-61227-949-7. First Printing. April 2020. Published by Black Coat Press, an imprint of Hollywood Comics.com, LLC, P.O. Box 17270, Encino, CA 91416. All rights reserved. Except for review purposes, no part of this book may be reproduced or transmitted in any form or by any means, electronic or mechanical, including photocopying, recording, or by any information storage and retrieval system, without permission in writing from the publisher. The stories and characters depicted in this novel are entirely fictional. Printed in the United States of America.

TABLE OF CONTENTS

Introduction 7
Louis Ulbach: *Doctor Sublimini* 13
Joseph Montet: *The Triumph of Science* 19
Maurice Montegut: *The Isle of Satyrs* 25
André Monselet: *In the Year 2000* 29
Gabriel Tarde: *The Bald Giants* 55
Alfred Capus: *The Bicycle-Man* 76
Gustave Geffroy: *The Immortal Man* 82
Maurice Montegut: *Days of the Future Year* 86
Maurice Montegut: *Another Planet* 91
Edmond Haraucourt: *The Two Augurs* 97
Edmond Haraucourt: *The Last Men* 102
Edmond Haraucourt: *The Point of Honor* 107
Edmond Haraucourt: *Memoirs of a Bacillus* 113
Edmond Haraucourt: *The Last Pope* 118
Pierre Mille: *In Passing:* Et Nunc, Et Semper 127
Pierre Mille: *In Passing:* Conte de Fées 134
Pierre Mille: *The Sirens* 139
Pierre Mille: *The Victory Song* 147
Albert Keim: *The New Race* 155
Edmond Haraucourt: *Memoirs of an Ephemeron* ...159
Adrien Vély: *The Ruination of the Anthropogenic Institute* 168
Louis Champeaux: *The Master of Death* 173
Albert Keim: *The Last Idyll* 194
Pierre Mille: *In Passing: Among the Tchouktchis* ...198
Pierre Mille: *A Futurist Story* 203
René Morot: Drosera Cannibalis 207
Maurice Renard: *Suzannah* 216
Maurice Renard: *The Future* 219
Pierre Mille: *In Passing: Interview With the Pole Star* 223
Maurice Renard: *Gardner and the Invisible* 229
Maurice Renard: *An Adventure in the Forest* 234

Maurice Renard: *The Dinornis Egg*......................................239
Maurice Renard: *Sirens* 243
Maurice Renard: *The Aerolith* 247
Maurice Renard: *The Enchanted Mirror* 251
Maurice Renard: *The Oysters and the Sleeper*.....................256
Maurice Renard: *The Scientific Adventure of Ambroise Peupiot*...261
Maurice Renard: *The Fantastic Eye* 266
Maurice Renard: *The Year 2000*...270

Introduction

This anthology collects stories belonging, at least approximately, to the genre of *roman scientifique* [scientific fiction], which were published in various periodicals between 1886 and 1938. Many of them were never reprinted in book form. A handful appeared in monthly periodicals that routinely published short stories of more than 2,500 words, but the majority appeared in newspapers, in slots that had a restricted word-limit, usually between 1,000 and 1,600 words.

Such short stories began appearing routinely in Parisian newspapers on the early 1880s, in slots that were approximately the same size as the "feuilleton" slots at the bottom of a page, in which most of the daily newspapers ran serial novels that were considered to be a useful device in encouraging customers to buy the same newspaper every day. A few periodical editors employed even shorter stories as "fillers" to help make sure that none of their available space went to waste.

The vogue for publishing short stories in newspapers did not last long; the heyday of the practice lasted from approximately 1887 to 1903, after which the habit tailed off sharply. Several daily papers, including the prestigious *Le Journal*, used short stores as the lead items on page one in the late 1890s, but once *Le Journal* had moved its "Contes du Journal" to page three, other papers followed suit, and there was a steep decline in the perceived importance of such short fiction as an asset to circulation after 1902. At the peak of the vogue, several newspapers had a stable of writers each contracted to deliver a story or article every week, or once a fortnight, but that schedule tested the ingenuity and stamina of authors to the limit, and few were able to keep it up for very long. The challenge facing them was quite different from that facing writers of daily serials, who merely had to continue the same story at great length, without any end necessarily in sight; the short story writers had to think of a different idea for every item, and bring each story rapidly to a conclusion of sorts.

The production of newspaper stories was lucrative while the vogue lasted, and provided the backbone of the income of numerous writers who were able to cultivate an expertise in the format; it was an attractive marketplace for any aspiring professional and it helped to made the fortune of its stars, who included Catulle Mendès, Guy de Maupassant, Octave Mirbeau, Jean Richepin, Edmond Haraucourt and Jean Lorrain, although their celebrity had to be cemented by publications in volume form, the newspapers themselves being essentially ephemeral. The temptation for writers producing such work on a regular basis occasionally to dabble in the exotic, in the interests of varying their output and cultivating novelty, undoubtedly had a certain strength, but it was offset by the fact that many newspaper readers—who came much closer to constituting a "mass market" than readers of books—were put off by material that was too odd or idiosyncratic, only wanting their habitual fare to be different provided that it also remained familiar. There were, in consequence, conflicting forces in operation at the potential entry-points of *roman scientifique* into the marketplace of newspaper short fiction.

In addition to the inherent paradoxicality of general reader demand, writers toying with the idea of writing futuristic fiction or stories of exotic inventions within a tight word-limit faced acute problems of explanation. Stories set within fictional worlds that are notionally identical to the reader's experienced world can generally fill in the particular background of a story with considerable narrative parsimony, but writers who have to introduce innovations into that fictional world, let alone writers who need to displace their fictional worlds considerably in time or space, have enormous difficulties of narrative economy to overcome, which put strict imitations on the kinds of *roman scientifique* that could be adapted to newspaper slots. That difficulty, and the tactics habitually employed to counter it, are very obvious throughout the present anthology.

In addition to the difficulties posed by accommodating the content of ultra-short fiction there are also problems of narrative form that affect items of *roman scientifique* with a particular acuity. In contrast to writers of feuilleton serials, who hardly had to worry about conclusions in the short term, writers of items that were complete in single issue, working within a narrative straitjacket, had enormous problems in finding satisfactory methods of closure and finding them repeatedly, not to say relentlessly. Not only are endings in long stories comfortably delayed, but their eventually form is largely determined in advance; it is a cliché that all nineteenth century novels should end with "a marriage and an inheritance"—the establishment of the hero and heroine, freed from separation, need and threat, with all the problems that constitute the plot of their story finally solved, if only by cutting the narrative Gordian knot with the aid of a *deus ex machina*. It is enormously difficult, however, to compress a schema of that kind into a vignette of little more than a thousand words. The utility of conventional "happy endings" is much less in short fiction than in novels, what is almost compulsory in the latter seeming undesirably anodyne in the former.

The most frequent strategy found by literary craftsmen to cope with that problem was, inevitably, to aim a short story toward some kind of "climactic twist" akin to those employed in narrative jokes, or a succinct summary observation, and many short stories do, in fact, simulate the form of humorous anecdotes quite closely. As all humorists know only too well, however, anecdotal twists have a limited lifetime; they soon come to seem hackneyed, and do not tolerate much repetition before eliciting a response of weary disappointment rather than admiration. As in jokes, the twists employed in short stories are generally ironic, tending toward cruelty. It was inevitable that an abundant genre of *contes cruels* would develop in short fiction, and that it would be particularly evident in the routinized ultra-short fiction required by newspapers.

There is no methodological problem in adapting *roman scientifique* to the *conte cruel* narrative strategy, in the same way that other varieties of fantastic fiction can be adapted to it with relative ease to form subgenres of "horror fiction," as demonstrated by such short story writers of genius as Edgar Poe, an enormous influence on the French writers who flocked to the newspaper marketplace. There is, however, a side-effect of that tempting ease which is a trifle awkward in respect of stories of innovation and futuristic fantasies, in that the logic of convenient story construction requires the vast majority of imagined innovations to go awry, and even to have consequences that are direly nasty. Seen *en masse*, therefore, short stories in the genre of *roman scientifique* tend to give the impression, to a considerably greater extent than longer ones, that scientific progress is a bad thing, at best an illusion and at worst a source of unremitting disasters.

Given that pressure, it is not surprising that the present collection contains very few utopian fantasies, nor that the most extravagantly optimistic item in it is the longest story, published as a short feuilleton serial and not as an item complete in a single issue of a newspaper. In a sense, the remarkable thing is that it contains any optimistic items at all; it was necessary to break the basic pattern in order to squeeze that one in. Tacitly—and sometimes overtly—the stories in the anthology, viewed as a collective, embody an attitude to the notion of scientific progress that ranges from the suspicious to the outrightly hostile, not because all the authors felt that way, but because their narrative format imposed it upon them.

In fact, the early stories in the anthology—which are arranged in the chronological order of their publication—were produced in an era of relative optimism with regard to scientific advancement, when the rewards of scientific research were widely seen as a cornucopia; but even where that notion is explicit within the stories, it is generally fitted with a compulsory irony. Attitudes changed, of course, over the timespan represented by the anthology, primarily because of the legacy of the Great War, which considerably eroded confidence in the future and provided a graphic illustration of the fact that technological advancement favored the power to destroy as well as the ability to construct. As the pattern of the stories in the anthology suggests, that shift in attitude helped to deter many writers who might have dabbled in speculative fiction before 1914 from involving themselves with it in the particular arena provided by the newspapers; the later stories are mostly provided by a single maverick writer who persisted in production long after his one-time fellow travelers had abandoned the game.

For these reasons, the present anthology is not a true cross-section of the whole genre of *roman scientifique*, but it is an exemplary showcase of a single sector of that genre, interesting by virtue of its idiosyncrasy rather that it typicality. Some of the stories are a trifle pedestrian, as might be expected of products of mass manufacture, but the best of them demonstrate that the limitations of the format permitted a certain artistry as well as ingenuity, and provided room for some interesting experiments in style and narrative construction. Some of the notions deployed in those experimental ventures subsequently became clichés, but were not at the time of their original publication, and deserve credit for their pioneering spirit, as well as their fast pace and easy readability.

Brian Stableford

*Louis Ulbach (1822-1889) made his name as a radical jour-
nalist, constantly at odds with the Second Empire and also
imprisoned under the Third Republic; he was the last editor of
the* Revue de Paris *before its suppression, and also held the
post of librarian of the Bibliothèque de l'Arsenal, where his
predecessor Charles Nodier had founded the crucial* cénacle
of the Romantic Movement. His most striking contribution to
roman scientifique *was the novella translated as the title story
of the Black Coat Press collection* Prince Bonifacio.[1] *"Doctor
Sublimini" was originally published in* Gil Blas, *20 décembre
1886.*

Louis Ulbach: *Doctor Sublimini*

I was having breakfast, and as I had no reason to admit
the public to the spectacle of my meal, even if anyone offered
to pay me the same price as to watch Merlatti eat,[2] I refused to
receive an unknown visitor who sent me his card. But, as obstinate as a traveling salesman of Bordeaux wines, the visitor
shoved aside my domestic, penetrated by force into my dining
room and sat down abruptly beside me.

"I've arrived just in time," he cried, and advanced his
hand to seize my glass.

---

[1] ISBN 978-1-61227-228-3.

[2] Stefano Merlatti (1865-?) was an Italian who briefly became
a celebrity in Paris by means of a public fast. In 1887, a book
was published by Marpon and Flammarion, signed by "Drs. F.
Monin et Ph. Maréchal" entitled *Stefano Merlatti, histoire
d'un jeûne célèbre, précédée d'une étude anecdotique,
physiologique et médicale sur le jeûne et les jeûneurs* [Stefano
Merlatti, the Story of a Celebrated Fast, preceded by an Anecdotal, Physiological and Medical Study of Fasting and Fast-
ers].

"What are you doing? Who are you? What do you want?" I asked him, preserving my glass as if in a petty game.

"What I'm doing," replied the importunate, "is attempting a decisive experiment on a man who appears to me to be an excellent subject. Who am I? Doctor Sublimini, a physician with diplomas from all the faculties of Italy, an incomparable professor of physiology, the inventor of cerebral fasting, a benefactor of humanity..."

He was about to continue the enumeration of his merits when I seemed convinced. I looked at him. His face was crimson; his lively eyes had flashes of genius. He was Fontanarose, the merchant of orvietan, but fanaticized, exasperated by contemporary nervousness.[3]

As I like lunatics, always expecting to discover that they are sages—which is to say, accumulators of sensation, I resigned myself to listening to Doctor Sublimini, except that I did not leave my table knife, blunt as it was, or my glass, within his reach.

"Monsieur," said the doctor, "I am convinced by long experience..."

I was surprised. My visitor did not appear to me to be old enough to attest a long experience. Sublimini saw my doubt.

"I'm fifty-two years old," he said, parenthetically, "but it's my system that keeps me young,"

At the same time, he took out of his pocket a phial, yellow in color which he shook, doubtless before making use of it in my presence.

"What is that liquid?" I asked.

"The universal cretinizator."

I smiled; I was sure of my fact.

---

[3] The charlatan Dr. Fontanarose is featured in Daniel Auber's opera *Le Philtre* (1831); the name was adopted subsequently by at least one travelling salesman of "miraculous" patent medicines. Orvietan was a term applied to numerous concoctions of that kind, hyped as panaceas.

"Yes," my madman retorted, encouraged by my smile. "I am convinced, by long experience, that what fatigues humanity is the continual exacerbation of ideas. Nature has invented slumber, that sublime repairer, but men abridge it, and mutilate it. Slumber is no longer sufficient."

"So what you're selling in that phial is a narcotic?"

"It's better than that, Monsieur. A narcotic does not suppress dreams, and dreams fatigue. I suspend the exercise of thought, or reduce it to a minimum that does not fatigue. One remains awake; one comes and goes, one writes and speaks, but I have put a muffler on intelligence, which creates a twilight in the mind. The man thus erased no longer has any disordered ambition of extravagant caprices. I have had the honor of applying my system in several States; I could cite you, among others..."

The physician Sublimini then named several governments reduced to mediocrity but very tranquil.

"You have nothing to do in France," I told the doctor. "There's no need to diminish the fervor of minds here."

"There are still men of intelligence," the good physician replied, with a caress of his gaze aimed directly at me.

"Oh, so few!"

"Enough, however, for that leaven to make the dough rise at certain times. My liquor is necessary for the pacific operation of your institutions."

"How do you proceed?"

He moved his phial, but I closed my glass with my hand.

"I pour a few drops into a glass of wine, water or beer—it doesn't matter which."

"Even absinthe? That's a waste of your liquor."

"Absinthe kills; my liquor vivifies. One doesn't experience any apparent modification of the appetite or reason; except that superb ideas are put in storage. One lives a positive life; one drinks, one eats, one can even read one's newspaper and understand it. In any case, newspapers put on my regime are not difficult to understand."

"Have you already carried out trials in Paris?"

"Oh, trials of no account. I've made a Naturalist novelist, a Decadent poet and a senator drink it."

"And what are you asking of me?"

"You know politicians, Academicians and artists. Can you not serve as my introducer?"

"No, Monsieur. It would be as difficult for me to designate for you among my acquaintances those who need to have fewer ideas as it would be dolorous for me to name those who practice your regime without knowing it. You admit yourself having applied your universal cretinizator as a supplement. Believe me, you won't make a fortune in France."

"In France Monsieur, one can make a fortune with anything, even when that anything is nothing. I shall announce publicly that I can create imbeciles in perpetuity, and many men of intelligence will come to offer themselves, asking for a guarantee of immutability. Only my liquor procures a waking slumber, from which one emerges, but which one can reenter easily. I do not destroy intelligence, I veil it, I temper it."

"It scarcely needs to be tempered further."

"However, your political assemblies..."

"Ah! It's not by virtue of an excess of intelligence that they are at fault. On the contrary, if they had more truly eloquent orators, more intelligent patriots, they would be better able to conduct the affairs if a nation that has need of enthusiasm to act and admiration to obey. We suffer from stupidity and ignorance. If a great poet comes along, like Lamartine or Victor Hugo, or a great statesman, of whom France has had so many in its history, or an artist of genius, I assure you that I would be perfectly reassured regarding the Republic, internal peace and the future."

At this point, my medicinal buffoon had a smile finer than the others, which only goes to prove that in Italy, the lunatics are diplomats.

"Monsieur," he said to me, politely, "The milieu makes great men as much as nature. By leveling for a time, the majority of intelligences, I raise up those who make use of my regime. I believe like you, that superiorities are necessary, but when there are none to dispute supremacy, mediocrity multiplies; the others reign and everything goes well. As for truly great men, those who have genius themselves draw it from humanity. They take more than they render. They leave a twilight behind them, having been luminous for too long. With my system one has superior men who are not inconvenient, and once again, humanity does well. I'm not excessive, like Merlatti or Succi;[4] I don't preach absolute abstinence from intelligence, I recommend a diet to prolong animal life, and you have seen in the urgency of the curious that the need of abstinence for the flesh, as for the mind, is a present tendency. I believe, after the avid file before Merlatti's platform at the moment when everyone hoped for his definitive cretinization, that I can count on a great affluence. I shall host banquets of the Grand Hotel, if you will do me the honor of presiding at one..."

"Never! I would rather go to the one that will doubtless be offered to Nègre-Gargantua, who consumes so much in order to produce so little! The awakening of appetite in everything, that's my theory. Let us drink, let us eat, in order to live a great deal, in order to love well, to hate without discouragement, to work without fatigue, to have all the vision of genius that every man glimpses in the warmth of digestion. I'm not your man for a trial; I won't be your accomplice for your experiment."

"I recognize, in fact," said Doctor Sublimini, with a superb expression, "that I was mistaken in addressing myself to you, and that I have made a vain step."

Was he saying that I was already sufficiently mediocre in intelligence to have no need of its diminution by his means?

---

[4] Giovanni Succi (1853-1918), a charlatan selling a patent medicine that he advertised as a cure for hunger, launched the fad for "endurance fasting" that Merlatti imported to Paris. Franz Kafka wrote a story inspired by his strange career, published posthumously in 1922 and translated as "The Hunger Artist".

He left, but I believe that while I was ringing to have him shown out, Doctor Sublimini had found a means of pouring a few drops of his liquor into my glass, for after his departure, I found myself quite bewildered, and since his visit, I feel a trifle stupid, as one can see by this very article.

Joseph Montet (1852-1919) was a graduate of the École normale supérieure who became a philosophy teacher and edited Le Drapeau, *the newspaper of the Ligue des Patriotes; he published several books of humorous short stories in the last two decades of the nineteenth century. The present story was the first item of fiction published in the popular science magazine* La Science illustrée, *billed as a* fantaisie humoristique *rather than* roman scientifique, *the label employed subsequently by editor Louis Figuier to describe the fiction he featured routinely thereafter until the turn of the century.* "The Triumph of Science" *was originally published in* La Science Illustrée, *25 & 29 décembre 1887.*

Joseph Montet: *The Triumph of Science*

"Monsieur Louis Vernet of Paris?" said Nathaniel Simpson, looking at a visiting card. "Wait!"

He took an address-book from his desk, through which he riffled rapidly.

"All right! Send him in."

Our friend Louis Vernet came in.

"You remembered my name?" he said, shaking the hand that the Yankee held out to him. "That's admirable."

"Not at all admirable. On the contrary—very simple. Look." And the American pointed out to his visitor a line written in his address-book: *Louis Vernet of Paris. Invited to dinner when he passes through Chicago.*

"With this," he said, slapping the book with the flat of his hand, "I'm certain never to forget anything!"

"Even an encounter as brief as ours. For, after all, how long were we acquainted?"

"One evening, no more."

"And then, around a very lively table, where you were vigorously swilling champagne in honor of Foxhall, the winner of the Grand Prix de Paris!"[5]

"Shh!" said the American, with a smile. "Here, I don't swill anything at all, except for the fresh ink of my account-books. Austere here, very austere…in a little while at dinner, we'll catch up."

"Ah! This is the sanctuary of work. What are you doing? Are you still in railways and paper?"

"No, I gave them up a long time ago. Steel is attracting some very underhanded competition nowadays. I've found a new specialty: alimentary substances. Much more profitable. Only one competitor to fear: Nature. She's not very strong."

"Really?"

"It's proven. In three years I've made three million. One was from making butter without milk, the second from making meat extract without meat, the third with a factory I set up last year."

"What are you manufacturing?"

"Eggs."

"Without chickens?"

"Obviously."

"You're joking!"

"I never joke about business."

"Well, I'd be curious to see that!"

"Nothing simpler. We've got half an hour to spare. That's enough to take a look at one of my workshops."

And the American, opening his office door, preceded his friend along a long corridor to a vast room, into which he introduced him. Large crates filled with superbly white eggs were stacked along the walls. The industrialist opened a second door. A rather sharp chill gripped Louis Vernet, who turned up the collar of his overcoat.

---

[5] The American-bred and British-trained racehorse Foxhall won the Grand Prix de Paris in 1881.

"Here we are," said Simpson, "in the manufacturing workshop. You see that vat? That's the yolk. And that other vat? That's the white."

"And what's the yolk made of?"

"A mixture of maize flour, starch extracted from wheat and a few other substances."

"And the white?"

"It would take too long to explain; the result is chemically identical to the white of an authentic egg."

"Perfect—but what about the shell?"

"Turn around. They're being made before your eyes."

"And how do you put your yolk and your white inside?"

"The art's in its infancy, but look—there's the machine. You'll notice that it has several compartments. The first contains the yolk, the second the white, the third the white pellicule of the egg, the fourth the gypsum scale that will form the shell. Did you notice the change in temperature as we came in? The cold is necessary—you'll see why. The yolk is poured into the first compartment in the form of a thick flour; it takes on a round form and congeals there—after which, it passes into the second compartment, where it's surrounded by the white and takes on an oval form by means of a rotatory movement; it congeals too. Then it passes into the next compartment, where it's coated in a light skin, and finally into the last, the scaler, where it completes its costume. The egg is made; it's placed on these drying trays here, where the shell is abruptly dried while the interior is unfrozen—and there it is. A chicken couldn't do any better."

"Nor as rapidly."

"Nor as rapidly. Look, here's one that's just been cooked for your benefit. Taste it."

Louis Vernet emptied the half-shell in one go.

"Exquisite!" he declared. "Well, that's what I can deliver at three dollars a thousand—just over seventy francs. Show me the chickens that can work on a regular basis at that price!"

"And for how long can your artificial eggs be kept?"

"Indefinitely. The one you've just eaten was a year old. Look, the date's marked on top. Another advantage: the shell is much thicker and harder than that of a natural egg; that's a guarantee for transportation. Hardly ever any breakages."

"And you're the only one operating this *tour de force*?"

Nathaniel Simpson's face darkened. "The only one? No—I have a competitor."

"As strong as you?"

"Stronger than me. He's found a means of giving the eggs, at will, the taste of goose-eggs or duck-eggs. That rogue Campbell is a clever one! But that's all right; sooner or later, I'll sink him. It's an obsession. In the meantime, let's eat."

*

"Naturally," said Nathaniel Simpson to his guest, as they got up from the table, "You've come to Chicago for the Exhibition.[6] What do you think of it?"

"Very interesting. The phonophotostenotypobiograph, especially, excited my admiration, and I confess that I stood open-mouthed in front of the instrument—which, in less than a minute, on being asked a simple question, gives you your photograph, the sound of your voice, your sentence in print, a facsimile of your handwriting and your date of birth."

"Pooh! Edison's latest creation…it'll be obsolete within a year. But did you see my eggs?"

"No."

"We'll go see them."

A quarter of an hour later, Nathaniel Simpson and Louis Vernet were standing in front of a display case in which several dozen eggs were displaying, between a double row of labels, the immaculate innocence of their rotund forms.

Beside them, in a second display case, other eggs were exposed, but these were of various sizes and with a greater

---

[6] Presumably the Inter-State Industrial Exhibition held in Chicago in September-October 1887, some years before the great World's Fair Columbian Exposition of 1893.

luxury of labels. Three placards hung over them, bearing the following indications: *Hens' eggs; Goose eggs; Duck eggs*.

"That's that rogue Campbell's display-case," Simpson said. "Needless to say, he'll win the prize!"

"I say," said Louis Vernet, "there's a ray of sunlight shining directly on your eggs. You aren't afraid that it will spoil them?"

"No, they're guaranteed to hold good. Anyway, it's winter—the sun isn't very fierce. If the Exhibition Hall weren't heated, we'd be freezing. Isn't that so, Jim?"

An attendant approached. "That's true, Mr. Simpson," he said. "The heating isn't superfluous."

Louis Vernet was still in front of the display-case, his chin in his hand, as if plunged in profound meditation. Suddenly, he raised his head, with a smile.

"I say," he said, taking Simpson's arm and drawing him into a corner. "How much would you give to sink your competitor?"

"Campbell? Any price at all."

"A thousand dollars?"

"A pittance...two thousand, if necessary."

"A thousand will suffice. Will you give me that credit? I'll answer for the success."

Nathaniel looked at his guest. "I don't understand," he said. "But that's okay—it's a deal!"

"Good. Just give me five minutes I'll meet you at the exit."

As soon as Simpson had drawn away, Louis Vernet summoned the attendant with a gesture. After three minutes of whispered conversation, he took out his wallet and gave the man a few banknotes.

"The rest in a few days, at most," he said to him, as he went away.

A week later, as he was reading his newspaper, Nathaniel Simpson leapt from his armchair so suddenly that he nearly knocked his desk over.

This is what he had just read:

THE TRIUMPH OF SCIENCE

Last night, at the Exhibition, the most extraordinary phenomenon of the century occurred. Everyone has noticed the curious display-cases of the artificial eggs of Messrs. Campbell and Simpson. Now, in the latter's showcase, this is the truly stupefying spectacle that was seen this morning: one of the eggs was partly broken, and through the opening of the shell came the head of a genuine living creature. The meticulous precautions taken for the accommodation and preservation of the exhibited products leave no room for the hypothesis of some impossible trickery; only one conclusion can be drawn from this marvelous fact, which is that Mr. Simpson has taken the imitation of Nature to such a point than he has stolen her last secret. There is no doubt that a splendid reward will consecrate this truly prodigious result of scientific genius, which is destined to begin a new era in the annals of humankind.

The newspaper fell from Nathaniel Simpson's hands. At that moment, Louis Vernet came into his office, holding a copy of the same paper.

"The attendant Jim," he said, "is a good man, who has earned his thousand dollars. The hen's egg that he slipped into your display-case didn't cost him more than three cents, to be sure, but he can keep the difference. As for your American sunlight, it's an idler that doesn't know its business, and without a small capture of heat taken from the heating duct, you'd still be waiting for your fantastic chick, Monsieur Simpson!"

Nathaniel Simpson burst out laughing.

"Diabolical Frenchman!" he exclaimed. "Only you could have such an idea. Except that you're going to have a dead man on your conscience—that rogue Campbell, will surely die of chagrin!"

Maurice Montegut (1855-1911) was a prolific poet, dramatist and novelist, who adapted readily to the market for short stories that opened up in the newspapers of the 1880s. "The Isle of Satyrs" was originally published in Gil Blas, *17 juillet 1891.*

Maurice Montegut: *The Isle of Satyrs*

My distant cousin Georges Trédorn died in Senegal three months ago, of a bout of malaria, it was said aloud—of alcoholic delirium, it was said in whispers.

He was a lieutenant in the navy. No one knew the sea better than him. He had a horror of firm ground.

Via the ministry and the consulates the family has received as a heritage three trunks, stained, patched and mottled with labels, which reek simultaneously of seaweed and sandalwood.

Cousin Georges had strange tastes; in all the countries he visited he applied himself to collecting images, sculptures, trinkets and the most...natural emblems. He had brought back horrors from Japan. As everyone knows that, it is me who is charged with opening the trunks, making and inventory—and suppressing the indecencies.

And among those vague embalmed things coming from the eighteen points of the world I have found yellow papers, steeped in salt, ragged and forgotten, and I read:

Indian Ocean 15 September
I've returned aboard trembling at what I have seen...I alone have understood... my six matelots are brutes... simpletons, at least. I've lost my head...

It's necessary, however, that I find it again, that I write down this nightmare...oh, it's frightful! Have I really seen it? But no, there's no doubt about it, and it's only up to me to bring back, willingly or by force, a specimen of those monsters. Barnum would pay me a million for it; it would be enough to make all the men in the world vomit.

This is it.

This morning, I was sent on reconnaissance to a group of previously unknown islands, omitted from the charts. They're in the open sea, two hundred leagues from any other land. In a launch, I had my usual six oarsmen. It was amusing: a map to draw, a sketch to make, and the Geographical Society in prospect, awarding me a prize on a day of full session next year…or another.

I approached a volcanic soil…these islands can't be very old. It's one of the last sighs of the old planet that has pushed them there…desolate, chaotic country, sparse vegetation, marine flora here and there.

"Heave to!"

A bleak shore, landslides of granite, gray and red. The water around it is deep.

The largest of the isles is only two leagues around; this will be quickly done. We enter into that virgin nature…

Virgin? Oh!

No trees, no birds, a great blue sky over white soil.

"Dirty little place!" says a matelot.

We advance. Suddenly, we hear bizarre cries, previously unheard, terrifying; and there, racing away at a gallop, twenty paces away from us, is a troop of nameless beings, the rapid vision of which chills…any yet, we're hardened, we seamen.

"Monkeys!" says one.

"No!"

"What, then?"

"Goats!" affirms another.

I keep quiet myself, for what I've seen doesn't resemble anything known…except, perhaps, mythological satyrs, and even then with extraordinary variations.

An immense curiosity grips us, and we run after those prodigious animals, those inexplicable phenomena.

The chase is hard…the monsters flee recklessly, still crying; and in their howls there are human voices. Finally, by means of surprise, we drive them toward the sea; before the waves they stop, frightened, and face up to us; in a large circle, we approach, also shouting, and, believe me, all very pale.

At a hundred paces I order: "Halt!" and we consider the enigmatic troop. There are twelve, all dissimilar, but all offering a hideous composite of humanity and animality, of goat and human. Some run on all fours, others walk upright. I see one of them that is very tall and hairy, which would be a true goat if it did not have human feet, almost white; but the two most horrible, assuredly, are that goat with a human head and that man with the head of a goat, with inverted horns.

And all of them, terrified by our presence, are weeping, lamenting, moaning and sobbing, with the tones of desperate men, women and children.

An immense frisson traverses my marrows.

I recoiled, my men too.

"Dirty creatures!" said the novice.

As we recoiled, our circle broke, and the twelve creatures, led by the man with the goat's head, passed through our midst and then disappeared into the rocks with caprine bounds, a fantastic agility. It's thus that a bad dream vanishes.

In silence we went around the mass of rocks and returned to the interior. I drew up my maps and traced my sketches, from the top of a hillock, and I gave the signal to depart, in haste to escape the mystery.

In our path, in the granite landslide, there was a cavern. One of my men penetrated into it at hazard; and from a distance I heard him utter a loud "Ah!"

"What is it now?" I responded, dolorously, weary of prodigies.

There was a human skeleton, a real one, on the dry sand of the grotto; it was lying very straight; next to it were a sailor's knife and a hatchet. In one corner, the calcined stones gave evidence of ancient cooking, a makeshift hearth, burning in this desert on cold nights. The man must have died naked; not a scrap of cloth subsists in the vicinity.

Then I had the disgust of understanding. I have reconstituted the shipwreck: the man throwing himself into the sea, naked, like the matelot of Virginia, his knife in his teeth, a hatchet bound to his waist. Alone on this island, alone with a goat or goats, perhaps arrived from the same ship, perhaps born there, as once were born throughout the earth the archetypes of various races, the primal individuals of living species. And I remembered the crime of bestiality punished by Moses, the monstrous couplings of humans with animals of which legends speak, with poeticize everything.

I had the key to the enigma, and my heart was sickened. A rage gripped me; I wanted to avenge humanity, soiled by that unpunished death, to suppress the evidence of the crime, those hideous human beasts, those demonic products, those creatures of nightmare and folly.

I had the rifles loaded, and again we searched for the ignoble troop. But they were no longer to be found; the horrible creatures had gone to ground, vanished; the isle was silent, nothing was moving there any longer.

Then I thought that bastard creatures, mules and leopards, remain permanently sterile, and I was consoled.

They will not be perpetuated. They have lived, but after them, silence will fall again over their existence, stolen from the laws of nature; and if their bones are ever rediscovered, they will be classified among the prehistorics, the antediluvians, of the epochs lost in the mist and dreams...

André Monselet (?-?) was the son of the journalist, novelist, playwright and gastronome Charles Monselet (1825-1888), whose memoir of his father was published in the same year as the present novelette. He had previously written a number of vaudevilles. "In the Year 2000" was originally published in Gil Blas, *24, 25, 27, 28 Sept & 1 Oct 1892.*

André Monselet: *In the Year 2000*

I

The scene is taking place in the great lounge of the Orient Express Balloon of the General Company of Aerial Transport, via Paris, Athens and Constantinople.

"One of my supposed ancestors was made famous by a voyage to Greece accomplished in antiquity, of which a French writer, Abbé Barthélemy, published a complete account in 1789, on the eve of the Revolution."

"Hang on: *The Voyage of Young Anacharsis!* So you must be..."[7]

---

[7] Anacharsis was a Scythian who traveled to Athens in the sixth century B.C., where he allegedly and built a reputation there as a "barbarian" philosopher, a forerunner of the Cynics; he was granted Athenian citizenship and named by some later writers as one of the Seven Sages of Greece, but none of his writings survived, save for a few fragments that are probably apocryphal. In 1787 the Jesuit antiquarian scholar Jean-Jacques Barthélemy (1716-1790), published a four-volume *Voyage du jeune Anacharsis en Grèce dans le milieu du sixième siècle*, the protagonist of which relates in old age how he made an educative voyage to Greece in his youth. The text was intended as a popular introduction to ancient Greek culture, art and mores.

"In person, or rather, Anacharsis junior, travelling in his turn to France for his personal pleasure."

"And it's in the year 2000 that you're accomplishing this little voyage?"

"Would you expect me, too, to look back from my epoch, to cast an ecstatic gaze over the past, to linger over voluntary memories, to study the people and things of another era, interested in what has disappeared? That's an old game. Everything has been said, and I'd arrive after everyone else. No, no, forwards, forwards. The best thing is to march with one's century. Is one very sure, in any case, that in talking about the present one hasn't been surpassed?"

"How's that?"

"Isn't Sébastien Mercier, for example, a contemporary of Barthélemy, the author of a story entitled *In the year 2440; a dream if ever there was one*, in which he predicted, in 1770, in the milieu of a figurative slumber, the benefits of the Revolution to come?[8] Yes, I know, that's only pure imagination, whereas I'm not dreaming, I'm marching wide awake, among all sorts of marvels; but I don't want to give the impression, nevertheless, of being four centuries behind the times—which makes me hesitate to set forth."

"Bah! Who would perceive it, such a long time in advance?"

"Perhaps; what if my impressions, my notes of the voyage, were to seem out of date?"

"Have no fear; nothing is more agreeable to the French, at present, than *Sensations*, printed abroad, in which Parisian life is found mingled, if only for a moment."

"Are you certain of that?"

"Convinced—and, if I dared to ask you for the first fruit of those sensations, for..."

---

[8] Louis-Sébastien Mercier, *L'An 2440, rêve s'il en fut jamais* (1771; augmented in subsequent editions; tr. as *Memoirs of the Year 2500*).

"Excuse me...in my turn, to whom do I have the honor of speaking?"

"It's only fair: Joe Boxton of Sisteron City, Connecticut, member of the American Journalists' Club, correspondent of the *Splendid Standard*, travelling the world in search of the up-to-date and the unpublished. All right!"

"Put it there, as they say in your homeland. I've always liked America—both of them—and I'll readily consent to reserve for your compatriots the first fruit of my..."

"Sensations."

"Yes, sensations is very good. Anyway, to be printed in the New World—for it's always new, isn't it?—is, if I'm not mistaken, the surest means today of being read in France."

"Bravo, Monsieur Anacharsis."

"Junior, Mr. Boxton."

Alone, at last! I let myself get caught up in his dialogue. But it's in the old style, that, my good man, it's what was once called an interview. And I desired to travel—I'd forgotten to take account of the rage for information in the two continents—incognito!

In a balloon, here I am in a balloon. Who would even perceive it? No oscillation, not the slightest shock. No more doubt, I've set forth, truly departed for the twenty-first century.

"Will Monsieur be dining in the dining room or on deck?

"Eh! People eat on balloons now!"

"*À la carte* or *table d'hôte?*"

"On the deck, certainly...oh, a simple chocolate; I still have a little air-sickness, and I have no appetite."

"As Monsieur pleases."

The waiter went away, testifying to some surprise; his smile gave me to understand that I give the impression of being behind the times.

Shortly thereafter I found myself comfortably installed in the open air—in a manner of speaking; we were in the clouds—with a cup containing a liquid of immaculate whiteness before me, on an elegant table.

"But this is milk, waiter!"

"No, Monsieur; it's just that the chocolate has turned white in aging."

"Bah!" I raid, with a hint of astonishment that I tried to disguise this time. *It's necessary to expect*, I thought, *that I'll see many others*.

"And where are we now if you please?"

"Between two thousand and two thousand five hundred meters above the Pont-Neuf. We've just crossed the Alps at three thousand meters, a little while ago. A fine spectacle, but Monsieur hadn't yet got up.

"I regret that, of course."

If this breeze continues, we'll be in sight of New Paris City within two hours. Monsieur is staying at the Central Hotel like everyone else?"

"Like everyone else. I intend to do that. Tell me one more thing, waiter, I beg you…we're arriving from…"

"Monsieur is asking me where he's coming from?"

"Oh, a simple item of information, to put order in my thoughts."

"Monsieur is joking? Monsieur no longer remembers boarding the balloon yesterday afternoon in Athens, in the hall of the General Company of Aerial Transport? Monsieur is, however, well known in Athens—the new Athens!"

"Oh yes, yes. I remember now." Privately: *Damned if I remember*. Aloud: "It's sleep that has troubled my intelligence slightly.

"In fact, Monsieur has been asleep since the departure.

Privately: *Of course, I was even sleeping the other slumber*. Aloud: "In sum, it's always good to know where one is coming from when one doesn't know exactly where one is going!"

After a turn around the walkway of the balloon, in the midst of strangers of mark, I mingle discreetly with the general conversation, interrogating Boxton in particular; behold:

New Paris City is, it appears the new designation of the capital of France, since the latest social Evolution. The Universal Federation—the Council of the representatives of the various States—chose that different designation in order to efface even the memory of the old and barbaric city, the ramparts of which have been razed following the general peace. But the former designation has subsisted even so, so deeply rooted was it in minds. And I, who, plunged in my posthumous books, was still in the old Paris of the nineteenth century...Gods, how hard it is to be in a century that is not exactly your own...

All the passengers are on the deck now, with their elbows on the rails and leaning over, aiming their binoculars and telescopes in all directions; a general rumor warns me that we are over New Paris City.

I approach in my turn. The amiable Boxton hastens to join me and direct my gaze. The bird's eye view of the capital is a marvelous spectacle, in which the gaze embraces a gigantic panorama.

The suburbs of the immense city presently extend all the way to the horizon, bordered by hills: a city that extends from Versailles to Vincennes in one direction, and from Saint-Denis to Villeneuve-Saint-Georges in the other, with an uninterrupted sequence of houses between those extremities; seen through the clouds of smoke that envelop it, one might think it the crater of a semi-extinct volcano.

A slender thread of water traverses it in zigzags; that is the Seine, but much enlarged, it appears, the bed of which, profoundly hollowed out, permits the access of ships of heavy tonnage. New Paris City—I definitely prefer saying Paris—is still partly circled by a channel that links it directly to the sea, cut in all directions by railways on which electric trains circulate, served underground, I'm told, by a Tubular of compressed air, and, above the houses—ten-story houses surmounted by terraces, an Electric Métropolitain linking together all the stations of that vast modern Chicago...once one would have said Babylon! Old, so old!

In Paris today one no longer swears except by the Metro or the Tube. And yet, above the Metro, aerostatic lines still function, very busy, since those marvelous dirigible machines transport you with an unprecedented rapidity from one country to another.

Thus, stronger than our fortifications, Mont Valerien has become a country dance-hall. In fact, what good are ramparts when all danger of war has disappeared, permanent armies have vanished at the signal given for a general disarmament, when only natural frontiers still exist, and when foreigners, whoever they might be, are no longer anything at present but our neighbors from over the mountains or our friends from overseas?

Today, everything is free, vast, open, limitless, grandiose and colossal!

But we're going down. Aboard the balloon, the bell is agitated, the passengers are getting ready, the luggage makes its appearance.

What am I going to see on the ground, having already learned so much from above? The conversations to which I lend an ear allow me to suspect many other surprises. Everything is colliding in my mind. What do you expect? To fall thus, in a single bound, into the middle of a civilization, in the very heart of enlightenment; to witness the dawn of a century that sees yesterday's hallucinations and utopias becoming realities: there is enough in that to trouble the best equilibrated brain.

We are still descending, slowly; around us, on the contrary, by virtue of a well-known phenomenon, everything seems to be rising, and the first monuments and the first constructions perceived seem to be departing for a distant voyage.

"In five minutes," says a balloon crewman, "we'll touch down."

I lean over one last time, and I distinguish, pell-mell, cutting the azure, electric wires of all dimensions, forming, so great is their number, a kind of network above the capital.

Seen from this height, Paris resembles an immense cage in which a host of microscopic vibrions is agitating.

"And to think that those vibrions are the giants to whom the new world is owed!

II

This time I really am a Parisian—of the twenty-first century—to judge by the costume; the transformation was easy. A modern tailor drapes very cleverly, but there are no more heavy fabrics and no more burdensome collars; the tight fit has also had its day, amplitude is in fashion—long live amplitude! Hence the epithet of "balloonish" to qualify the skin-tight clothing of old.

The stockings and shoes, the short culottes, the lace ruff over the open waistcoat and the Ange Pitou hat,[9] alias the Evolution hat—such is the generally adopted clothing.

Fashion is liable thus to return to the past. But what is a more modern sign of present times is that, thanks to new laws, women dress, for the most part, in masculine costume, to which they have added powdered hair. It's Diana replacing Venus! After all, nothing therein is disgraceful, and one soon gets used to that new transformation.

Indeed, I think that, thanks to what I see, what I hear, and what I read, I shall end up occidentalizing myself. The Central Hotel, where I reside—Courtyard A., Staircase C, Corridor 12, Room 17A, is the most modern expression of the new comfort; it has been constructed on the site of the two lakes in the Bois de Boulogne, which the city filled in after an epidemic of malaria. Instead of that liquid mass, a Mutual Insurance Com-

---

[9] Louis Ange Pitou (1767-1846) was a counter-revolutionary journalist fortunate to avoid the guillotine, whose celebrity was increased when he became the eponymous protagonist of *Ange Pitou* (1850-51 as a feuilleton in *La Presse*) by Alexandre Dumas, the third part of the series *Mémoires d'un médecin*.

pany against unemployment has had a splendid building erected, linked by a private service of electric trams to all points of the city, provided, in sum, with al imaginable necessities and superfluities—in a word, what our ancestors called the *nec plus ultra.* But try to make use of such terms today!

Everything has been assembled in the Central Hotel, in fact, for the greatest comfort of travelers: a music chapel, a gymnasium, a swimming pool, a hippodrome, a tennis court, a garden restaurant, a concert terrace, a theater, and also gaming rooms—for gambling has finally been liberated in France, the salt of all liberties, and the tax on gambling has rapidly become one of the most important national revenues.

Thus, without displacing myself, I was able, the day after my arrival to attend a sermon in the morning by the Reverend P. Bridon, the best orator of the Oratorians, and after lunch to applaud on the Concert Terrace the charming divette Angelina in her latest summer creation, *The Legend of Mont Nichon,*[10] of which I would cite one or two couplets if I did not fear making one or two American ladies blush, Can you imagine that in France, censorship has been abolished.

Five o'clock—the hour for a promenade.

A crowd is besieging the paths of the Bois, everyone attempting to be seen in an uninterrupted file of electric carriages, for a horse-drawn carriage is a rarity now. The file extends from the Avenue Alphand to the Franco-Russian pavilion near the Central Hotel, along the Seine via the new pathways that lead to Saint-Cloud and reenter Paris under the dome of verdure known as the Boulevard Zola, in the recent and delightful quarter of Les Bâtis-Neufs.

Deserting society and the noise, I escape, unperceived, and, spotting one of the light electric cabs guided with a truly surprising skill by a "boy," I am transported into a new corner of the great city.

Note that the competition between these cabs has overturned any horary and kilometric tariff previously in use.

---

[10] *Nichon* was a slang term for a woman's breast.

Henceforth, there is a struggle between the boys for the journey. The cab is therefore the method of locomotion that I employ for preference to visit the marvels of the new capital. The cab is full of advantages: its wheels, enveloped with pneumatic rubber, slide over a superb parquet of glass, which has succeeded wooden pavements in the principal streets, and conducts you without the slightest shock.

Oh, the ground of New Paris City has been tranquil for a long time! No more blocked streets, or dangerous precipices established along streets for all purposes. That floor, in large frosted sheets of glass on an iron framework, covers half the sidewalks and three quarters of the causeways, considerably broadened, which has permitted the establishment of a subterranean Paris, very bright and vast, where the Tubular circulates at its ease, and where electric wires are also installed for lighting, and the wires of different communication—telephones, theatrophones, etc., etc., as well as gas pipes for the public heating of the city and water pipes from the springs of Dhuys, Vannes, Avre, Eure, etc.

It is the underworld of New Paris City!

For the repairs that all of that necessitates, junctions are established at intervals, and where ditches were once dug, it is only necessary to lift a lid and go down a staircase; the effective work is carried out underneath without the circulation being interrupted for a moment.

Go down one more level, and you find yourself in further subterrains where the different services of drainage arc channeled, from Paris to the sea, with stations. Paris is thus now situated on a second floor, a second floor aerated, illuminated, heated and watered by astonishing means that seem the simplest in the world.

Let us mention, finally, the circulation of vehicles and pedestrians, which no longer offers any danger, thanks to galleries suspended like balconies or terraces at the height of the first floor, forming in every broad and spacious street a new causeway with as many shops—which is to say, movement, splendor and light. Underneath, are the sidewalks where, in the event of rain, everyone immediately finds a refuge, while having the leisure to continue on their way.

Oh, the elegant footbridges from one side to the other, giving pedestrians every facility for waking in complete security, leaving the roadway free for vehicles.

My cab, at the regulation speed—fortunately limited, like the capital of a financial society—is still carrying me too rapidly. I scarcely have time to perceive in passing the Governmental House where the delegates are lodged for the maintenance of the administrative organization, a task much simplified; the Hôtel de Ville—for there are no longer any palaces—where the Maire of Paris meets with his forty-three deputies representing the forty-three arrondissements, since the annexation of the suburban communes; the Hall of Books, which I certainly intend to visit, and the most recent monuments erected in commemoration of Universal Peace, the Alliance of Races, Social Conquest, etc., etc...and the statues elevated to the memory of the unarmed combatants who struggled pacifically to renew and transform everything, and who finally succumbed to the task.

So, it has taken more than a hundred years to arrive here—two centuries, in fact, in practice, for theoretically, Jean-Jacques Rousseau...there, good, once again my watch is going backwards! I'll never belong to my new century!

III

I've done everything I can, but in vain, to obtain a ticket for the gala spectacle to be held next Thursday at the church of Sacré-Coeur, on the summit of Montmartre, for the benefit of the émigrés of French Sudan.

The program is magnificent: the first performance of *The Wedding at Cana*, a lyrical intention in four periods, words inspired by Monsieur Adam and musical translation by Madame Pondé-Semper, with the collaboration of artistes from the Grand and the Petit Lyriques, and the choirs of the interns of the Conservatoire. In the twelfth tableau, the Last Supper, a living reproduction of the famous painting by Paolo Veronese. which a certain critic of the nineteenth century did not fail to call the "*cène à faire*."[11]

The price of places has been raised considerably; the "prayer armchairs" are fifty francs, the "lower boxes" a hundred francs and the "work-benches" twenty-francs. The personnel entries have been suspended by exception. Only the critic-advertisers of the newspapers of the arrondissement will be admitted on presentation of their cards.

Well, if that's the case, I shall pay for my place in the church!

It appears, in fact, that the abuse of complimentary tickets has, in recent times, diminished receipts of churches in a disquieting manner, which, since their separation from the State have made enormous profits. Such a state of affairs being capable of harming the prosperity of Catholicism, the general syndicate of the directors of worship has hastened to put things in order by publishing a recent edict relative to those abuses. Henceforth, the church managers and chapel-masters can no longer deliver free tickets or notes of entitlement, under penalty of a fine.

It is necessary, on the other hand, to take into account that the rights of the poor are eroding diocesan profits considerably, so the church is threatened with what once happened to the theater, with the same menace of complete ruination.

Formerly, the Public Assistance Tax was levied on the net receipts of spectacles; today, more reasonably, the same tax is levied on the number of spectators—which has immediately caused the disappearance of free tickets, a largesse that had become harmful overnight—but which demonstrated at the same time the scant success of certain works previously reputed to have "exceeded capacity," according to an expression of the epoch. But the Church still refuses to accept tax

---

[11] This wordplay links "cène" [supper] with the conventional phrase "scène à faire," referring to the "obligatory scene" that completes a generic play.

inspectors at the entrances in order that the number of the faithful can be established; in that, the Church seems to us to be in the wrong; its public, as elsewhere, ought to be considered as composed of lovers of spectacles, as its strength originated from the very weakness of the theater before the theater belonged, as it does today, to "free authors."

It is a verity worth recording that the Church, like the Theater, in abusing an excess of liberty, and thus sinking into ridicule or scandal, has elevated the dramatic art, just as. in olden days, it had, in a sense, created it. The Church has hastened therefore in the present epoch to open a new outlet to veritable art: librettists and composers, artiste and musicians, immediately precipitated into it.

The time is long gone of mysteries judged by the dramas and operas performed at present, and the religious theme is no longer the unique thought of the Church, but all its works have an incontestable value; the public still recalls the marvelous and truly magical staging of the *Garden of Olives* at Notre-Dame, and the unrivaled voice of Mademoiselle Dupin "bringing down the house" every evening, as the newspapers say, while Mademoiselle Pickunsoldt, the Illyrian around whom there was such great rumor, did not attract a cat to the Grand Lyrique.

There is, therefore, no reason to be astonished that the subscribed faithful of our premières became, at length, veritable faithful subscribed to the Church. Going further, one can add that the diocesan performances have greatly influenced morality; a diva, for example, is delighted at present to be heard by the crowd, and believes in all sincerity that she is bringing the contribution of her talent in exchange for absolution. The sacristy is cluttered with artistes; it is no longer recognizable.

More than that, religious tours have been organized, in the example of dramatic tours, with the goal of bringing to the solemnities of petty provincial parishes the precious collaboration of distinguished talents; let us add that the success of these enterprises has been very considerable and very legitimate everywhere.

The temporary weakness of the theater, therefore, has enabled the strength of the Church—which does not prevent the defects once arising in theatrical administration being renewed in the direction of church halls, and that is why the general syndicate of the directors of Catholic worship has been led to take measures of an excessive but useful rigor.

But, you might say to me, the rights of the poor thus levied on the receipts of the theater and the church must form a considerable revenue today. Considerable indeed. As for the perfectly natural question: where does the money go; it is easy to respond that the sums this collected are applied to the extinction of pauperism in France, a goal that has almost been achieved at present, for, let us say it loudly, charity is the great word of the new century. Thus, many charitable works have been founded in recent times: the Abandoned Little Tonkinese; the Orphanate of Decorative Zincs; the Fiancés of the City, the Invalids of Health, the Retreats of Poverty, etc., etc.

The results are tangibly felt, it appears. Thus, the last signpost, two hundred years old, has recently been removed on which these words could still be read, half-obliterated by time: *Begging is prohibited in the département of the Seine.*

IV

Perhaps it would be good to say a little about the Government, although people no longer talk politics in France, since everything runs smoothly. That is because things have changed greatly; there is no more President of the Republic, no more Senate or Chambre des députés.

In their place, twelve General Commissioners preside over the progress of affairs: the Interior; the Treasury; Foreign Relations; Commerce; Industry: Roads, Canals and Railways: Agriculture; Education; Liberal and Decorate Arts; the National Militia; Marine transport and commerce; Justice and arbitration.

It is, in fact, a governmental committee, with a president elected by secret ballot. Beneath them, the départemental committees sit in their respective départements, headed by a president equipped with the full powers of the ancient prefects. At a lower level, arrondissement councils have been subsisted, along with municipal councils, for district councils in big cities, constituted in the same fashion.

The primary elections, called municipal or district elections, are held by universal suffrage, the other two elections by restricted suffrage; finally, drawing lots decides the appointment of governmental commissioners taken from among the presidents of the départemental committees.

Those different elections are called primary, secondary and tertiary; they are held every year for one of the levels; there is, in consequence, a perpetual turnover, which is known as the administrative mechanism. The meeting of the presidents of the départemental committees for the drawing of loots for governmental commissioners takes place, in consequence, every four years, and is the pretext for an imposing ceremony at Longchamps, also known as the Champ de la Féderation.

That political system, of which I can only indicate the broad outline here, satisfies the population of the cities and the countryside completely, and seems very reasonable, so that new order of things has rallied all support and has caused the disappearance of all coteries.

How many benefits have been owed to that new regime! The care of the poor classes, the amelioration of individual lots, equity in the division of the land and fortune are the great fundamental principles of that government issued from the last popular movement.

It is thus that the licensing of armies has permitted, among other things, the repurchasing of the old railways lines from the various companies of "exploitation"—that is the appropriate word, employed until the present day—and the possibility of immediately relegating to some gallery of horrors the frightful carriages that made the fortune of famous financiers for a long time. Progress has substituted electric trains for the old steam engines.

Finally, Agriculture no longer lacks arms (O Venus de Milo!) Having returned to the hearths, our brave young soldiers—I am saying *our* now, as if I were naturalized—whose formidable inutility has been fortunately recognized after so many centuries, have returned with ardor to the land; instead of permanent professional armies, a simple council of representatives elected by the different nations—for, needless to add, there are no more kings and princes—is sufficient to settle amicably any difference that arises between neighbors of such a pacific humor.

There are no more Pyrenees now!

A certain number of soldiers has retained the honor, nevertheless, of conserving their uniforms and going to serve France in the colonies; by the same token, a colonial army has been created. Other volunteers have been employed to form a National Militia, the only troops existing today with the objective of ensuring the maintenance of order in all the cities; the départements have nevertheless conserved their fine gendarmes, whose cadre has even be reinforced. The elegant uniform of the soldiers of the Republic of Monaco has finally been adopted for the militia.

It results from all these perfections that the service of order and security is marvelously organized today—that is a justice to render to the General Committee. This time, everything is quite tranquil: sleep easy, Parisians!

One odd consequence of the new regime: the navy, presently unburdened of its heavy contigent of warships, has too many large and small ships, and, not being able to use them all for transport and commerce, has made the wise decision to hire out a certain number to rich individuals—a few still remain—who make use of them for pleasure trips. Thus, it is possible to travel the world aboard a first class cruiser at a rapid sped, and even, for small purses, to hire a torpedo-boat with a view to an excursion or fishing trip.

Another excellent thing: the separation of Church and State, in suppressing any religious budget, has finally permitted the suppression of tollbooths, so impatiently awaited. Come on, Jacques Bonhomme, you can bite the grape!

Other important reforms have also followed in consequence, such as the limitation of private fortunes, in order to avoid cornering and speculation; the return to the communes of property in land exceeding certain proportions; the liberty of cultivating all terrains, etc.

Finally, the French language, which was already the diplomatic language, is on the way to becoming the universal language. Gibberish will therefore disappear.

And the Law, my friends, what a shipwreck!

A veritable Code has recently been drawn up, responding to present day mores and needs, the text of which, conceived in a clear and precise language, has replaced the horrible and pretentious jargon previously in usage. The Code is finally within the reach of all; it is in the same format and the same style as the bourgeois cookbook.

Is there any need to add that the death penalty has been definitively abolished, in consequence of a plebiscite, and it has been decided to employ recidivists in African colonization.

And in the midst of all that, you might ask, what have the people done?

The people, in their gratitude, utilize all the marble and bronze to immortalize the features of their heroes. Brumont, entitled the liberator of territory, already has his statue. Why should he be treated any differently from Louis XIV and Monsieur Thiers?

V

My quality as a foreigner of distinction (hold your head up, Anacharsis) has enabled me to be introduced to the General Commissioner of Liberal and Decorative Arts, one of the twelve governmental commissioners—a charming man!

An odd thing, which proves that political direction no longer depends on anything but a lottery, the General Commissioner of Liberal and Decorative Arts is today a Lutecian of Lutece—which says everything, or, at least, that he is interested in art and artists.

I went with him to visit the Hall of Books and the Painting Market, the two latest artistic conceptions of the epoch, which are intended to cast a vivid light upon contemporary literature and painting...but let us proceed in order.

Who would believe, to begin with, that in the fatherland of Voltaire and Diderot, only three hundred men of letters still exist? Yes, three hundred writers constitute, it appears, an intellectual nourishment sufficient for the France of the twenty-first century, but three hundred recognized, official, patented writers with shops on the street, all crowned by the Académie! And that scarcely a century after the deluge of octavos in which the literary ship of the nineteenth century nearly sank.

That is because the book has also suffered its little crash, and sleeping novelists, Mesdames, had a narrow escape, exactly like simple dramatic authors.

In the duel to the death between publishers and booksellers on the subject of storage, commission and discounting—read "Japanese salad"—the situation of the novelist became, to say the least, critical.

But what did the readers have to say? What, no more *petit Charpentiers* to get their teeth into? What would become of the lovely Madame X*** if her favorite novelist was suddenly lacking?

The situation became untenable when the writers judged that the moment had come to unionize; there were scarcely any who were not. In addition, they interested the government in their cause to such a extent that the latter, desiring in good faith to come to the aid of literature, took their defense in hand and had constructed for their benefit the Hall of Books, a magnificent rotunda with a crystal roof, in which each author possessed his stand and exposed his volumes, which he sold himself.

Gavroche, who still exists, immediately nicknamed those new booksellers the "latest publications."

The public, for its part, is very assiduous at the Hall of Books, located on the site of the old Bourse, which it was necessary to relocate because it was no longer central enough. But, the Hall of Books only having been constructed for three hundred display cases, it was decided that no one would enter that new Académie except on the death of one of the stallholders; the candidate is nominated for choice by an *ad hoc* committee chaired by the General Commissioner of Liberal Arts—the decidedly charming man—to whom a delegation of immortals is adjoined, for form's sake.

There exists in France, therefore, a multitude of candidates for a literary boutique, but there are, in reality, only three hundred authorized vendors of literature. Some of those abandon the Hall of Books before the due time in exchange for a good minor position in forest conservation, the administration having finally recognized that that position conserves much more literature that the dusty bookshops in which it was previously enclosed. Has not La Fontaine proved already, in the time of Louis XIV, that a fabulist is not unworthy of that post, and of all conservers of forests he is, I believe, the only one whose memory has been conserved.

As for booksellers and publishers, they only remained in pairs, like two china dogs, the former ordering from the latter new luxury editions of the dead authors of the twentieth century –which hastened their common ruination.

And that is how this liberal regime, so attentively devoted to everyone, was able to give a new impetus to literature.

I come now to the Painting Market, which is one of the most attractive curiosities that is has been give to me to see.

Oh, it is not exhibitions that painters lacked a century ago—at least they could put their talent on show—but there too there was a plethora, and if France no longer produced artists like ancient Greece and Italy, what is very flattering is that it was still necessary for those artists to be able live agreeably under a beech tree—which they would hasten to paint.

But how could every painter be given a beech tree, or even a living?

The annual Salon, considerably increased in size, no longer being sufficient, there was recourse to a perpetual Salon, open all year round, the canvases of which were changed every three months. It was already a progress when an artist had an idea of genius: to divide the Salon into for classes: the "outside competition," the "medals," the "mentioned" and the "nothing at all"—consequently indicating the possible value of their paintings, in accordance with the appreciation of the artists; only they can judge such questions well.

The first Salon thus organized obtained a great and real success for an entire year; the "nothing at alls," principally, were disputed as the artists of the future, but at low prices.

The goal did not appear to have been completely attained, however, when, in a further meeting of liberal and decorative trusts, the project was proposed of a ambulant Salon.

An ambulant Salon!

Yes, you understand, a Salon that tours every year, after two months of exhibition in Paris, all the great cities of France, and subsequently even abroad, during the summer, in the season of holidays and festivals.

The idea of the ambulant Salon was immediately adopted unanimously; it was only a matter henceforth of foreseeing its success.

Was it permissible to doubt, in the twenty-first century, that an architect could accomplish a *tour de force?* No, it was not permissible. Except that it was a carriage-maker that executed it. In the following month of May, throughout the extent of the Republic, a succession of salons could be seen, shaped in varnished wood—fir, bamboo and old pitch-pine—mounted on carts, seeming to form a single whole but easy to dismantle and transport with the aid of a small road locomotive powered by electricity: in sum, the model of ancient fairground caravans, but improved. This time, the success was unprecedented.

The interior of the artists' cabins—artistic exhibitions—was much admired; their accommodation was, moreover, very comfortable; everything was anticipated there for the voyage. The painters were grouped together by camaraderie—the only school that still subsists today in painting.

The departure of the ambulant Salon took on the proportions of a popular event; an ovation was given to the artists who accompanied their canvases, like cashiers traveling with their cash-boxes. In the provinces there was delirium; the populations ran to see our national celebrities; the receipts were superb and the sale went marvelously. The vogue of the ambulant Salon soon surpassed all expectations, to the point that song and caricature gave themselves to it wholeheartedly.

In brief, the painters came back to Paris with their Salon empty, and immediately returned to install themselves under their beech tree—what am I saying? under a forest of beeches—until the following year.

"That's what Art is in France, Monsieur!"

"Monsieur General Commissioner, permit me to address all my felicitations to you. But one question imposes itself, however: what about Sculpture? What has been done for Sculpture?"

"That's fair enough. Sculpture was about to travel with Painting, but when the signal for departure was given, the lack of equilibrium of the Venuses and Danaës caused a general breakage. We are seeking at present a means of avoiding the recurrence of any such disaster, and everything permits the hope that those ladies will hold together better at the next Salon.

VI

A few current observations:

What was once astonishing in France was the number of decorated individuals that one encountered at every step; one was literally walking over légionnaires and trampling them underfoot, not to mention officers of the Académie; the Mérite agricole still had that of being more hidden; as for foreign Orders, they were like bouquets of flowers—or fireworks—in the lapel of every frock-coat. People were seen in ceremonies who made cravats and lifebelts out of them. A new regime, based on rigorous equality, could not tolerate such a state of things, and at the same time as it abolished titles of nobility, the twenty-first century suppressed multicolored rosettes and ribbons.

As it was necessary nevertheless to think of recompensing splendid actions and works of all kinds, it was decided then to accord the quality of *honorable* to every citizen to be particularly distinguished. Above that flattering mark, much sought-after, which did not spoil buttonholes, there is now only the "Sèvres plaque," which crowns a well-filled career worthily, but which is very difficult to obtain.

"The Sèvres plaque," Monsieur Prudhomme would have said, "is the sword of honor of the ancient royalties."

There was once much joking with regard to the famous phrase: "The administration that all Europe envies us..." Nothing is more exact today than that sentiment, not only in Europe but the entire world, with regard to our bureaucracy; there too, it is good to add, great progress has been accomplished. But one chapter would not be sufficient to describe in detail the ameliorations that have been realized. My sensations can only be fleeting notes in this voyage by electricity—steam has had its day—so let us simply say that the inflated salaries accorded to petty bureaucrats have been the principal cause of a complete reform.

All journalists!

It is no longer a profession. Journalism has been absorbed into information, reportage into announcement or advertisement. The public, increasingly demanding, desires so much to be informed, that its members have ended up gradually, without perceiving it, informing themselves, addressing themselves to newspapers in accordance with their needs, for reportage, news, demands or advertisements. and Interviewing one another

But if journalism is dead, if the last journalist has gone to the other world to ask after the health of Monsieur de

Girardin,[12] the newspapers themselves are very much alive and their name is legion. They pullulate. There are not hundreds but thousands and tens of thousands of them, which grow underfoot, arrive via post-balloons from the four corners of the world, in every format, etc., etc. They come from Belleville as from Kamchatka!

Let us, then, put a little order into this confusion. Already, for a long time, every arrondissement has had its Universal Monitor or public Bulletin, under the direction of the delegates of the quarter, and *La Ville*, a daily of eight pages in an exceptional photogravure format, appearing in the evening at seven o'clock, is the veritable official voice of the capital, summarizing everything.

It is necessary to see Paris at the moment when everyone is unfolding that immense standard.

"Look, they're laying out the tablecloth," some wit never fails to shout.

But newspapers no longer only appear in the morning and the evening; some have three or four different editions; they also appear at night, since the brasseries and restaurants have the liberty to remain open. There are the *Nuit,* the monitor of noctambules, the *Aurora*, the organ of street-sweepers, and the *Cordon,* aimed at concierges—but with a small circulation, for concierges have been replaced almost everywhere by electric bells or letter-boxes.

Every corporation, moreover, possesses its particular bulletin, published under the direction of its syndical committee, responding to its needs and defending its interests. They include the *Mouron*, which is given away free in schools, the *Étal*, the butchers' journal, the *Lait Chaud de Paris*, the organ

---

[12] Émile de Girardin (1802-1881), the great pioneer of the popular press in France, founder of the cheap daily newspaper *La Presse*, and a renowned polemicist, who naturally went into politics and became the leader of the permitted opposition during the Second Empire.

of dairy-workers, the *Flûte*, the bulletin of bakers; the *Mont-Doré*, a specialist sheet for cheese-mongers, etc., etc.

Certainly, journalism is no longer as influential in that fashion, but it is within the range of everyone; it will no longer aid in making a revolution, but it has nothing more to do in that regard, and the petty sheets I have cited at random certainly serve private interests, and even more, for wrapping merchandise.

Other, more important publications, respond to general needs: there are the *Reveil-Matin*, the *Précurseur*, the *Petit Resumé*, the *Vingtième Siècle*, the *Franc-Parler*, the *Tantôt*, etc...

In the midst of that deluge of print, in that enormous number of various rags, my choice was borne immediately toward the *Inutile*—the newspaper of tomorrow—with this inscription in its editorial: "The need for a new newspaper not being felt, we have hastened to found this one."

The news in the *Inutile* is nevertheless in accord with its title; it is the accumulation of everything that is utterly indifferent to the public, published by all the newspapers in the world. I assure you that the organ in question is well-filled. As for the qualification, "newspaper of tomorrow," there is nothing astonishing about that, for the majority of dailies adopted it a long time ago. It is from the excess of information that tomorrow's news is born.

The liberty of the press and the ever-increasing number of newspapers has, therefore, transformed the nature of journalism and, in making the profession of journalism disappear, has made it the profession of everyone; the chapter of indiscretions has gained in particular.

As for the direction of newspapers, which can no longer be individual property today—no fortune would suffice—it depends uniquely on associations.

It is insurance companies, the importance of which has increased considerably in the midst of increases in capital, that have taken the direction of the most authorized newspapers, in making them serve their interests better.

Insurance in fact, took a great step forward on the day its price, much reduced, was included in another obligatory expense, such as rent, railway tickets, etc., etc. The various insurance companies, fusing into a great General Society, were able to insure tenants as well as travelers, without the slightest supplement in the price of the rent or the journey, and, by the same token, make the insured as many subscribers to the various newspapers they controlled—hence the enormous importance obtained in such a short time by insurance policies. Their domain has increased further, the State having authorized the General Society to take charge of recruitment and maintenance of corps of fire-fighters.

The result is marvelous, and everything progress today with assurance!

VII

"Some romance, if you please!"

What, in this rapid voyage , after having hastened to see everything, in order to describe everything, in broad outlines, I have not said a single word about women, thus allowing it to be thought that women no longer exist, and do not count in the twenty-first century!

No women in this marvelous century? Do not be deceived.

But then, murmurs a charming voice in my ear, how is it that you, Anacharsis, a descendant of Adonis and Antinous, have not encountered any petty romance? Not the slightest adventure, damn it!

It's true; I have not yet mentioned women, although they have been, since my first step, the objects of my attention and my curiosity; but perhaps I had a reason for that; I was not sure that they are so enormously similar to what they once were.

Let us understand one another; there are the same assemblages of brighter, silkier fabrics, more scintillating than ever, with, here and there, a few diamonds and precious stones that heighten them further, and diaphanous complexions and costly cosmetics, under an envelope as rich and perfumed as they might be, but does the heart of Chloë, Marion and Virginie still beat in the same manner, I wondered? Is Amour, in this materialistic century, still the same; given the progress accomplished, is it not the case that certain...ameliorations have been brought to it, or at least attempted? In brief, has Amour not had difficulty in remaining the natural sentiment of Adam for Eve, after the apple?

Gods, what if Amour had become artificial?

I saw in woman therefore, as in everything gravitating around her, the ultimate expression of an advanced civilization, a new conception of education and mores, such that anxiety began to take possession of my mind and a poignant doubt suddenly seized me.

Certainly, she is no longer the *précieuse* that Molière criticized, although she is more scholarly than ever; however, while remaining the companion of man, she has also declared herself his equal, and has claimed numerous rights. While man, in fact, drew her to repopulation, while giving herself to physical exercise, woman, by dint of patience and activity, with an incomparable science and prescience, thanks to unaided will, slowly increased the circle of her empire, preparing slowly for her own evolution.

And gradually it has been possible to see woman taking possession of all professions, sliding into all employments, and attaining all positions. The commerce of luxury—clothing and jewelry, lingerie and fashion—of which she had understandably taken possession at the outset, seemingly having been created for her, was soon no longer sufficient; she needed enterprises to negotiate, bargains to conclude, in sum, the realm of business. Then she entered, superbly, into the realm of numbers, leapt over the counter, and, as before and as everywhere, with a perfect method and an astonishing surety, she succeeded marvelously.

Today, woman triumphs all along the line; she reigns over the Arts as over the Sciences; she writes, she paints, she engraves, she sculpts, she sings, she composes—just as she rides horses, drives carriages, plays the stock market, handles capital, signs treaties, treats diseases and pleads in court.

Does she not still dream of casting the vote and taking her place in the chair of State, as she already has that of Mid-Lent? And with that, I thought to myself: *Damn! Amour seems to me to be in peril in that turbulence. In what place here can Amour lodge? Ahoy, Cupid!*

And I went to look for him in all societies: among the "occupied," who are the socialites of today, thus named because they are always visiting and can only receive in the homes of others, the homes of the "inclined," who are the beautiful youth of old, with a lorgnon, style and conversation as well. A pity—they were so adorable when they were bewildered!

Finally, in despair of the cause, I addressed myself to God and the Devil; it was the Devil who replied.

As, of old, the Lame Devil led Don Cleophas by night over the roofs of Madrid to show him, through partitions of glass—if Lesage can be believed—what was happening in the homes of the inhabitants, a very similar stratagem succeeded for me...

Thus, the reader can be reassured with regard to an old formula; the twenty-first century has not affected Amour! Truly, I was wrong to be alarmed. Amour is of all centuries and all lands, immutable and eternal, without progress being able to attain him. Any metamorphosis is possible, but Cupid's arrows will never be taken away.

After that, and as nothing more remained for me to see, that same evening my preparations for departure completed, I took my place in the Orient Express Balloon, which set me down a few hours later in Athens, my fatherland, without my escapade having been perceived in the necropolis.

Gabriel Tarde (1843-1894) was a criminologist and social psychologist, an early proponent of the idea that crowds sometimes manifest a kind of "group mind" because of an innate human tendency of imitative behavior. His Fragment d'histoire future *(1896; tr. as Underground Man) was a more elaborate exercise of the same kind as the present story, but less farcical in its satire.* "The Bald Giants*" was originally published in* La Revue Bleue, *novembre 1892)*

Gabriel Tarde: *The Bald Giants*

It was in the year of grace 1992. One can trace back to that precise date the initial seed of the most marvelous revolution that has regenerated our species. On a fine day at the end of April, an illustrious philanthropic agronomist, animal-breeder and reformer named Samuel Zède was walking in a seigneurial park in the south of France.

France was then employing the unexpected leisure of a long peace fruitfully, compensating itself with luxury for a few petty civil wars; divided into a dozen universal republics, it had returned, in the name of communal liberty, to feudal vexations. But the French, ever intelligent, were rejoicing in being avenged by the great Czar Nicolas V or VI, who, after having taken Berlin by assault and vassalized the Empire of Germany, had extended his domination all the way to the banks of the Rhine.

More careful of our true interests, Samuel was meditating while walking on that Muscovite deluge. He was paying scant attention to the songs of the birds, the purity of the air and the sky, and the limpidity of a beautiful river that was passing the foot of the château, carrying large ships in its course escorted by a file of small boats—for the gradual destruction of the railways, the result of territorial fragmentation, had rendered river navigation its former prosperity.

Our doctor was not very poetic, although a dreamer to the highest degree, and even rather chimerical. That day, however, he seemed more struck than usual by the beauty of nature. He had just taken his habitual turn around his poultry-yard, his barn and his bed of rare flowers. He had cast a gaze of paternal admiration at his beautiful cattle, so fat that they were stifling, at his racehorses, as thin and spare as the horse of the Apocalypse, at his magnificent pigs, so buried in their paunches that only their little spiral tails served to make them recognizable. He had also darted a glance at the aviary, where the most beautiful hybrids in the world were putting on flesh, and on his kennel, where running dogs with ears so long that the made a noise like Spanish castanets while shaking off their fleas were howling from time to time. Finally, his tulips, his double roses and his extravagant dahlias, all sparkling with the foam of sap and life poured out in iridescent cascades by his flower-beds, had obtained a smile of satisfaction from him.

But having seen that, he became thoughtful again and wandered into the forest. When he arrived in a clearing he stopped next to an eglantine. Before him opened one of the pretty flowers, so simple, of the thorny bush; a pure corolla with five petals, scarcely pink and, in the language of the poet "as pale as a cheek of which amour has drunk the colors," timidly offered him its light cup, as the sky often presents to the most unfortunate along the path of life. For the first time, the learned dreamer appeared to remark that uncomplicated beauty; comparing it to his double roses, he reflected profoundly, and from one idea to another, from one comparison to another, I shall tell you the route that his thought followed.

"Such, then," he said to himself, "is the original theme of all the variations of horticulture; this rose, so pale and virginal, is the mother of all our opulent and provocative roses. When I compare it with those roses that I was observing just now, however, what a contrast! All trace of parentage has disappeared. There is a world, an infinity, between them. And now, if I draw another parallel, if I compare myself, a literate scientist, to that ignorant rustic peasant with whom I was chatting before coming here, let us be frank, is the interval between him and me equal to that between the two flowers, one of which is cultivated and the other is not? Immensely less, surely. The stamens of the simple flower have been transformed into petals in the double flower, but that is a prodigy; it is as if the arms of the peasant were transformed into a pair of cherub's wings attached to my flanks!

"Now, there is no doubt about it, I cannot fly, and I have reason to think that, save for a few differences to his advantage, that natural man is conformed like me, a son of culture. If he is doubtless more envious than me, and I am perhaps a little more egotistical than him, in spite of my philanthropy, that comes from what I possess and what he would like to possess; and that is of no consequence. He believes in witches and I have believed in turning tables. His agriculture is a little more backward than mine, but in compensation, it is much less ruinous. In sum, the two of us are very nearly equivalent. The power of education thus has a much more restricted effect on us than on other beings, and the transformations that humans can operate on themselves are nothing compare with those they operate around them.

"But let us go further. That wild duck I can see over there differs strangely from the ducks in our poultry-yards, its relatives. It differs more than I differ from the peasant in question. On the other hand, it differs less than the eglantine I have before my eyes differs from the double rose in my flower bed. In pursuing these juxtapositions I believe that one can easily arrive a formulating a law: the more distant a living being is from humans—the duck is doubtless less distant than the rose—the more radically humans can transform it; from which it follows that, of all living beings, human are the most difficult to transform.

"Nevertheless, it need not be thus. And that law is only a warning addressed to our revolutionaries. Who could help laughing, in fact, on confronting their pretentions and their bombast with their results? Would one not think that they had already endowed us with Considerant's additional eye because they have substituted their personalities for other nullities on the governmental seats?[13] There is no advocate's secretary, restored by a revolutionary stroke of his employer, who does not believe in good faith that his homeland has been regenerated, in sensing himself slightly remade. With all that, we still walk on our two legs, with gout, and all our successive regenerations, which are represented to us as transfusions of blood, have never been, in essence, anything but effusions, alas.

"The truer revolutionaries are those who have invented the trowel, the mill, the printing press, the telescope and the locomotive; they have introduced into our existence and our condition, if not into our nature, a few rather notable and considerably exaggerated changes. And again, what is that—iron knives instead of flint scrapers, locomotives instead of diligences—when I think of the stamens of my eglantine becoming petals in a double flower? If one calls those industrial modifications progress, the passage from one world to another, the gradual divinization of humankind, how can one qualify the vegetal revolution in question?

I consent that people swoon before the cabalistic figure of 1789 and think of everything that preceded it as antediluvian, but tell me what is paleontological in the skulls of my ancestors, and how the transformism of our scientists applies to that somewhat overrated revolution? Revolution is a pretentious word applied to changes in the shirt of the human species. They are like more-or-less useful baths, sometimes baths of Pelias,[14] but more often Turkish baths accompanied by vig-

---

[13] Victor Prosper Considerant (1808-1893) was a utopian socialist and ardent follower of Charles Fourier, whose own writings echoed many of Fourier's extravagant futuristic speculations.

[14] In Greek myth, King Pelias, who sent Jason to search for the Golden Fleece, was invited by his daughters to step into a cauldron, which they had been tricked by Medea into believing capable of rejuvenating him; instead, he was boiled alive.

orous massages; apart from scratches, the skin does not change, or hardly changes, at all.

On the day when humans were derived from apes, if one admits the thing, there was truly a revolution worthy of the name; but since then there have only been pastiches. When one thinks of the timidity of our radicals, one is amazed. Moses teaches the Hebrews circumcision, Mohammed teaches the Arabs ablutions, Lycurgus teaches the Spartans to eat gruel—and they are the most radical reforms. The principal human evolutions have certainly been operated in costumes, and from the thigh-guard to trousers there is undoubtedly a much greater distance than from Barbarossa to Emperor Wilhelm, may God have his soul. One wonders why shirt-makers, hatters and tailors have never been called to play a political role.

"It is evident that, in spite of all those abortive attempts, human nature is a raw material that no one has yet been able to manufacture. We have made the tour of it; it has been attacked indirectly by education—the boldest and the greatest have proceeded in that fashion—or simply by a modification of the political, alimentary or intellectual regime, but who has taken the bull resolutely by the horns? Who has treated human stupidity, human imbecility, our incurable wound, a one treats a fever with quinine—which is to say, directly and by means of its specific? No one, I repeat, no one...

"With the result that the brain—that flower of our souls, that delicate corolla, of which our skull is the thick calyx and our vertebral column the gross stem—still awaits its horticulture! Lycurgus purified the race, but in a roundabout manner, by means of an artificial Darwinian selection of the most handsome children. Gall—a precursor, that one!—has envisaged the problem but he has not solved it;[15] he has divided up the brain into plots like a kitchen garden, but apart from the fact that there is much to retouch in his mosaic, is he preoccu-

---

[15] Franz Josef Gall (1758-1828), the popularizer of the pseudoscience of phrenology, which expanded the physiognomic studies of Johann Lavater (1741-1801).

pied with the essential point, knowing how to cultivate each of those plots, with the means of developing artificially the bumps that he has discovered? Do you think so? He would not have dared, even if he had been able to do it! And there have been poets scandalized by the boldness of the *audax japeti genus*![16] What! All scholars have found it very simple for a long time to admit that the skull is the result of the suture of a few vertebrae, but we despair of being able to inflate certain parts of that organ slightly? When will we occupy ourselves with searching for the key to that strong-box of our thoughts and our souls?

"A prodigious thing! A miserable insect, a cynips,[17] which has not made the anatomy of an oak-leaf or the stem of an eglantine—I see a justice in this—has only to bite that leaf or that stem and secrete a little liquid thereinto, and in a few days it swells, swells visibly, become enormous, I nearly said hydropic. And we, who have dissected the brain, who can even fabricate mechanical brains, have not yet distilled in our laboratories the precious liquid that, poured into one of the bumps of the skull, would lend it a sudden tumefaction, accompanied by an extraordinary development of the corresponding mental faculty

"I am mistaken; we have found something approaching it: coffee; but its effect is nether localized nor durable. Is it not good that it gives us a legitimate hope of finding something better?

"Well, if it is thus, what do my barns and my poultry-yards matter, my kennels and my hothouse; ought I not to blush at knowing how to swell the shoulders of my cattle and the bellies of my boars, and lengthen the ears of my dogs, if I

---

[16] Literally, "the audacious children of Japhet," but the phrase was used by Jean de La Fontaine as a poetic description of the human race and caught on as a conventional way of referring to an anonymous crowd.

[17] *Cynips quercusfolii*, the gall wasp.

am impotent to develop by half a centimeter the least of the cranial protuberances of one of my children?

"Will I be told that the long centuries that have gone by without any cerebral transformation are an obstacle to a sudden regeneration of the human brain? But that is nothing. Analogy responds to the contrary. For millions of years, the primrose of China remained simple until the day when, in the last century, a gardener had the whim to double it and vary it, and in a few years it was no longer recognizable. There is many a family of farmers who, since the Roman Empire, transmitted its ignorance and inveterate rusticity from father to son; put the child in college today, educate him appropriately, and he will metamorphose into a petty clerk without the slightest difficulty, into a scribe or a clubman, and handle words or a pen as well as his father handled the plow.

"Oh, if I could! O Gall, Lavater, Fourier and all, might I merit being your pupil! And you, little flower, can you have suggested to me the great idea, without comparison, of this century and all centuries!"

From the day when he made the preceding reflections on the social problem, Doctor Samuel neglected agronomy entirely. Buried in absolute retreat, in the midst of a collection of skulls of every sort—which he enriched incessantly, like Bernard Palissy[18] in the midst of his enamels—he delivered himself day and night to experiments on living animals, including dogs, cats and monkeys. An obsession hallucinated him. He departed from the ancient observation that the skull of newborns is soft, flexible and easily malleable, so he experimented on mammals, the heads of which he reshaped.

In addition, he had composed certain drugs, as tonic as coffee but much more specialized in their effects, the action of which he combined with that of metallic molds, which served

---

[18] The sixteenth-century Huguenot engineer and craftsman Bernard Palissy, who spent many years attempting to imitate Chinese porcelain.

his experimental subjects as coiffures. I shall not go into the details of his procedures, which have, in any case, been lost, like the secret of Greek fire.

What is certain is that hazard served him marvelously and that he obtained from the outset, extraordinary results. A monkey molded and drugged by him became intelligent enough to take the place of his valet de chambre, even combining with his qualities a penchant for the drunkenness of which he died. Two of his dogs learned to read, and a third, having escaped, was taken for the devil in person by the local inhabitants, who fled the château like an inferno.

Encouraged by the success of his first operations, the great philanthropist resolved to consummate his work. He was heard pronouncing strange words. His ill humor against pseudo-revolutionaries increased by the day. "Our forefathers were irrational," he often said. "Their politics consisted of cutting off the heads that inconvenienced them. That was cutting down the tree to reach the fruit of concord. The politics of the future will consist of making heads, of grafting heads. The best means to reach an understanding is to manipulate brains; it will suffice to pinch the interior mechanism, and the sovereign will think whatever you wish. That is what can be called a new era."

In fact, in that era the doctor became a father, and the father of a sturdy son who looked at him so stupidly, wept so foolishly and suckled so awkwardly during the first hour of his existence that he was judged idiotic unanimously by the entire chorus of midwives and nurses. Samuel seemed delighted with those marks of stupidity, which would put all the more in relief the efficacy of his discoveries. Immediately, notwithstanding the opposition of his wife, who fortunately died of the consequences of childbirth, he set forth on the work of mental transfiguration. His first concern was to enclose the nursling's head in a hemispherical steel mold of military appearance. A new-born thus coiffed in a helmet, in which he slept, suckled, etc., giving him a rather amusing military appearance, had not been seen before. It seemed at first to be a mockery addressed to certain braided and deep-rooted kepis of the local national guard, so no one suspected what that martial coiffure was nurturing.

Isaac—that was Samuel's son—owed to that initial education being bald all his life, bald-born, in a sense. He also retained a few stomach upsets. On the other hand, he grew on his forehead two mound-like eminences, which swelled with age, gradually tattooing it with interlaced furrows and hieroglyphics.

At the age of two, his father judged that the helmet could be removed. "I am," he said "only the spur of nature; now that she is on the right path, let us allow her to do her work." He was not to repent of it.

I shall not recount the successive prodigies achieved by young Isaac to begin with; it was not his least merit to rectify the opinion of his nurse regarding his faculties, and later to stupefy his teachers and comrades. Suffice it to say that, endowed with two admirable bumps, that of calculation and that of play, he became the greatest calculator and the greatest gambler—which is to say, the greatest capitalist—the word has ever seen. At ten years of age he laid siege to his college and obliged his headmaster to capitulate. At eighteen he commanded a corps of sharpshooters and found the means, with his volunteers, to accomplish exploits—notably reconquering Algeria and Senegal, lost more than fifty years before after an Arab and negro revolt—to the benefit of our civilization.

At twenty, the twelve or fifteen universal republics of France having succeeded in agreeing (once is not custom) to declare simultaneous war on England, which then threatened us, he was nominated by acclamation generalissimo of our armies on land and sea. One cannot imagine the ideas he had in that immortal campaign. He put Caesar and Napoléon definitively into oubliettes. He took up the Napoleonic project of an invasion of England, but with what engines!—not with a fleet of nutshells but with an immense squadron of improved submarine torpedo-boats. Every torpedo contained a battalion and a month's food-supplies; it was equipped with a rubber tube, the extremity of which floated invisibly on the surface of the sea, where it drew the air necessary for respiration. The torpedo-flagship was linked to all the others by an ingenious system of telephones.

Imagine the stupor of the English when, that terrible army having traversed the Channel and sailed up the Thames, they saw rising from the water in the port of London myriads of little crystal edifices, which reminded them of their ancient exhibitions, At the same moment, in fact, at a signal from the admiral, all the soldiers had given the river bed a vigorous kick and had returned to the surface. Clinging to the flanks of the vessels that filled the port, climbing up and capturing the entire fleet, was the affair of a moment. Before the end of the day, the capital of the British Isles was in our hands, and England capitulated. There was not a lady in the realm who did not moan henceforth about the decadence of English mores and the forgetfulness of good manners, the unique cause of the great reverse.

In the meantime, the Czar, aided by his vassal the Emperor of Germany, took advantage of our invasion of England to invade us: a grave imprudence, which permitted General Isaac to give his full measure. Within two months, by virtue of the cares of that artificial Moltke, incomparably superior to the other, neither Prussia, nor Germany, nor Russia existed any longer. He had invented a species of telegraphic artillery, the details of which escapes me, by means of which, tranquilly sitting in an office armchair in the telegraph office in Paris, he was able to bombard Berlin and Saint Petersburg at the same time. Informed by molded swallows, which served as scouts, of all the movements of the enemy, and endowed in addition with a prodigious strategic skill, he captured two million prisoners and such a great quantity of cannons that a pyramid of steel was built subsequently on the bank of the Seine.

Needless to say, Doctor Samuel had kept his secret hermetically. He had only confided it to his son. The entire world admired the prodigies of that genius fabricated by the human hand, and no one suspected the methods of fabrication. The complete baldness of Isaac had been noticed, but only as one analogy more with Caesar; and that was not, let it be said in passing, one of the least reasons, aided by his ugliness, why it was so difficult for him to combine with his triumphs other more gracious conquests.

Isaac loved women with the passionate and unfortunate amour of spoiled children for the stars and cyclopes for Galateas. However, he found a Delilah, alas, and it was his undoing; for she was paid by Nicolas V or VI, and was only too well able to fulfill her mission. The Czar, then a refugee in Constantinople, had expedited her from Circassia, once the seed-nursery of sultans. She descended from the mistress of Mohamed whom the dying prophet begged to stand upright before him in a state of maximum undress, and to fill his eyes with ecstasy before closing them.

As soon as he saw her, the conqueror forgot absolutely the map of the world, the marvels of genius and the prodigies of heroism, the death he had confronted, the fortune he had made, and the awakening after the victory; all of that no longer appeared to him as anything but an inverted shadow of human happiness, at the aspect of that miracle of beauty. He was subjugated in his turn, submerged beneath the waves of that blonde hair. She was blonde with dark eyes, the perfidious woman. On the faith of those great dark eyes radiant with ebony lashes, what human mistrust would not have gone to sleep, like the mistrust of a pilot on the faith of the stars in the sky?

So, as she was caressing her illustrious lover's prominences one day, not without suppressing a slight smile, she asked him where his strength came from.

"You're holding the key to it," he replied, enigmatically, and not resisting her insidious persuasions supported by sweet promises, he told her that, unlike Samson, he owed his power in part, to his baldness; and finally, he confessed everything to her; he explained the geography of the brain, the form of the

65

molds and the recipe for the drugs. She was stupefied, but did not forget anything.

She was careful, as one might imagine, not to inform Nicolas alone of the confidence she had received. She instructed secretly, by turns, unknown to one another, the kings and emperors, dethroned or not, and the presidents of all the republics of Europe. Each of them paid very dear for the virginity of her secret.

Experiments were attempted everywhere, and they succeeded everywhere. So in every city and every village, before long, a patented molder was established, whose design often brought improvements to the initial discovery. A few States decreed molding free and obligatory; others left it facultative. All, however, abandoned to the father of a family the choice of the bump that he preferred for his children, provided that it was not the bump of criminality and murder, but that of industry, eloquence, music, painting, mathematics, physics, etc.

Sixteen years after these measures, the entry to all careers was closed to those who could not produce, along with a certificate of vaccination, their diploma of molding in some category or other: commerce, music, eloquence, etc. It is notable that, the operation never having succeeded with women, it was necessary to renounce it in their regard

Each of the States possessing the secret was considerable disappointed when it perceived that neighboring principalities or republics were similarly populated by men of genius. However, there was no lack of publicists to point out the advantages of the new state of things.

"Henceforth," said one of them, "Babeuf's dream is realized and we are founding a true republic of equals.[19] The equality of all is the superiority of all. When there are no long-

---

[19] François-Noël Babeuf (1760-1797), alias Gracchus Babeuf, was a political agitator of the Revolutionary era, considered too radical by the Directoire and guillotined after allegedly plotting its overthrow, and is nowadays regarded as an important precursor of Communism and Anarchism.

er any but eminent men in the world, universal suffrage will cease to be an absurdity. For it is necessary to recognize that our forefathers were scraping the bottom of the barrel when they gave the same weight to the vote of a rag-picker as to that of Thiers,[20] however backward the latter appears to us now."

"Sun, sun, veil your face!" cried another, one of those bulged with lyricism. "Eclipse yourself before the splendor of fraternal genius! We are all kings, we are all gods. It is not merely pantheism but panarchy. O Prometheus, where are your chains? Rejoice, you are victorious!"

These hymns were nevertheless a trifle premature, and a few slight inconveniences began to make themselves felt: to begin with, the exaggerated influence of the molder in each commune. It did not take long to excite the legitimate jealousy of the schoolteacher, the maire and the barber. How could a man be contradicted who could not only make up his own mind but those of others?

In the second place, genius having become as common as badges of rank, was considerably diminished in value. In addition, the choice of fathers of families did not go beyond five or six privileged bumps, which soon formed plagues of Egypt. For instance, many chose the bump of the bar, but not one the bump of quibbling, so there was a swarm of advocates and no litigators.

But the principal cause of conflict was the essential distinction that was established between the States that had decreed the obligation of molding and those that had tolerated the admixture in the ranks of society of natural heads. The latter possessed an enormous advantage over the others; the inferior population of raw brains worked the fields, swept the streets, did the cooking and maintained the literary, scientific

---

[20] Adolphe Thiers (1797-1877), the first president of the Third Republic, who failed dismally to follow through on the radical ideas of his youth, and was widely regarded as a turncoat after his brutal treatment of the Communards of 1870-71 and their successors.

and autistic leisure of the manufactured brains. By contrast, people were dying of hunger in countries that were entirely decretinized, no molded man ever consenting to work the land, and the number of monkeys that they had thought of molding for domestic chores being insufficient.

That was not all; for reasons that will be divined in due course, the women of all countries showed a marked inclination for the hairy and un-retouched apes who still persisted in usurping the title of human beings, while the reviewed and corrected exemplars of humanity had difficulty obtaining their favors. Thus, an irresistible female emigration was produced toward the cretinist States—which is to say, those in which men could still be found stupid and vulgar enough to have been an Academician of the eighteenth and nineteenth centuries.

The jealousy of the entirely progressist States dared not show itself nakedly. Cleverly, it took on a philanthropic color, which scarcely fooled anyone. It formed a protective society for cretins, destined to their amelioration and to rid them of their outmoded hair, which gave them headaches. Congregations were also established for the diffusion of molds and the conversion of gentiles.

Eventually, war broke out and arms were taken up. What a war! And what further progress was accomplished in the military arts! Let us skip over the details; it is sufficient to know that the cretinist States were defeated and that the progressist States, far from abusing their victory, were content to impose humanely the desire to emancipate all their inferior brethren without delay, by means of molding applied to all heads of all ages. There was no objection to raise against that charitable goal, except that, the youthful flexibility of skulls being the essential condition of success, the majority of those undergoing the operations died within a week and the others within a year—which caused the philanthropists to shed many tears.

"What is the point of so much lamentation?" objected an excessively frank Darwinist. "It is the mission of superior races to absorb the inferior. Since we're rid of those inept rivals, it only remains for us to subject Asia, Africa, Oceania and America to the same fate, as the world belongs to the strongest, and strength to intelligence.."

As soon as it was said it was done; progressist Europe invaded the other four continents of the world and exterminated everything that did not resemble it.

Then the poets had a right to celebrate the rediscovered Eden. There were no longer more than a few million men in the world, but they were men of genius, served by a few billion improved monkeys. Those men, occupied in painting, making music, speeches or verses, embroidering metaphysical systems and epic poems that relegated Homer and Plato to the rank of nurslings, appeared due to enjoy a perfect happiness forever.

Happiness can, in fact, be defined as genius, according to Goethe: genius is fecundity. The joyful light of the sun is joyful because it is fecund; running water is cheerful because it fertilizes. How can a man support without sadness the sight of nature, inexhaustible in its creations, if he cannot oppose a comparable force to it, an equally creative imagination? Such is the man of genius: he struggles with nature, reflects it and tames it; he pushes it back into the shadows by means of the splendor of the very images and inspirations that he borrows from it, a kind of extraordinary Archimedes who, with the flames of his ardent mirrors, eclipses the sun from which they emanate.

The misfortune was, in past ages, that the great man, always alone, raised like a palm tree in the desert or the isle of Saint Helena in the middle of the ocean, had only spoken to his brethren through death and the centuries that separated him from them, like cocks responding to one another at a distance by moonlight. But in these better times, melancholy ceased to be the indelible shadow of grandeur, and nowhere was any longer heard the sublime plaint of Moses: "Lord, you have made me powerful and solitary; let me sleep profoundly in the earth."

Genius, in brief, was everywhere, and genius was happy.

And yet, as I have already said, the end of the world—by which I mean the end of humankind—stemmed from that. That felicity was brief.

To begin with, it was troubled by another great war, the most formidable that the sun had contemplated, which closed the mouths of the theoreticians of perpetual peace for a few years. With the cretins exterminated, all *casus belli* seemed banished forever, all the more so because, for some time, nationalities and frontiers no longer existed, and in suppressing heroism and patriotism it was believed that the temple of Janus had been definitively closed. But, the distinction of fatherlands having been abolished, and the distinction of classes consummated, the distinction of bumps remained. There was one important bump that was lacking to all the musicians, dramaturges, novelists, painters, etc., which was the bump of admiration. Everyone wanted to be admired by everyone, but no one was disposed to admire anyone else. No one found auditors, readers, or spectators—a public, in sum.

And as two even more essential bumps were also lacking, two bumps without which, in my humble opinion, social life is impossible—I mean those of Generosity and Respect (also known as Resignation)—this is the plan that our Olympians imagined. They founded international societies of the protuberants of each category. All the individuals endowed with the same bulge agreed to constrain the other protuberants to admire them.

The project was violent and the method no less so. Astonished humankind thus had the war of the bumps after those of religions, fatherlands and classes.

It was in that epoch that the wigs of the era of Louis XIV were brought back in order to disguise a baldness that was becoming perilous. The enemy was, in fact, recognized by his apparent bump, and it was as imprudent to appear with one's head uncovered in certain companies as it had once been to show oneself in a black frock-coat at certain public meetings.

The wig, therefore, became a shield, but means were always found to evade that defensive weapon. One passed a hand negligently, without seeming to be doing anything, over the cranium of one's guest, and if one discovered the hostile signal, look out! A revolver was applied to the fatal bump, and he was given the choice between admiration and death.

People fought again, therefore. The number of men having diminished considerably, auxiliary militias of orangutans were recruited. It was the first time, since the fabulous battles of the Ramayana, that our species was seen to have recourse to alliance with monkeys. Those intelligent quadrumanes were not, however, much more ridiculous than others with a saber at the side and a kepi over the ear.

In spite of the ravages inflicted by the war of the bumps, it was not the principal cause of the extinction of humankind; the parties did not take long to perceive the extreme preponderance that armed struggle gave to possessors of the bump of military art. A congress was held in Vienna; a Holy Alliance of Bumps was concluded; it was decided that admiration would be a public duty that would be successively incumbent on each party. People would take turns to admire, in the fashion of mounting guard. Everyone resigned themselves to it.

Thus, a profound peace was enjoyed for a long time. But then, a very serious flaw inherent in the cranial operation was revealed, of which Doctor Samuel of venerated memory had not thought. He had nevertheless been struck by the fact that the eglantine, the first object of his sublime meditations, had lost an important faculty in becoming a double rose: the faculty of reproducing itself. An organism has a budget of forces; one can only operate a diversion of force to the profit of one organ to the detriment of another. Alas, events proved that only too well.

I have already noted the lack of inclination that women manifested for the bald geniuses. One can commence to take account of that antipathy by the preceding general reflection. Nature has its compensations. Of men so fecund in paintings, operas and masterpieces, there was not one who was able to glorify himself in being a father, at least after the elimination of the cretin population. A woman who became pregnant was cited as a miracle; but she gave birth to a monster. That is because, when stamens change into petals, there are no longer any stamens. That should have been foreseen.

Humankind, fearfully, perceived its imminent end. After having proclaimed its immortality and divinity so loudly, it cost it dearly to admit its imminent disappearance. Everywhere, the ranks were thinning out; painters exhibited in deserted museums, preachers sermonized in empty temples; great captains only commanded a few orangutans.

Ten years went by, and no more than a few hundred men remained in the world. Ten years after that, there were no more than ten. And after a further ten years, only two remained.

Of those two, one was a very distinguished journalist. Devoured by the passion of writing, he had not discontinued sending his copy every morning, on politics, on the colonies to exploit, on reports of capital and labor, etc., to the offices of his newspaper, which still appeared, printed by monkeys and distributed to empty houses. When one is a protuberant, in fact, one no longer belongs to oneself, one belongs to one's bump. He responded to himself in another public sheet, and maintained in that fashion a courteous polemic, enameled by mutual compliments, but extremely lively and interesting.

The second of the survivors of humankind was an eminent advocate endowed with a admirable oratory protuberance, marvelously swollen and bulbous. He went to the Palais de Justice every day and, in spite of the redundancy of the role, put on his robe, his collar and his wig, and perorated for hours on end, sometime in the criminal court and sometimes in the civil court, to the great amusement of his friend the publicist, who never ran out of epigrams on that innocent mania. For his part, the advocate mocked the writer as well, sometimes comparing him to the enraged grammarian who, on the point of death, pronounced the last words: "I am going away or I am leaving, for both mean what is meant." The writer had no difficulty in replying, and as he had an excellent memory he loved to interrupt the pauses of the orator to quote him an ancient forgotten strophe of the poet Barthélemy on Monsieur de Villèle:[21]

> If the star of sinister augury
> That Arago sees on the horizon,
> With a hair of its tresses
> Changed our globe into an ember,
> Villèle, encrusted in his place,
> Would be the just man whom Horace
> Indicates so calmly in his verses;
> And scorning the errant comet,
> He would still quote the price
> Of the debris of the universe.

But the last advocate took the joke poorly, and often, carried away by habit, responded to the hack in a tone of offended dignity: "Posterity will judge us...," or "History will say...,"—which made his opponent laugh loudly.

The journalist died first. Alone then, and liberated from an importunate satirist, his interlocutor could deploy at his ease the exorbitant self-importance that began and ended all his remarks and now filled the entire world. Having always believed himself to be destined for a great political role, he abandoned the Palais de Justice for the Palais Bourbon, where he listened to himself speak with rapt attention, and then for the Hôtel de Ville, where he convinced himself that he was presiding over a republic, which only lacked republicans. But he had a quantity of monkeys.

---

[21] The Romantic Republican Auguste Barthélemy (1796-1867) collaborated with Joseph Méry (1797-1866) in writing satirical verses, including an "Épitre à M. le Comte de Villèle," addressed to the ultra-Royalist statesman Joseph de Villèle (1773-1854).

The intoxication of such an exceptional position did not take long to deprive him of his remaining reason. He got it into his head that he could revive the dead by means of his eloquence. Thus, he had himself transported to the bank of a great river, and in a place where the bones of a large number of people were accumulated, whom a great plague had once struck simultaneously and who had not been buried for want of arms. He placed himself on a trestle, which seemed quite solid and gave the impression of a throne, but which was neither. There, upright and proud, inspired by the beauty of the location, the sight of the waters, the majesty of the ruins, and the bones that covered the ground as far as the eye could see, he made a gesture; and at that sign a great drum-roll was sounded by marmosets. Then he raised his voice and preached to the dead a mass revival, in the style of Ezekiel.

"Rise up," he said to them, "rise up, my people! I tell you to rise up. Have you not slept long enough? Do you not recognize the appeal of the drum, national guards of times past? Is it possible that one forgets in that way what one has heard so often? Rise up, I tell you, the fatherland has need of you. Rise up as you can, some with all their bones, if they can find then—that is doubtless the surest way—but the others must come too; let them replace their missing bones with pieces of wood and fragments of iron—old rifle-barrels, whatever comes to hand—articulating them as best they can. Come on, courage! Have no fear, one cannot die twice! Rise up, regenerated bones!"

The skeletons did not interrupt, but did not budge. And, more and more excited, the entrepreneur of resurrections cried: "To arms! To arms!" This time, he went completely mad. From time to time a passing flock of crows came marauding, making a great racket of which he seemed proud. Nothing resembles applause so much as cawing, Crows and monkeys, the former cawing and the latter drumming, maintained his madness. Convinced that he was being acclaimed, he paused momentarily, wiped his brow, drank a glass of sugared water, and with a frantic gesture repeated: "To arms! To arms!" And the crows cawed again, and the monkeys drummed, And he resumed again: "To arms! To arms! To arms!"

But as he was gesticulating, the worm-eaten plank on which he was standing suddenly cracked, and, precipitated from his throne into a cavity, he fell dead. By virtue of a singular good fortune, he had buried himself; the cavity was very deep.

Such was or very nearly, the death of the human race.

The museums were overflowing, the libraries were full, the cities stuffed with artistic riches of infinite value. The human habitat was intact; only the soul was missing.

But the earth did not cease to rotate, the sun to shine, the birds to sing; creation did not seem to have perceived that its king was dead. Passed thus from monarchy to republic, it rejoiced greatly, although the citizen wolves still ate, as before, the citizen sheep. Only the monkeys had gained from the event. They hastened to distribute the vacant places in the public monuments, to put on the uniforms of the dead, and they appeared to take pleasure in that macabre pantomime.

I ought, however, before finishing, to reassure my readers. The human race did not disappear irredeemably. A few cretins saved from the general massacre dared to show themselves again after the definitive death of the bald men. Being Auvergnats, they formed numerous families, and gradually, the world has been repopulated.

Alfred Capus (1857-1922) was a prolific humorist who capitalized on the reputation southerners had as tellers of tall tales. In 1914 he became editor of Le Figaro *and became a fervent patriotic polemicist.* "The Bicycle Man" *was originally published in* Les Annales politiques et littéraires, *5 mars 1893.*

Alfred Capus: *The Bicycle-Man*

There was once a fellow from Provence named Marius. Ever one knows that the region in question produces men of extraordinary strength in quantity: wrestlers and phenomena of all sorts, and it has reached the point when a human serpent who is not from the Midi has, so to speak, no chance of acquiring any situation.

Not only was Marius from such a family, which went back, father and son, for several generations, but he also showed from a very young age that he was endowed in an exceptional fashion for bodily exercises. In that era the bicycle was enjoying a fabulous vogue, and had ended up replacing all other modes of transportation almost completely. It played an integral role in the education of young men of the bourgeoisie; the lycées and colleges had professors of cycling, and the second part of the baccalaureate *es lettres* consisted of a Faculty course and examination in cycling.

Marius was given a bicycle when he reached his fifteenth year. On perceiving it, and without being given the slightest indication, Marius leapt upon the instrument, and after five minutes, none of the mysteries of the bicycle was foreign to him. His family marveled, and understood immediately that he would be one of the masters of the sport one day.

Instead of opposing his vocation, as parents are all too often accustomed to do, Marius' father allowed his son to abandon himself to his natural instincts. The child had, moreover, a rare intelligence, and while cultivating the bicycle with fervor, he did not disdain purely intellectual exercises. Between two records he learned to read and a little arithmetic, and he was not sixteen years old when he already knew how to read, write and count as if he had been doing it all his life.

The most flattering successes rewarded his elevated capacities. In 1900 he won the great Paris-to-Kamchatka race organized by the French press in honor of the end of the century. All the nations had sent representatives to that solemn proof; the English only arrived in second place, more than fifteen hundred leagues behind Marius, and that magnificent success further augmented the prestige of Provence in public opinion.

To see the young southerner mounted on his bicycle, one would have sworn that the bicycle and he were only one and the same person, and one could ask the question of whether it was Marius who guided his bicycle or the bicycle that carried Marius, so easy, ample and harmonious were their common movement.

You know the story of the famous acrobat who arrives in the family dining room one day walking on his hands. On perceiving him, his daughter murmurs: "Oh" Papa's walking with his feet in the air and his head down; he must be preoccupied." Similarly, when Marius was not on his bicycle he acquired a gauche air; he was visibly lacking something. It had even reached the point that he needed the instrument to accomplish the simplest actions of life, to go from one room of his apartment to another, or to go to table, and he only slept peacefully with his bicycle between his legs.

At the age of twenty, however, having exhausted all the joys that the bicycles of this world can procure, he was seized by melancholy. He murmured: "I'm the strongest of all known cyclists; everything that one can do with a bicycle, I've accomplished, and more. I've traveled the five continents of the world. I've emptied the cup of triumphs. What remains for me to do? Oh, humanity is very limited!"

And he uttered long sighs over the vanity of all things.

One morning, after having ruminated those sad reflections, he mounted his bicycle mechanically, and set forth into the country.

He did not take long to experience a strange sensation. He had been rolling with a vertiginous rapidity, but he no longer had any notion of effort or fatigue. It seemed to him that the bicycle entered into him, so to speak, becoming an integral part of his individuality. His hands were directing the handlebars mechanically, as if they were his own fingers; his feet and the pedals were confused to the point that he no longer knew where his flesh finished or the bicycle commenced. When his wheel collided with a sharp stone he had the same pain as if he had walked barefoot over stones.

"That's odd!" he exclaimed. He moderated his speed, stopped, and tried to dismount; but the he thought that madness had taken possession of him, or that he was the victim of some unusual nightmare. He tried to pinch his earlobe with his fingertips in order to wake up, as is the fashion in Provence, but he could not take his hands off the handlebars. He tried to take his feet off the pedals, but they remained implacably fixed. He tried to raise himself up, but his backside and the saddle of the bicycle were inseparable from one another.

Prey to the most bizarre presentiments, and tormented by an inexpressible anxiety, Marius went home and explained to his family the supernatural phenomenon of which he was the victim. His relatives made fun of him at first, assuming that it was one of the practical jokes that southerners have the habit of playing on one another.

"Get off your bicycle, idler!" cried his little brothers.

Marius had to shed abundant tears in order for anyone to consent to begin to take his adventure seriously.

"What! You're stuck to it!" said his father. "Wait, I'll get you off it, simpleton."

But whatever efforts Marius' father made, he was incapable of detaching his son from the bicycle. Then, understanding that something fantastic was happening, the entire family got down on their knees and addressed prayers to Heaven, sobbing. Then they went in quest of neighbors, who were frightened and made the sign of the cross. The rumor soon spread throughout the district, and a great crowd gathered outside the door of Marius' house.

"It's necessary to exorcise him," murmured a worthy lady, and ran to the curé of rhe parish, who came in all haste. But he threw holy water over the unfortunate Marius in vain; he and the bicycle remained intimately united.

"It's not a matter of religion," said the curé. "I advise you to fetch a doctor."

The man of science, a skeptical man who did not believe in miracles, refused at first to disturb himself for such a stupidity. "Your Marius is a joker who wants to put one over on the doctor," he declared, authoritatively, but they insisted so much that he consented to go to his house. He took his pulse, ausculated him and put his head against his chest

"Come, my lad there's nothing wrong with you," he concluded.

"There's my bicycle," moaned Marius.

"What! You want to make me believe—me!—that you can't get off it!" cried the doctor, indignantly.

"Try," said Marius, "You'll see."

The doctor shook him terribly.

"You're a hothead, an impostor! Science demonstrates that when a man has mounted a bicycle, he must necessarily be able to descend from it, and it isn't at the commencement of the twentieth century, after all the progress that we've accomplished, that you'll change the laws of mechanics.

Marius uttered lamentable groans. "But I tell you that I can't, Doctor. Don't abandon me, I beg you.

Touched by the tone of sincerity of that supreme prayer, the doctor, who was not fundamentally a bad man, examined Marius again, interrogated him about his life, and asked whether anything similar had ever happened to anyone in his family.

"I never heard mention of it," said his father.

"Then we're not in the presence of a case of atavism, and I don't understand it at all."

He prescribed a potion at random, adding: "I'll come back tomorrow, and if things are still the same, I'll summon two of my colleagues in consultation, and we'll send a report to the Académie de Médecine."

Marius, on his bicycle, did not close an eye all night. In the morning, the three doctors arrived and were extraordinarily embarrassed. They ended up declaring that Marius' case did not concern medicine and that it was necessary to summon surgeons from Paris.

Two days later, five of the most renowned masters of the art were assembled around Marius' bicycle, and their unanimous advice was that the bicycle and Marius could no longer be separated, except by means of a surgical operation that would cost the life, if not of the bicycle, at least of the man. One of them even wanted to carry out the autopsy immediately, in the interests of science. He only renounced that idea with difficulty, which was keenly combated by Marius and his family.

"You've become a bicycle-man," concluded the scholars. It had to happen some day."

"Can we live like this?" asked Marius.

A new discussion began, from which it resulted that one could live perfectly well, on condition of taking precautions and avoiding draughts.

Meanwhile, the newspapers had got hold of the affair, and Marius, interviewed more than two thousand times, became the most famous man on Earth.

Poor Marius ended up becoming accustomed to his strange situation. He even found a certain charm in it, something piquant and unexpected. He received flattering visits, countless tributes, and compliments that tickled his self-esteem. Women who had disdained him when he was a man like any other, fell in love with him, and he had the cruel joy of rejecting them in his turn. Several of them choked on their despair.

Needless to say, the most brilliant propositions were made to him by American impresarios, but he refused energetically to exhibit himself on a stage, and wanted to remain in the bosom of his family, in his native town, of which he was the pride. He also refused to stand for parliament, in spite of the certainty of being elected by his fellow citizens. No political ambition held him, and he did not even hide his disdain for public functions. On the fourteenth of July, however, he consented to be appointed as a chevalier of the Légion d'honneur.

Finally, one day, a princess as beautiful as the day passed through Provence. She went to visit Marius, like all tourists, and fell madly in love with the young man. She declared to her royal father that she would never have any other husband than him.

The king began by refusing, but, his physician having told him that his daughter would die of chagrin if she did not marry Marius, he allow himself to be persuaded. The wedding took place after the legal delay, and in a sumptuous fashion.

A year later, the princess gave birth to a son, mounted on a little bicycle of flesh and bone, as it was easy to foresee. Thus was born among humankind, at the beginning of the twentieth century, a race of bicycle-humans analogous to the centaurs of antiquity. That race was fertile in ingenious minds, and cast a little distraction into humankind.

Gustave Geffroy (1855-1926) was a journalist and art critic nominated by Edmond Goncourt's will to become one of the founding members of the Goncourt Academy. "The Immortal Man" was originally published in Le Journal, *27 novembre 1897.*

Gustave Geffroy: *The Immortal Man*

There was once—and only once—an immortal man.

Was he born in the time of the days who surrounded the cradle of a newcomer and adjudged to each little wailing being qualities and faults, virtues and vices, marvelous gifts of success and insurmountable bad luck? Was it a benevolent or malevolent fay who had endowed him thus with the impossibility of dying? Or had he found the elixir of endless life, keeping his precious secret for himself alone, living eternally among the innumerable crowd of ephemerae?

At any rate, when he arrived at the full physical strength of his individuality, there was a sudden arrest in his manner of being. At the moment when others commence their decline, he was fixed forever. He no longer changed. Not one of his functions was subject to the slightest deterioration. None of his hairs went white. His sight did not weaken. His teeth remained intact. He was not hard of hearing. His alert and vigorous body only knew good fatigue, productive of profound and peaceful slumber. At dawn he woke up buoyant, animated by a legitimate appetite. His mental labor retained its acquired ardor and regularity,

He had reached the plateau of life, after a light climb; he traveled that beautiful expanse in all directions; he saw others climb, out of breath from the ascension, and descend again— or, rather, tumble down—the rapid slope, the slope of death.

That immortal man experienced the most vivid interior joy and the most powerful hidden pride when he acquired the absolute certainty that he was not aging and probably would not die. He saw the days succeeding one another, and then the years, and then the centuries; he saw flowing before him, passing and disappearing, like rivers toward the sea, individual adventures, the destinies of peoples and the movement of races. He watched things born, develop and die. He devoted himself by turns to the ardor of action and the curiosity of the scholar. He took pleasure in preparing experiments, putting plans into action and awaiting the results. He was simultaneously a creator and an observer.

He gave himself the luxury of all existences. He wanted to know everything about humankind and its genius As he had eternal time before him and experienced like a presentiment the dread of running out of the unknown, he constrained himself to long patience and made increasingly hard apprenticeships.

Before serving the humble and deciding social action, he traveled the world, and learned all servitudes, all miseries, all mental weaknesses. As a statesman, orator and governor he had the joys of magnificent momentary successes and the disappointments of irremediable collapses. At various points he founded harmonious civilizations that were ruined by unexpected pressures from without. He became a conqueror in order to subjugate and pacify the earth, but he only experienced the desolation of having destroyed and the bleak ennui of solitude. He escaped into art, became a painter, sculptor, musician, giving himself the task of consoling humankind. He wrote admirable books, he enabled an elite to emerge, as all great artists and great writers do, and conceived the hope of changing the brain of the instinctive being by that means.

Without that glimmer, he would have become disinterested in life. While he had the thought within him that the human race was going toward the conquest of its own mentality, of consciousness, of its superiority over the material world of which it was the issue, he devoted himself again to existence, refusing to become the bitter and desperate philosopher who witnesses the perpetual recommencement of what has been and the permanent announcement of what will be. At the same time, however, he had an exact idea of the measure of time and the necessary slowness of the progress of beings. He recognized that his genius and his immortality were utterly useless to that collective work of humankind's self-creation. He observed that every generation adopted its task, presented itself with its compact and laggard army, always preceded by forerunners.

He therefore plunged back into anonymity with delight, recommenced voyages already accomplished, but not in hectic courses across the world; everywhere there was a pause, a long sojourn, the complete knowledge of a region, a language, a way of life, everywhere the joy of living for life's sake, enjoyment of all aspects, of all manifestations, sensing the muted labor of intelligence. The immortal man, thus hidden, conceived the possibility of witnessing an expansion of human consciousness, coinciding with the apogee of terrestrial force. And he felt himself invaded by the serenity of wellbeing, at the idea that he would witness the supreme blossoming in question.

It was while he was in that state of mind that he met the woman that he loved amorously. She was petite and beautiful, naïve and passionate. Her face was reminiscent of a summer rose; her dark velvet eyes had the innocent gleam and wild mystery of the eyes of gazelles. Her mind was all spontaneity and her divinatory ignorance burned within her like a flame of poetry. She told the man she loved all the secrets of joy and dolor that were within her; she incarnated for him, in her innocent person, a temporary force, a joy of being, and a moving melancholy of termination; and when her hour had come, she went away into death.

The immortal man is alone. He has tried to rediscover a creature similar to the one that disappeared, but in vain. The formation of that charming being was a unique phenomenon. It shone once, and then vanished, and would never return. The immortal man now finds that life is long, that death would be a welcome repose, and that it is necessary to flee with his memories. The entire accumulation of past centuries weighs upon him as a terrible burden, an infinite sadness. The past is no longer anything but a confused night in which the black fire of gazelle eyes burns, a formless ruin in which the regret of a voice sings

The immortal man has tried to kill himself. He collided with the inexorable refusal of death. He has retrenched himself from the world by departure; he has lived in the desert, motionless, devoid of desires, inanimate. Always, the sweet phantom has reproached him for surviving that which should have been his lifespan. He understands the extent of the torture that has been inflicted upon him: of having become a god, a fixed and immutable being among all those who are born, pass and go away. He aspires to the common fate; he would like to become a man like the others, a man who has lived, a man who has loved, a man who is dying.

With what impatience he waits for the human race to complete its destiny! What crazy hope is within him that the planet will cool, weaken and finally bear away his sad immortality into the icy abyss of oblivion.

Originally published in Le Journal, *1 janvier 1898.*

Maurice Montegut: *Days of the Future Year*

No, no, Science is not bankrupt, as some of us once claimed; Progress continues, and is affirmed—in the sense that it is aggravating, complicating and perfecting our human dolor and pushing it to paroxysms unknown to our ancestors. Why complain, then?

The present story, implausible in our epoch, will certainly be a banal reality a hundred years hence, by which little children would not be surprised. It is, therefore, around the year 2000 in which the scene occurs.

Above all, do not prejudge by what follows that our unique character, "Monsieur Lhomme," is an exception, a rare individual. Not in the least; among his contemporaries, he will count—or rather, he counts, since we have turned the clock of the centuries forward singularly—thousands of fellows; every bourgeois with a little fortune lives like him, partaking of the same joys, vibrating with the same emotions.

It is the first of January. Monsieur Lhomme is alone at home; he is no longer young; he is alone because he has seen disappear over the years, first his father and other, and then his brothers and sisters, and then his wife and children, not to mention sincere friends: all his affections. An exceptionally tender heart, he has lamented every time, wept and wanted to die. However, he has lived. Why? He has no idea.

For the first day of the year that is commencing, like everyone else whom the abuse of dreaming has rendered oversensitive, he is looking back over the days that he has lived, their joys and the suffering. Alas, it is the joys above all—the old joys, the dead joys—that draw the hottest tears from his eyes. It is our destiny that it is necessary to expiate one moment of happiness by years of increasingly bitter regrets. We all know the sadness of Monsieur Lhomme…although poignant, they are vulgar…thus far.

But wait a while; Science has made progress.

Monsieur Lhomme has just rung; a domestic appears.

"Pierre…is the Evocation Chamber ready?"

"Yes, Monsieur."

"Good. I want to be left alone there…don't let anyone come in, even if you hear me cry out."

Pierre bows silently. He knows the order. It has been the same for years, every first of January.

And now Monsieur Lhomme is in the Evocation Chamber. He is holding out his hands in an affectionate gesture, and his voice, already trembling, murmurs very quietly:

"Greetings, my beloveds!"

Is it to spirits, then, that he is addressing himself? Is it shades that he is evoking, by means of spiritualist methods? No, there is nothing supernatural here; the anticipated phenomena are in the realm of exact science, of pure mechanics, but moving nonetheless.

The room, which is very large, is obscure and baroquely furnished. In the center is a large armchair, into which the old man lets himself fall, overwhelmed by anguish. In front of him, in a large frame, a luminous white screen extends, on which nothing appears as yet. Beside him, on a table, stands a kind of metal trumpet in the form of a funnel. He applies his ear to it, presses a button…and suddenly, on the screen, images are designed, while distant voices speak beside him.

Yes, you have guessed it; it is a cinematograph or biograph, a phonograph that functions for the voluntary hallucination of the attentive old man, but so far from their first expression, so perfected, that it revives past scenes with precise gestures and true color, repeating the dead voices with a terrifying fidelity.

Who does not know the melancholy that one feels in leafing through old albums of pale photographs? What sadness there is in that review of companions of old—but imagine that, having abruptly grown to human dimensions, colored and palpitating, those phantoms agitated and started to speak with familiar voices. Then, the distraught soul would doubt life and death, the distance between the real and the unreal would seem to be abolished. Everything mingles, verity is complicated by dementia, and in the indecisive moment, times are reunited. What a provision of incessant, renewed, eternal dolors there would be in that passive apparatus, those instruments whose inert matter dares to imitate life! What a precious discovery for those who have never suffered enough! Who could deny Progress?

The first picture: Monsieur Lhomme sees a scene from his childhood depicted on the luminous screen; it is the family dining room. Here is his father, still young, and his mother, still beautiful...and here he is, but so small that the maidservant comes to install him on his chair. Friends are still around the table, and voices rise, laughing: the voices of happy people, content to respire the odors of good cooking, and to see old bottles lined up on the sideboard. Lhomme perceives, in a silence, the sound of sliding crockery, of silverware colliding with porcelain; and, over there, on the screen, his mother inviting him to eat with tender words, that he hears—and at which he weeps. Then the gestures become animated, the conversation becomes noisy, grave subjects are broached, and they talk about well-known, very important persons, whose names no longer say anything to him. And he sees the little child he was falling asleep on his chair, bored by the political talk.

The second picture: again it is a family gathering, but his father has a white beard, his mother gray hair; he is a young man, his brothers and sisters are no longer children. They are all silent in the large drawing room, as if they are waiting. The door opens; a young woman appears with her parents. Words of welcome are pronounced, but he and the young woman are looking at one another with profound eyes. She is going to be his wife.

"Oh, how pretty she was!" sobs the old man.

The third picture: they are married. She is next to an open window. And in the apparatus, her voice rises:

"Jacques, Louise! It's necessary to come in, children; it's starting to rain..."

Outside, doubtless in a garden, laughter bursts forth, and abruptly, two beautiful children come in pursuing one another; they are robust, splendid, made for life. Alas, alas, they have not lived...!

And the old man, at that vision, straightens up in his armchair, extends his arm and cried, in a sob:

"Jacques! Louise!"

There are other pictures. He sees his friends again, all disappeared; each has his story...mad, suicide, killed in a duel, perished at sea, struck down before the enemy...dead before growing old. He hears their voices, recognizes their attitudes, their gestures. Horror—some of them are singing songs; and that gaiety frightens him, he who knows how they will finish, or how they have finished...since past, present and future are mingled and confused.

He sees young women who are now old, he sees himself again, everywhere, declining gradually from one picture to the next, under the weight of misfortunes and the burden of the years. But what does that matter to him? What does his decline and his decrepitude matter? What does it matter that he was once strong and is now weak, was once handsome and is now ugly? What is frightful is to hear his children laughing, who are dead, to read the tenderness in eyes long extinct; to watch the spectacle of old embraces and to think that those arms, those hearts and those lips—O God!—are no longer anything but nothing.

With a determination to suffer, the old man passes repeatedly over the excessively faithful and poignant scenes; he fills his gaze with them, intoxicates his thought... His father, his mother, his wife, his children... Them, again, again, always... Go, live, speak, affirm yourselves, escape the tomb and reenter into life...!

But suddenly, the torture is too much. Monsieur Lhomme slides from his armchair, falls heavily to the floor, where he remains extended, motionless; and while that pale living being has the appearance of a dead one, the dead over there on the screen come and go, gesticulating, laughing, singing, with blood in their cheeks—like the living.

Originally published in Le Journal, *5 octobre 1899.*

Maurice Montegut: *Another Planet*

Yesterday evening, when I went into the laboratory of my illustrious friend, the marvelous astronomer Gallas Merrickh, I was struck, as soon as I crossed the threshold by the sadness of his face and the dejection of his attitude. I was immediately certain that an irreparable misfortune had overtaken him.

Now, I like Merrickh as much as I admire him. That old man of seventy is the most complete human being I have ever known; in spite of his science, his daily excursions into the sky, he is not disinterested in sufferings on earth; everything human moves him profoundly; unlike many others, the development of his magnificent brain has not diminished in the slightest the extensions of his generous heart; the pettiness of human beings compared with the multiplicity of stars has not made him scornful of the species—far from it.

Furthermore, I know that all of his words are serious, that he only announces a fact in full certainty, and what he affirms to me I believe blindly, even though, in general, I am not credulous.

Because of his expression and posture, I dared to interrogate him. "What has happened, Master? You have the marks of disaster in your features, and you, the omnipotent, appear desperate..."

He tried to smile, and then replied in a weary voice that I hardly recognized: "In fact, my child, I have had a profound disappointment, which has made me regret the labor of my entire life...which, however, has been very full."

I could not retain an exclamation of surprise, and also chagrin, and spilled out vague words.

"What! You regret, you! From any other person, that affirmation would seem to me to be banal and comprehensible, for few lives are worth the trouble of having been lived—but not yours! You have dared everything, you have interrogated infinite space, which has responded to you; you have tackled the most formidable problems, and you have resolved them to your satisfaction. Memorable discoveries are owed to you of which scientists are proud; you are the scientist—slightly mysterious, like a divinity—whose words make the law; you have overturned and renewed astral science, and opened immeasurable pathways through space...and you're doubting yourself?"

He shook his head, and replied: "Alas! I don't doubt; I regret, I tell you; that's all. You'll understand...and when you've understood, perhaps you'll shrug your shoulders, in spite of your respect for me, before the puerility of an astronomer's soul. But I too am made of flesh.

"Listen, then: you know that since my early youth, for fifty years, always, at the same time as other, less arduous, less complicated and more immediate work, I've pursued the dream of communicating directly with the inhabitants of the planet Mars, a planet that is not far away, comparatively speaking, and which offers real or supposed similarities to our poor Earth. I don't want to give you a lecture, I'm simply stating a fact. To that study, I've sacrificed all that human life can offer of consolations. For forty years, I've spent my days and nights studying texts and aiming telescopes, improved over time, at the object of my cult.

"Full of a profound, indisputable faith—and the faith of scientists is only comparable to the law of true priests—I forgot present time in my confidence in the future. I was certain that our destiny did not end with death, which is only an obscure transition, and is continued by evolutions in new worlds. Our first stage, after the Earth, was Mars, I thought, and I was convinced of it—and you'll see shortly how right I was.[22] And

---

[22] This story was published shortly after the publication of Camillle Flammarion's best-selling *Uranie* (1889; tr. as

I added: *On Mars I shall make up the time lost; I'll live for myself, without thinking about later.* Man proposes...

"And, in that fashion, I have never known joy; I have been the solitary man in the crowd. Although fair of face and proud enough in manner I have not known women, I have not known amour—and I'm sixty years old!"

Gallas Merrickh paused momentarily, stifling a sigh that resembled a sob; then he went on, in an ill-assured voice:

"Mars! The more I contemplated and considered that strange planet, the more serious my conviction became that transformed beings lives there, former inhabitants of our Earth, who remembered, and by virtue of the religion of the past, were interested in us. With anyone other than you, I would not use such language, for fear of being treated as a madman, but I know you and you know me. On Mars, often, strange gleams appear, which can be seen from here, like great fires of joy or advertisement, on high mountains: perhaps signals, I thought at first; signals for sure, I can respond at present.

"Having admitted that, I multiplied a hundredfold the tension of my effort toward the sister planet where our future destinies must unfold. What has happened is not explicable, any more than telepathy, magnetism and even electricity, all manifestations proximal or distant, physical or occult. Know that three days ago, I established communication, indubitably, with those former humans in a changed world. The Martians have understood me and responded to me.

"The Marians do not speak; perfect in the organism, they comprehend thought—which suppresses lies, the first progress. And it is my thought, extended and projected toward the fraternal star, that finally encountered half-way, in space, the thought of an inhabitant of Mars anxious about the Earth. That distant thought clutched the psychic tentacles launched by my being, and in that way, slid into my brain, penetrating and lu-

---

Urania), which includes an account of an astronomer's reincarnation on Mars.

minous. Once that coming and going was established, we were able to exchange ideas…the fact is accomplished…"

I have told you that what Gallas Merrickh advances is for me a prime verity, that I believe what he says, blindly. I stood up in great enthusiasm.

"Master, great master, unique master, first among masters, I'm passing from astonishment to astonishment…your discovery is sublime, you're equal to the gods. You've surpassed the Earth, suppressed Time and Space, vanquished the Mystery, diminished Infinity. No man, down here, has ever attained such summits, realized such miracles. You are the glory of the world, the greatest benefactor of humanity. Thanks to you, humans will no longer fear death; you have assured their destiny…honor to you! But how is it that after this prodigious, supernatural result, you remain morose, prey to sadness and discouragement"

The old man let his bald forehead fall into his fleshless hands with a dull plaint, and continued his astonishing confidence, his dolorous confession.

"Child! The Martians are superior humans. They have conserved none of our weakness, our errors. But at what cost! They are not born in their new world; no, they continue there; they put on their ancient form there, purified of vile or damnable organs…

"No birth—you seize the implication—hence, no amour. Not even sex. All similar, purified in their flesh, refined in their soul; the law is logical, for to suppress amour is also to suppress lust debauchery, envy, jealousy and hatred, the most ferocious passions by which humans are labored. Woman is assuredly, among us, the greatest engine of discord, the principal cause of our hostilities. For one noble goal that amour proposes, how many crimes does it generate every day? What part does thought, in spite of the false rhetoric of poets, have in amour? Very small, in truth. Amour is uniquely the work of the flesh. Civilizations have travestied, prettified or uglified it, but, in spite of formulae as glosses, it remains what it is— which is to say, the impulsion of an animal instinct, the brutal certainty of the conception, the creation and the safeguard of races, for the continuation of the wretched species. And that is why, in the superior planet, amour no longer exists, any more than reproduction. Up above, there are only sages, the mind dominates, the body is nothing but an appearance necessary to individuality."

Gallas Merrickh paused again I took advantage of that to say: "Well, Master, what is unfortunate about that? You've said yourself that there is more to criticize than to praise in amour and woman. All our furies, or at least the majority, are born of that bestial need. So much the better if it doesn't survive the Earth, if it's the guarantee of a purified existence; for my part, I adhere to it with joy."

The old scientist stood up, his knees tremulous. And now, in a quivering voice, he cried, crushing me:

"Idiot! Uncomprehending idiot! But for me, I've been robbed! I've sacrificed my terrestrial life to bitter science, with the mental restriction that I'd be compensated, and largely, later and higher. I've placed my repose and my felicity in the future. Oh, you hold the pleasures of the Earth cheap, you who are saturated with them to the point of disgust, of scorn. But what about me? Amour is perverse, women are perverse, it's true—I concede that. But amour is sweet, and also vivifying. Women are also radiant; I only know them from afar, those damned magiciennes, but enough to know that their eyes are like my dear stars; that their mouths are the flowers of a perfumed Eden; that their supple and fresh arms hold the secret of embraces, and their white and delicate hands the mystery of caresses. I have savored none of those sensualities! And I have learned that henceforth, I can no longer count on them! I'm seventy years old; everything is irreparable. Yes, thrice yes!

"I would exchange my science for the youth of a drudge, the discovery of the inhabitants of Mars for the murmur of an ardent mistress on a beautiful summer night. What has sagacity made of me? I have not lived...and in any case, sagacity is knowing how to savor one's share of intimate joy in the succession of existences, the duration of the moment, through the worlds traveled. I have missed my happiness on Earth; I have allowed my sap to dry up in my sterile branches. My passage down here will only have been dupery, deception, monstrosity! And that is why I'm weeping before you, weeping in the regret of my virginity; why I'm striking my breast, confessing that I have marched outside the true path, a stupid creature, hallucinated by pride, forgetting his true ends and sole reason for being. I haven't been a man, but a phantom; I haven't loved!"

And that marvelous scientist, who had just discovered a world, wept, with great sobs, having passed over the Earth ignorant of the kiss.

Edmond Haraucourt (1856-1941) was a poet and novelist of some distinction, although he made his living for much of his life as a museum curator. Black Coat Press has published a collection of his speculative fiction, Illusions of Immortality *(2012)[23], and the episodic novels* Dieudonat *(1906; tr. 2018)[24] and* Daâh the First Human *(1914 as* Daâh, le premier homme; *tr. 2014)[25].* "The Two Augurs" *was originally published in* Le Journal, *13 January 1900.*

Edmond Haraucourt: *The Two Augurs*

Draped in white togas, their heads wrapped in veils of plush linen, arms naked and feet shod in sandals of woven rope, two men, fresh-faced and rosy-cheeked encountered one another on the edge of the swimming bath, and smiled. Both had clean-shaven faces, and their blissful bellies extended before them with satisfaction. The taller one had sea blue eyes that could see into the distance; the other had small dark sharp eyes, which saw into the depths.

The two men, draped in whiteness, after having looked at one another for a moment, burst out laughing.

"Friend, is that really you?"

"You haven't changed."

"In twenty centuries!"

"You were seen for the last time at the ford of the Capitol."

"You were descending the Sacred Way."

"I find you again in the Rue des Mathurins."

"We went to the Thermes together."

"We saw the Hammam together."

---

[23] ISBN 978-1-61227-075-3.

[24] ISBN 978-1-61227-777-6.

[25] ISBN 978-1-61227-355-6.

"I love this place of peace and meditation, with its beds of repose, and the sound of the singing fountain, to remind me of the antique age."

"The bath makes the flesh supple, and one limps less."

They talked, and then lay down on the low beds, while a cubicular slave enveloped their feet in dry cloths and a Syrian negro disposed agreeable beverages before them.

"Do you still exercise sacerdocy, handling the rod without knots that traces temples in the sky?"

"You're joking, friend! The profession is no longer worth anything, and Pliny was the last one able to say that we were paid from the public treasury. I no longer prophesy."

"Nor me—and yet I perceive things to come."

The man who saw distantly asked: "Are those things distant."

The man who saw deeply replied: "Very distant and very close, and I see an entire century that will last half a decade, for humans will move henceforth much more rapidly than time."

"That's true," replied the other, "and I too have contemplated the future event."

"Speak, my brother, while I listen to you!"

Having spoken politely, the man with dark eyes turned his head away imperturbably, in order to smile without being seen, and his colleague, who could see the future, could not see the present. With confidence, he continued, and his eyes fixed upon the rose of a great multicolored stained glass window.

He said: "We're entering the new age. A little war still, in order to finish the bellicose era of Mars, and now we're in the century of Mercury. Commerce is a god. The Bourse is a temple, at the same time as a battlefield, and people deliver combats there. International exchange has brought people closer together, but the struggle is hard nevertheless. People fight with products. Transaction reigns over the animate world. The telegraph carries the news of skirmishes to the four points of the world. Rises and falls, victories and defeat! A crash is the failure of a nation; it languishes momentarily, gets up again and sets forth. It launches its traveling salesmen across the globe, who are the last conquerors. The inventive genius of humans, more fecund because they devote themselves entirely to discoveries, creates, invents. multiples force, multiplies expansion tenfold, covers the earth, displays itself, and triumphs. To the most industrious, glory, and to the indolent, defeat! People no longer kill, but they kill themselves; the vanquished go home and blow their brains out, discreetly."

"That's distant," said the other.

"That's close, and the hour has come."

"Are you forgetting that there's fighting in the Transvaal at present?"

"The last blood, and I say that it's being shed for nothing, for the definitive result will be the same, to whomever the victory belongs. The English victors will have exploited commercially the land that they wanted to take, and, vanquished, they'll exploit it all the same. When the Boers have proclaimed the independence of their land and founded the United States of South Africa, the English will say, phlegmatically, "All right!" Then, tranquilly, as if nothing had happened, they'll install their shops and send their products; at first they'll only have the second place, because the Germans, better welcomed, will have occupied it first, but in the end they'll predominate, as always, for the God of Business, whose reign has come, has deserted the south to go northwards, and Mercury is presently called Business."

"What? The Latins, our ancestors..."

"Will march behind, and will be outdistanced. The latitudes of force are being displaced; The valor of Venice, Genoa and Madrid is rising toward London, Berlin and New York. Brother, can you not see already that America is avenged for Christopher Columbus, Ferdinand of Spain, and has taken its revenge. They will do less than the Saxon races; they do not know how, the Latins of Spain, Italy and France...

"Of France? Will not the Exposition in preparation be the triumph of Paris?"

"A city of celebration, a city of joy! Paris remains the dance-hall of the world; people go there to laugh and seek kisses! The Champ de Mars is now a fairground, but it is no longer a market."

"The city will earn gold and renown."

"It will pay dearly for it. Benefits for all, because peoples have encountered one another again and drawn closer; the Exposition will do Paris good for a month and harm for three years."

"You see blackly."

"I see clearly."

"And what do you see?"

"Three words harnessed together in the Exposition of 1900, the Epidemic of 1901 and the Revolution of 1902."

"Ah! A sinister augury, my brother..."

"On the soles of their boots, in the creases of their garments and in their breath, those passing through will bring death. In the tents that are set up and the carpets that are laid down, death is hid, and death rises in the dust. It falls back and incubates in the warm mud. The Exposition of '89 killed more people in France than the war of '70; a new disease fell upon the city and never quit it. For three consecutive years death worked so hard that life in France could no longer compete with it, and for three years the number of births did not equal the number of deaths. The past shows the future. If you have a cottage in a forest or on a mountain somewhere far away, and if you can live there, run away."

"I'll stay, in order to see."

"After heart-breaking hours, you'll see tragic hours; for history ought to inscribe in red the date 1902."

"Why is that?"

"Count with me, Brother. Under the lilacs of 1900 visitors will arrive; in autumn they will leave and winter commences the dismantling of the great bazaar. Thousands of arms make heaps with plaster; in the air of 1901 microbes scatter, which pullulate in spring. Heritages are numerous but are not kept for long. Thousands of thousands of arms dig holes and fill them in, in the devastated fairground, during the spring and summer. 1902: the winter is cold and hungry and the thousands of thousands of arms no longer have scaffolding to demolish or holes to fill in. Let us give them the ditches of the ramparts to fill in and the walls of the enclosure to demolish. Here is spring and heads affirm. Men have come, too numerously, to the city and voices say to the arms: 'Are you not going to rest?' Strike ! Strike! And everywhere, strike! The so-called Proletariat stamps its feet, striking the earth! Then it strikes people, and as '93 became pink, so 1902 is crimson!"

"You're exaggerating."

"Ninety-three was against the nobility and royalty, a few heads; nineteen oh-two is against the bourgeoisie, millions of heads. They fall, they fall, and cities burn! Watch them rise, the yellow flames into the blue sky; watch it flow, the red blood in the green grass, and look at the dead with violet lips! I can see!"

Hallucinated, the augur extended his rigid index finger toward the yellow and blue, red and green, and violet rose.

His colleague replied to him: "You're showing me the sunlight on a stained-glass window."

"No, I'm showing you the future..."

He let himself fall back on the divan, apparently very weary, as if exhausted by effort; but, having slid a thin thread of gaze toward his colleague he saw a sniggering mouth and two little dark eyes mocking him.

He turned his head frankly, and the two augurs, looking one another in the face, burst out laughing.

Then they smoked a cigar in the calm of the large high room, while the fountain murmured in its basin of white marble.

Originally published in Le Gaulois, *2 November 1900.*

Edmond Haraucourt: *The Last Men*

Pilgrimages of regret travel toward cemeteries, and the living remember the dead. Humans disappear and we think about them; but families have disappeared and we do not think about them; peoples have disappeared and our attention scarcely cares; races disappear, but what does it matter to us? The world will end, but that is a long way off.

Let us go to the cemetery of those who are not yet born. This is what I have seen.

Centuries had passed, so numerous that nothing any longer remains on earth of us and of our work—nothing visible. The generations of the time were so far from ours that they only had, at the most, the slight notion of our aspect and our mores that remains to us of our prehistoric ancestors. Not that those last men were ignorant of everything; on the contrary, our modern science, compared with theirs, would seem infantile; but they arrived so far behind us that, in the perspective of the ages, we became for their eyes the contemporaries of those who lived in caves and forests and who carved the first flints.

They only recognized anthropoids in us, and worried about us as we worry about the populations that doubtless trod the double region of the poles, the only one habitable in the epoch in which the first hardening of the planet began, when the continents in formation whined in a vapor of steam and the equatorial soil burned like red hot iron.

Now, the globe was no longer the same. By virtue of the weakening of the Sun and the consequent anemia of the Earth, everything had changed. The world map presented a new configuration. Europe was frozen, and Asia, and three quarters of

Africa, as well as Oceania, and of the two Americas, nothing remained by a horizontal strip extended between the tropics.

The cold had progressed further and further; the poles, in enlarging, had progressed toward one another; the two ice-caps, tending to join up, had petrified everything and restricted life to the ribbon of the equator.

It was dying, and the rest had disappeared. A bold explorer who risked himself in the hyperborean ice of Span or Algeria would not have been able to tell, beneath the motionless ice-sheet, what was continent and what was ocean, and the mild Mediterranean, with its frost-covered waves, was fixed in a cold of which the present winters in Greenland can only furnish us with an approximate idea.

One thing, however, still testified to our vanished existence, and that was three Egyptian sphinxes and two pyramids; a recent exploration had discovered them under the mass of ice and snow, and scientists analyzed with amazement those vestiges of a giant humankind lodged in colossal dwellings, of which the head of the sphinx gave the frightful proportion.

Thus, that world of finition, strangled between the tropics, only comprised the Guianas, the Guineas and a third continent of recent creation formed by alluvia that had come, five thousand years earlier, to weld together the Antilles. That part of the globe, the youngest, was also the most fertile, fertilized by the detritus of the dead north.

In spite of that relative wealth of the last humus, animal and vegetable life only continued there with difficulty; poorly protected by the excessively thin layer of the atmosphere, terrestrial heat radiated into space and was lost; the exhausted soil no longer produced anything but wretched plants that consented to grow without warmth or water: pines and maples scarcely hoisted themselves above the grasses, stunted in the dull air, and forests of birches and oaks only attained the height of our wheat fields.

The sun, impotent to evaporate the frigid waters of the sea, traveled in a wan sky devoid of clouds; the rain only fell at secular intervals, and streams and rivers dried up. The ground, no longer being furnished, became rough and friable. In the places where virgin forests had been, glaucous lichens carpeted the tropical plains, and in the shelter of greenhouses, the most truculent of flowers was the timid edelweiss.

There was little wind, because of the uniform envelope of cold, condensed around a planet devoid of contrasts, but sometimes there was a light invasion of frost, so slow that one could not perceive any breath, so glacial that it vitrified the stems. Nothing moved; a wan light blanched forms, and the shadow of things was pale.

The races of wild animals, without shelter and without nourishment, gradually became extinct, except for reindeer, wolves, a few bears and condors.

Domesticated species had disappeared less promptly, thanks to human protection, but the most vivacious had become etiolated, and now none remained any longer, except for rare bison reduced to the stature of mastiffs, and a few mountain dogs scarcely as large as cats.

Humans had suffered less.

Enclosed in dense cities, clad in furs, they defended themselves better against the cold, and science had delivered chemical aliments that permitted them to struggle against the insufficiency of natural resources.

Since time immemorial they no longer ate; they only nourished themselves. Official laboratories sent bottles of pills and essences to domiciles destined for common alimentation; by reason of its rarity, water was distributed more parsimoniously. In spite of the surveillance of the authorities a tendency had been observed many times, perhaps hereditary, to squander the precious liquid, and the supreme laws policing society were intended to restrict those abuses; factories making artificial water were carefully guarded and its subsequent distribution effected with a strict severity, which occasioned revolts. The rich were reproached for fabricating considerable quantities of water at home, which they employed for ablutions and other superfluities. Nevertheless, the troubles did not last long and everything returned to order, thanks to the mathematical organization of those peoples, detached from all abstract ideology.

For we would be wrong to imagine that those ultimate shoots of the race were similar to us; time, the climate and all the urgencies had modified their thoughts as well as their needs, and the functions had even transformed the organs. Their stature, far inferior to ours, had participated proportionately in the diminution of the habitable world, in all respects.

The strongest scarcely attained the dimensions of a child of seven years, but their heads were equal to or twice the size of ours, and oscillated incessantly on thin and fragile necks. Their limbs were very small, thin and short, inappropriate for walking or labor, and the feet infimal; but the twelve fingers, long, thin and spatulate at the ends, by virtue of the habitude of pressing keyboards, were manifestly more apt than ours in the manipulation of delicate instruments. Since machines accomplished all material labor of motion and locomotion, those beings, dispensed of effort, not acting themselves, not eating, and always sitting before their machines, had narrow chests, flat bellies and enormous articulations, knotted by congenital arthritis.

Their whole body was pale and glaborous, as if dusty. Their bald heads and faces bore no trace of any down, and their epidermis, even in youth resembled silk paper that had been crumpled for a long time. The useless teeth had disappeared and the inferior jaw, no longer used, was reduced to being no more than an imperceptible projection, a vestige of a chin that faded away below the mouth; the latter was narrow with thin lip, and the nose was similarly reduced, with the consequence that the eyes were in the lower half of the face, sunk beneath an enormously developed forehead. Those bulbous eyes, with pupils that were very large and very bright, widened or blinked by turns in the perpetual desire to see or to comprehend.

Those monsters quivered incessantly, shaken by furtive little spasms, and slept little, a slumber agitated by dreams. Thought never left them any repose, but their hearts were dry, emotionless and pitiless, inexorably egotistical. They did not love anything and did not believe in any afterlife. They had suppressed all passion, as a useless expenditure of energy—which is to say, a waste, and, in consequence, a danger. They lived chastely and impassively, not fearing death and not enjoying life.

Their day and nights, haunted by figures and lines, were spent in calculation; their considerable brains had attained a capacity for work and production by comparison with which we, today, are embryonic beings, and the conquests of their mind would be unimaginable for ours.

Science furnished everything, and humans had nothing else to do except think, in order to discover and augment endlessly the patrimony of their force—the employment of which, however, would come to an imminent end. As soon as an unforeseen necessity was produced, an immediate invention responded to the need.

The cold itself seemed vanquished, at least temporarily; for eight hundred years it had no longer advanced, dammed by human genius, which had draw to the surface of the terrestrial crust, for its own usage, he last frissons of warmth still vibrating in the core..

In the heart of the planet, the work of decrepitude continued nevertheless, slowly but surely. As long as a calorie remained in the entrails of the globe, however, it had to belong to the sickly tyrant, in order to prolong the agony of his race and to slow down the death of a celestial body. And that is why, in the depths of space, in the host of ever-twinkling stars, the sun, already habitable, could still perceive the supreme scintillation of a world that persisted in remaining visible and alive, because death had just encountered an obstacle there: human thought.

Originally published in Le Journal, *4 septembre 1900*

Edmond Haraucourt: *The Point of Honor*

In the early years of the twentieth century duels became rare. It was no longer considered as a social duty to murder a living creature in order to punish a misunderstanding; the hereditary concept of murder for the sake of honor was no longer in accordance with the skepticism of modern philosophy, and, obsolete since the Revolution, it already seemed vaguely ridiculous.

It is appropriate to add that the terrible crisis of 1902, which had shed so much blood, bore minds to a forceful reaction against any idea of homicide, and the new generation remained profoundly impressed by it. Respect for life became a fundamental principle of sociology; everyone was in accord in order no longer to kill without urgent necessity, and murderers found themselves definitively considered as afflicted with aberration by virtue of degeneracy. In 1918 capital punishment was suppressed from the penal code; for several years, in any case, it had only been a theoretical formula that did not frighten anyone, because the law was no longer applied.

It was, therefore, not admissible that the death penalty, abolished for murderers, should remain in vigor against ironists or adulterous lovers, and that a deceived husband or a mocked citizen still had a right usurped from the executioner. However, no complementary legislation intervened against the duel, since it was already prohibited by the letter of the law, and the care of completing the work of the legislator, over time, was left to mores.

It was not necessary to wait for long; the insignificant result of ordinary encounters increasingly discredited that bellicose method, and the moment soon arrived when a gallant man dared not risk himself in such an adventure, which no longer seemed anything but an attempt at publicity and renown. The administrators of newspapers finally understood that the majority of duelists only aspired to attract attention to themselves, their names and their books, in order to create or augment a political or literary situation without paying the expenses of advertising; in consequence, it was decided that documentation would only be inserted in exchange for money, like other advertisements, and that fortunate innovation suddenly diminished the number of quarrels. There was no longer any mention of the number of bullets exchanged without result.

Idle persons continued, for hygienic reasons, to take fencing lessons, and in establishments of hydrotherapy it was acceptable to let off steam for a quarter of an hour before taking a shower. In 1930s, seized by a romantic resurgence, women became enthusiastic for exercising with swords and short culottes came back into fashion during all seasons. In 1932, however, a Minister of War having forbidden the duels that were still obligatory in barracks, the ladies followed the example of the soldiers and laid down their arms with a common accord. Only those who worked in circuses continued, because they were exhibiting themselves for money, and supplied their alcoves by means of the presentation of their figures.

From 1933 to 1937 there was no mention of any encounter with either swords or pistols, but a clever man suddenly thought of the benefit that might be obtained from that silence. He had the idea of rejuvenating the duel, of renovating it and transforming it in conformity with the tastes of the day; there were considerable profits to be made, and the opportunity was good.

Precisely in that era, violent diatribes were excited by the celebrated Cleophat affair, and excited minds divided the country unto two distinct camps; the press polemics rose to previously unknown heights, and Monsieur Dicks, the impresario, thought of rendering visits to a few publicists of the two parties. He proposed to them to organize a series of encounters; he offered the hall of the Pandemonium, the most select in Paris, and a purse of forty pounds sterling, forty pounds per adversary, a name in large print in the posters and tickets for the spectacle, in order to allow the elegant public to arrive at leisure.

The representations at the Pandemonium were a fabulous success. It was necessary to double the price of seats and the service; people ran from the provinces and abroad. Wagers were laid enthusiastically and the stakes were often considerable. Before the spectacle the odds were shouted in the hall and outside the theater. Swashbucklers were at a premium. The taverns around the Pandemonium were encumbered by punters and bookmakers. The program, renewed every day, presented new performances every evening.

As soon as they came on stage the crowd acclaimed the champions frenetically, and the latter fought well, excited by their own passions and the cheers of their supporters. Some of them were occasionally whistled, because of a sudden pallor or because they retreated to the wings; but the gallery gave courage to the majority and the audience was able to contemplate the nobility of the attitudes that the combatants would not have had without it, in a solitary park.

Of course, the combatants did not come to these "rendezvous of honor" without having taken a few preliminary precautions, and one scarcely saw people there except those trained in the use of a sword or enraged by a fury that was more valuable than science. The maladroit avoided venturing on to those dangerous boards, and in order to dissimulate their prudence under the appearance of wisdom, they wrote eloquent articles against the savagery of a game worthy of the Middle Ages, renewing the barbaric epochs of Louis XIII and Duguesclin, intolerable in a civilized people. They criticized their colleagues for consenting to those exhibitions, invoking morality and sanitation, and urging the government to take repressive measures. That theme was quickly exhausted, however, and the homilies of pacifism were obliged to cease, for want of readers.

People had, in fact, acquired a taste for those generous spectacles. Philosophers who wanted to dine in town approved loudly of the reawakening of national energy, and all sensate people shared an opinion that was so clearly patriotic.

When people talk too much about energy, it is because they have very little.

In any case, those singular combats never presented a serious peril; as before, they were stopped at the fist blood, and the director of the Pandemonium never had to reproach himself for the death of a man.

One evening, however, the performance nearly turned out badly. One of the adversaries, in a moment of madness, had deflected with his left hand the blade that was menacing him and had run his man through with a direct blow. The poor devil was carried off and the quivering crowd howled. The partisans of the wounded man cried murder, banditry and conspiracy, accusing the entire party, and the petty benches were up in arms. Punches, slaps and cards were exchanged; the duel was restaged and the comedy of true combat was played in the audience. It was necessary to bring down the curtain, evacuate the hall, and give first aid to the victims of the brawl.

The next day, an edict of the prefect prohibited "encounters of honor" and closed the Pandemonium. But Paris was discontented. Demonstrations were organized in the streets to demand the reestablishment of the games. Monomaniacs ran the boulevards changing "Down with the prefect!" A queue formed at the theater door; the police were obliged to charge. The municipal councilors, wearing their sashes, made speeches, gesticulating; but the prefect held firm. A debate was scheduled in the Chambre; the Ministry fell; it was replaced by another, which changed the prefect but kept the edict. There were no more games, but at least the functionary had been sacked, and the city returned to order.

However, a custom had been created. Dicks' invention was quickly exploited by others. A cablegram from America invited the French duelists to give their performances at the Great Punch in New York and Chicago: three days at sea, all expenses paid, superb purses; the strait was crossed. France lost another industry and the Ministry, called to account, fell.

The movement took hold, it was now known abroad that Paris, the city of joy, could not have a monopoly on "encounters of honor." Immediately, they were seen everywhere, merchants of attractions organizing performances in the great centers of the two worlds. The success was universal. Europe and America were enthusiastic for those manifestations of human valor. Spain was the most ardent in propagating them.

For people, like individuals, admire strength twice in their existence, when they are very young and when they are very old; the former because they observe a beauty therein, and the latter because they contemplate therein what they no longer have. The Greeks had athletes that they saluted in the Olympic Games, and the Romans had gladiators whom they slaughtered in the circus. Young people rejoice in seeing strength in its blossoming, because they love it; old peoples take pleasure in seeing it laid low, because they detest it. For the former, it is a model, and for the latter, incapable of following an example of vigor, it is a revenge for their weakness.

Nevertheless, that new pleasure could not last very long; it lent itself too readily to the possibility of abuses, and was quickly deformed. To begin with, numerous publicists, lured by the importance of large purses and desirous of getting their hands on them, sought partners and challenged them, and the violence of the press became frightful. Then, the most malign or the hungry invented a further progress; contriving polemics in association, they feigned quarrels, arranged roles, agreed replies and regulated the combat.

The duel was preceded by numerous rehearsals and carefully staged by retired associates: the fashion of attacking, breaking off, returning to the assault, giving and receiving wounds, falling and getting up again, exchanging handshakes, waiting, pausing, talking and shutting up, gestures, intonations and facial expressions were all methodical and immutable. The costume of the wounded man included an ampoule full of a red liquid that simulated blood. But the play was often poorly acted, and the public did not take long to perceive the trickery. People whistled. The punters, duped, demanded her money back. Only the naïve consented for a while to risk betting against the bookmakers. Finally, they abstained, like the rest.

It was no longer possible to add faith to those combats; in fact, the showmen were now organizing tours; a duel was dragged from city to city, pitifully. Only inferior actors could any longer be found to play the roles, which were poorly acted and badly paid. Curiosity turned away from those nonentities.

Hopes of renewal were founded on the importation a new element, and encounters of honor were set to music, but the attempt did not succeed.

Only small towns and villages still deigned to be amused by the spectacle. Traveling troupes announced their next venue by means of illustrated posters but people hardly glanced at them and rarely came, and during the combat they laughed loudly.

The thing was exhausted. Dueling was dead. There were no more points of honor.

Originally published in Le Journal*, 15 August 1901.*

Edmond Haraucourt: *Memoirs of a Bacillus*

The story of my already long existence will probably not astonish you. But what will doubtless surprise you is that I have been able to write it, or at least to dictate it.. What will make you marvel is the analysis of my thoughts, the ensemble of my observations, my hopes and my ambitions. I am not an ordinary microbe. Recognize in me an elite bacillus, illustrious among his fellows, the author of a great work. I have done a great deal already; I shall do even more. For as long as God lends me life I shall pursue my task, with the aid of imbecile humans, and as long as a new Pasteur has not fund the means of destroying our powerful and prosperous race, the memory of my genius will subsist in the gratitude of my descendants.

I have worked on humans for a long time, nourishing myself on their substance in the depths of the lungs or the brain, with the consequence that I have been able to learn their language and their ideas, think with them and talk like them; I am infused by their science, and as for their soul, I have drunk it; I have drunk enough of it to guide myself and reason like a human.

I was born in the caverns of a scientist and my early childhood instructed me in everything that was being plotted against our race. Antisepsis preoccupied that learned individual; it was the object of his research and the theme of his discourse. I knew the danger and I learned to fear it; it was a matter, no more and no less, of killing all of us, of suppressing in society the spores of tuberculosis, and I soon understood that there was, between our species and the human species, a duel to the death, which would only end with the disappearance of one race or the other.

I resolved, for my part, to remain on my guard and to seek refuge in a less dangerous organism; so, when my education was perfect—which is to say, when I had acquired a full knowledge of the weapons employed by the enemy to arrive at our extermination—I installed myself comfortably in a convoy of the emunctory and I departed from the scientist; that same evening, I introduced myself into the more propitious universe of a less erudite poor devil, less careful of his person; in the name of spores I took possession of that empire. There I would be able to act, and from there to radiate, to conquer other bodies, establishing the center of an immense domination.

I must admit that events served me and, hazard—which I could, following the example of humans, call Providence—came to my aid. For among us, as well as among human beings, the plans of the greatest politicians and the most powerful dominators depend on occurrences that remain independent of the will; more often than not, external circumstances determine whether an idea of genius will bear fruit or not, and it depends on chance whether the idea is good or bad, profitable or harmful, and modifies History in one direction or another. God aided me! The fortune of events made me a sublime and glorious Bacillus.

In fact, the man I occupied was sent back by his doctors to his birthplace—in order to be cured, they said; in order to die, they thought. That was Bretagne, and on arrival, I had the joy of observing that we were penetrating into a region virgin of tubercular domination, where we were unknown, where no one feared us: a poor country, but healthy. The struggle was beautiful to undertake, the conquest superb to make. The pure saline wind would be a rude adversary for us, which would wipe out entire armies of my spores, but I sensed that I had the strength to renew our battalions, and I was counting above all on the collaboration of humans, whose vivacious imbecility is our surest ally.

The success surpassed my hopes. Humans are more stupid than one thinks, infinitely more stupid than a microbe can imagine to begin with. It is necessary to have inhabited one and eaten him away, like me, to succeed in conceiving the excess of their stupidity, which, in certain regions, is confined to that of brutes. You know that we work willingly in the bovine species; I know cows who resemble milkmaids, and milkmaids who resemble cows, who guide their beasts to the heath; the brains of the former are exactly like those of the latter, and even the instinct of the animals, compared with the immortal soul of the humans, furnishes a superior quantity of useful intelligence and natural prudence; the animals defend themselves against us, but humans second us, and I affirm that, without their aid, we shall never arrive at a definitive triumph.

Judge for yourself. My entry into Bretagne passed unperceived, as you might imagine. I was introduced to an island populated by a thousand inhabitants; you will find that double-diamond of land off the northern coast, two leagues out in the Channel. The ancient Isle of Breac'h seems to have been, as its name indicates, a Medieval leper colony.[26] I took a good augury from that appellation, and vowed to reestablish there the omnipotence of contagion and death. In truth, what was leprosy compared with me? Was it, like me, a national peril? That benign epidemic was not even contagious! I am the epidemic that can kill an entire people! I run and I float, I pass and I spread, and I go where I will, in the wind, where it wants to go and where we want to go, everywhere at once.

We arrived on Breac'h, and I rejoiced in seeing myself surrounded by water. The consanguinity typical of islands, where marriages are between close relatives and weaken the species, promised a propitious terrain. I did not pause to observe another cause of degeneracy from which I would profit: alcoholism reigned there, with all its heredities. The passersby, in dozens, were idiotic, goitrous, deaf-mute or coxalgic. I saw them file past, and merely by seeing them, I understood the right over them that their parents had bequeathed to me. That society belonged to me, and I took possession of it.

---

[26] The Breton *breac'h* means "spotted."

Certainly, it did not take long. As soon as the first visit of my host to the cottages of his numerous family, my plan was made. People looked at us, saying: "Yves won't grow old." They said that simply, with the grave tranquility of Bretons when they talk about death. Yves coughed and spat, producing a little of me almost everywhere; when we emerged from a house we left behind a little mortal saliva behind, on the beaten earth that replaced the parquet. My spores incubated there; afterwards, they rose from the ground, innumerable and invisible, entered into inhalations and installed themselves in individuals.

I had the good fortune to introduce myself into a few food merchants and poisoned their shops; they spat me out with their lungs and expectorated me into the atmosphere of the meat and the bread; people filed in there, in crowds, to buy death under the aspects of life. Ah, the beautiful days! How I laughed to see that stubborn horde bringing its money and paying to have the right to carry away to the cottage the death of the little children!

The young offered it to the old in a kiss; the old spat it at the young! I lived in untidy beards, yellow sheets, cramped beds. In the common spoon and the borrowed glass I circulated around. I went from mouth to mouth, hasty in my work; I captured springs to which people came to wash linen and draw water by turns; in the wash-house mud that completes wells, my spores awaited takers in thousands, and infiltrated the cisterns; from dirty laundry I passed rapidly to cups! Cows imbibed me at the trough, and I swam thereafter in the white milk and crawled in the golden butter!

All those vagabonds, poorly nourished, with depleted blood, fell beneath me. After five semesters I possessed twenty cottages. When I adopt a house, I empty it! I only leave the stones and the furniture standing, and woe betide whoever acquires them! The task is very easy for me to destroy entire families thus, for on the eve of the day that the gravedigger carries a coffin away I hasten to a new workshop, a new cadaver to make; in the death-bed, and often in the sheets, always under the curtains, someone comes to lie down, out of affection or economy, on the eve of the funeral. They don't leave me twelve hours of idleness! Even if I wanted to rest, it wouldn't be permitted to me. It's necessary that I kill! Every six months, the gravedigger comes to take one from the same bed. They want me to kill them; they order and demand it. I almost have the air of being their slave, and I supply them with a means of suicide.

Unconscious suicide, you might say, by virtue of ignorance? No, by virtue of stubbornness and stupidity. When they have been advised to the peril, when experience has shown it to them, when the cemetery cries out to them, they shrug their shoulders, smile disdainfully and carry on as before. I tell you that they want me, and I am the elect! In twenty years, the isle will be empty. It's mine!

Furthermore, it's very useful for me to have such a domain to my devotion, far from physicians, far from sanitary regulations and public powers, a lost land that is abandoned to me, which no ne defends against me. Prepared by alcohol, all of Bretagne awaits me. I shall take it.

Remember that I am announcing my conquest. I am an Attila, scourge of God.

Inscribe my name in History.

Originally published in La Grande Revue, *1 January 1903*

Edmond Haraucourt: *The Last Pope*

In the Vatican quarter, behind the ruins of St. Peter's, there was a house of rather poor appearance, and very old, for it bore on the stone of the fronton the date of the year 2077. That entire quarter of Rome, as you know, has retained its appearance of another age, and it constitutes an islet within the city of dilapidation and poverty, with sad streets of unsanitary dwellings. Many times, already, the Council has deliberated the project of demolishing the buildings, scarcely six stories high, in which only vagrants consent to live; but time passes and the hovels remain standing.

The medical profession brings us to see strange places; I was summoned there in order to visit a invalid, and I must confess that, in spite of my curiosity for things of olden days, I was venturing into that region of the city for the first time. A vile electric elevator stopped at the first floor and I wondered to what degree of poverty it was necessary to be reduced in order to live so far from respirable heights, so close to the ground, almost in the tomb already.

As soon as I entered the sick man's apartment, however, I was surprised to observe some wealth. It was cluttered with trinkets, several of which appeared to be very expensive, mingled with others whose only value was their antiquity. One could have believed that it was the redoubt of an antiquary or a scholar; at a second glance, I diagnosed in that little museum of sorts the mind and hand of a theographer. In fact, the pieces gathered there were of an exclusively religious character, but with the difference from analogous collections that this one only comprised items referring to the cult of the Christians, and, in a fashion more specialized, to the sect that bore the name of Catholicism; at least, I judged it thus, with a margin of error, for my erudition in theography is that of a man of the

118

world, and would not permit me to make a categorical judg-
ment regarding the attributes and subdivisions that a profound
study demands.

On the wall, a large ebony cross supported an ivory crucifix of beautiful workmanship; opposite, a panel painted in
oils—which suffices to indicate its antiquity—represented two
crossed keys under a tiara, with garlands of rope; silk chasu-
bles embroidered with flowers were visible in the shadow of a
partly-closed cupboard. In one corner there was a long crutch
in gilded wood, terminated at the upper end by entwined
branches of foliage. On a shelf, a white linen miter shone with
glassware; in a display-case there were cups, urns, vases and
candelabra in bronze that had lost its gilt, and, on a support of
the same metal, a glass lens surrounded by radii. A kind of
table or altar, wedged against the wall, supported colonnettes
of oak, sculpted caskets, imitation lace tablecloths, a thallium
crucifix and figurines of old men with the beards of adoles-
cents, which had wings. Near the door, a trunk with an iron
lock bore the inscription: *Saint Peter's Pence.*

I discerned all that with a rapid glance, in passing, for it
is not appropriate to our professional discretion to penetrate
the secrets of private life.

I was introduced into the moribund's bedroom and I saw
a bizarre spectacle: five or six aged individuals were gathered
around the bed in an inexplicable posture; the men in question—for there was no woman there—were on their knees, in
the fashion of upholsterers varnishing a parquet, but they were
not doing anything. They kept their hands joined, and were
speaking in low voices; they were not conversing but murmuring scarcely intelligible words in an unknown language, which
appeared to me to be Latin. They did not seem, in any case, to
be making any effort to listen to one another, since they were
all talking at the same time. They did not disturb themselves
when I came in, except for one, who got up and said to me:
"We're praying."

Then he stood aside from the bed and I saw the invalid.

He was a glabrous old man with a broad forehead and dark, shining eyes, illuminated by fever or thought; the brow ridges were energetically muscled, and the meager temples were hollowed out by the thumbprint of genius. He was gazing at the ceiling of the room and his lips were moving silently.

The man who had already spoken turned to me again and said: "Permit the Holy Father to finish his orison."

You are doubtless unaware, as I was unaware, of what an orison is; the word once served, it appears, to designate a kind of mystical monologue, which is improvised or recited, and in which the orator supposes that he is addressing the divinity of his choice.

As it is appropriate to lend oneself, to the extent that one can, to the whims of the clientele, I waited for the end of the orison.

After a few moments, the invalid lifted his head painfully, buried in the cushions, and then extended his right arm and made a mysterious sign in mid-air with two fingers, above the kneeling men. Then he met my eyes, and stopped moving.

He smiled and said: "I think, Monsieur, that science can do nothing for me."

I examined him. He only had a few more moments to live. I did not tell him that, but he responded to me: "I know it."

He tried to raise himself up on his elbow, but fell back. Then, while fully extended, staring directly ahead, not looking at anyone, he spoke.

"Thank you, Monsieur, for coming; and you, my brothers, adieu. Don't weep for me, but for them. I bless you, in the name of the Father, the Son..."

He wanted, I believe, to add another word, but he did not have the strength. One of the witnesses continued: "...and the Holy Spirit." In unison, they all replied: "Amen." They stood up simultaneously, and no one said any more.

I leaned over the dying man. His heart was still beating, faintly.

The witnesses interrogated me with their faces. With a sign, I made them understand that the end was approaching. They had an air of gravity rather than sadness, as if the disappearance of their friend would cause them a common embarrassment, not grief. The atmosphere around the dying man lacked amour. I sought to explain what bonds or what relationships could unite those men, who not only did not belong to the same family but quite evidently did not originate from the same country, or even the same race. Doubtless they were members of some workers' corporation? I noticed ribbons in their buttonholes and insignia similar to those that our ancestors adopted at the end of the Middle Ages, in the nineteenth and twentieth centuries, to distinguish between the various orders of chivalry. The ribbons were scarlet and the insignia silver, representing a flat hat with a wide brim, decorated with tassels.

Divining my thought, my first interlocutor approached me. "Monsieur," he said, "May I introduce to you the cardinals of the Holy Catholic Church."

I bowed, without understanding very well, and he lowered his voice to add: "Our Holy Father is at the last extremity, is he not?"

I did not understand how those men of disparate origin could have the same father, and he was evidently of much the same age as them, but I did not persist. I went into the next room in order to draw up a prescription. The one who accompanied me said: "It's a pity for the world, for His Holiness cannot be replaced."

I raised my eyebrows, in order to testify my impotence to prevent that misfortune, the range of which escaped me, and I resumed writing. But the man, desirous, I imagine, of informing me of his own importance, added: "Alas, Monsieur, you will have seen the last of the Sovereign Pontiffs die, before the last cardinals of the Roman Church."

Then I understood I had not known until that day that Christians still existed, let alone Christian priests. My surprise was acute. I am not one of those who are completely uninterested in ancient legends and vanished mores, and the dilettantism of my curiosity lends itself readily to opportunities for learning concerning the evolution of the human mind. The cardinal sensed that I was disposed to listen to him.

"Yes, Monsieur, the man who is dying in that room—may God receive his soul—was the vicar of Jesus Christ."

He saw that I did not perceive the exact meaning of his words, several locutions of which escaped my understanding. He made a gesture of condescension with his hand, and, shaking his head with a sad smile he added:

"Don't take us for madmen because we're small in number. The great things of humankind last longer than one thinks, and continue unknown to history. When they have disappeared from the light they are thought to be dead, but they survive in the shadows and prolong their agony there. The mission is concluded but the title persists; it is thus that freemasons were once seen who no longer practiced masonry, and who still deliberated, although there were no longer any cathedrals to build. Sârs and Mages were seen three thousand years after Nineveh and Babylon, and we know that in the nineteenth century there was a Grandmaster of the Templars. Thus it is with us, Monsieur. The Catholic Church, dispossessed of the Holy See, has nevertheless, as you can see, conserved its faithful followers, and pontifical elections have been able to perpetuate it, even though deprived of their splendor and their solemnity. It is necessary to admit that, from then on, the number of our followers diminished more rapidly. The abolition of ecclesiastical costume and the suppression of church bells were a terrible blow for religious sentiment, for the bells were God's publicity, were they not, and how can anything be maintained without a little publicity?"

"Historians claim that, in all times, priestly organizations have recognized the importance of publicity and scene-setting."

"They became more indispensable than ever, Monsieur, the moment we lacked them; the material means of attracting popular attention were withdrawn from priests at exactly the moment when that attention was withdrawing of its own accord, in order to be directed to other concerns. Peoples and individuals were then too occupied on earth to think any longer about the other world, and inventors did great harm to the Creator. The sense of the Beyond and the appetite for mystery withdrew from minds, and you doubtless know that the weaker religious sentiment is, the more numerous religions become. Each individual aspiration attaches itself to whichever solicits it the most, and when one god is about to disappear all the gods reappear. We had to struggle against an enormous competition, and we were then without arms for the battle. Theosophists and occultists were our most powerful rivals, and all souls curious about infinity went toward them or their cult offered the amusement of prodigies. What can I tell you? The indifference of peoples ended up going as far as forgetting us. But that forgetfulness happened so slowly, during the succession of days, that no one could say at what date it commenced."

I replied, charitably: "That is the law of the world, Monsieur, where everything progresses to the point of dying, even the best things. Whatever has force departs from nothing to rise to the supreme, and fall back into annihilation."

"You speak the truth, Monsieur! The first bishops of Rome wore mantles of coarse cloth, and the bishop of Rome became the Pontiff of bishops, and that Pontiff became a king, and that king was then the master of monarchs. Have you noticed the number inscribed on the door of the humble house where we are? It dates from 2077, a thousand years after the epoch when the monk Hildebrand made the emperor of Germany kneel in the snow of Canossa. Then, we were at the summit of power, and our will dispatched half of humankind against the other half. The tumult of adorations resounded in our temples of stone and we covered cities with our monuments and our corteges. But it was necessary for us to descend again, precisely because we were at the summit, and down here, nothing is stationary; the universal lord fell back to the rank of a petty prince, with a minuscule Estate; and as his realm was weak, the other kings took advantage of that to take it. He became, for the second time, the Pontiff of the bishops; it was granted to him to issue mandates, for want of commandments, and to offer advice instead of issuing orders."

"All theocracies end in that way."

"And all the religions that they bear, fatally, end with them! It's a great misfortune, Monsieur, that God cannot live on earth other than through the authority of men. When priests lose their social supremacy, the gods die; look at Assyria and Egypt, Olympus and Druidism. Peoples only believe in their divinities while they tremble before priestly power."

"God is compromised by introducing him into politics."

"What are you saying, Monsieur? You are belying your historical knowledge in supposing that God can be excluded from politics; he is the very principle of it, and all social politics was, for hundreds of centuries, nothing but the struggle between Humans and God, between the consciousness that emancipates and the law that forbids emancipation—which is to say, between individual strength and general strength. Will humans be free, or will they be led? That was the entire problem, for several thousands of years. The two most magnificent constructors of peoples ever seen on the face of the globe, Moses and Mohammed, in order to shore up their political work and make it solid, had recourse to God, without whom they would have been unable to do anything: they attributed their words and their dogmas to God, and nations gave the obedience to the word of God that they would have refused to the prescriptions of the Sage."

"Possibly."

"Our Lord did the same, Monsieur but, by reason of excessive generosity, his work was incomplete, and his edifice sinned by virtue of too much confidence in our idealism, on which it based everything; his work lacked coercion, and the Catholic Church gave it what it lacked. It was necessary, by order, to force humans to dream, to sing, and to believe themselves to be happy, for the day on which they doubt God,

Monsieur, they doubt their own happiness, and on that day, Monsieur, they suffer."

"One can't deny that successive gods have been useful, from different points of view."

"Consoling, comforting and purifying, they were useful enough, were they not, to be thought indispensable? The conception of an afterlife seemed inherent to the very essence of humanity. Is humanity any happier, alas, now that it has lost the appetite for the dream? Every absence is a loss, and you have impoverished yourselves by ridding yourselves of God. People wanted to shake off a yoke but they threw away a treasure, which is the dream, and suppressed a strength, which is the Faith."

A gasp reached us from the next room, but the cardinal, filled by his subject, did not hear it and continued:

"Were we, then, such terrible masters? Oh, Monsieur, kings committed a dire fault in dispossessing the Holy See of its temporal power. They disarmed themselves in weakening us, and when they sacrificed us, they condemned themselves by the same stroke. They wanted to emancipate themselves from priestly guardianship, which was the equivalent of divine protection! In order to deliver themselves from a judge they deprived themselves of a defender. Thrones only have force when riveted to the altar!"

"Destinies of the same species are linked together, and nothing in the social edifice falls with impunity for the rest. Kings had to disappear shortly after you--before us, since you can see that we still endure. A king deposed is no longer a king, even if ten thousand citizens regret his loss, but a god whom ten men worship remains indisputably a god."

The labored respiration of the moribund reached us through the door, which stood ajar, along with the murmur of prayers.

"But I haven't told you the end. It was slow, Monsieur. One after another, the nations turned away from us, and indifference to everything that is not material having gained almost everyone, there only remained in this world a few scattered

125

dreamers, still inclined to worship but difficult to gather together; first we were a few thousand Catholics, later we were a few hundred, then a few dozen. That lasted for two centuries. In the end, Saint Peter's pence were insufficient to maintain the Pope, who had to take on a métier, and the day came when the number of believers was reduced to the dignitaries of the Church alone. Gregory XX, who is dying—can you hear his death-rattle?—only found in the whole world two cardinals to appoint, and now that he is dying we are insufficient in number to constitute a conclave. He will have no successor."

At that moment we heard a cry, something feeble that wanted to be strong. I ran to the door.

The old man had raised himself up on his bed, extending his arm toward the ceiling, toward the sky; already, he was falling back.

Before I could get close enough to catch him, his head was dangling over the edge of the bed.

Pierre Mille (1864-1941) was a journalist, successful enough to have a prize named after him. He published several volumes of fiction as well as numerous books on current affairs. His short story "En trois cent ans" *(1922) was translated in the Black Coat Press anthology* Nemoville *(2012)*[27] *as* "Three Hundred Years Hence." "Et Nunc, Et Semper" *was originally published in* Le Temps, 27 décembre 1906.

Pierre Mille: *In Passing:* Et Nunc, Et Semper[28]

To plunge into the future, falling precisely upon the day that one desires; to be able to foresee the future or, rather and much better, to live it in advance? The Englishman H. G. Wells has given the means to the whole world with his Time Machine. No one makes us of it? Believe that that is by reason of horror of the slightest effort. But I am indefatigable when it is a matter of obliging you. You desire to know what will happen in the year 1907? I have departed on Wells' machine. A turn of the wheel, the kind of dazzlement produced by the furious rush through the days and nights mingled by the rapidity of travel, which blurs darkness and light in order to produce nothing but gray, gray and more gray. Finally, the abrupt and disconcerting halt...

I found myself in the same place, but a year more had gone by, and I only had to put a sure hand on the journal that I had written during that year, still non-existent for you. After which, I came back among you with my booty. The journal is incomplete, because of my idleness; numerous and regrettable

---

[27] ISBN 978-1-61227-070-8.
[28] *Et nunc et semper* means "now and always." It occurs in the Latin version of a familiar prayer prayer, usually rendered into English in the phrase "as it was in the beginning, is now, and ever shall be."

lacunae have been left therein; but such as it is, I yield it to you.

*

3 January 1907. The year is commencing under the most somber auspices. A well-informed person has just told me that we are going to have a terrible war with Morocco, and then with the other nations of the world, by reaction. The army of El Guebbas is camped in confrontation with Raissouli's,[29] and if it is beaten by that of the insurgent or allows itself to be absorbed into its tumultuous bosom, the troops of France and Spain will be disembarked in their turn. Then, it is affirmed, there will be a universal conflagration.

3 February. We shall also have a religious war. Nothing is less dubious; the Vatican wants to refuse the third law made on the separation. The most frightful events are to be anticipated. Today is Sunday and my neighbor has just departed for Saint-Sulpice. That is because she has been summoned to go to her persecution.

7 March. An old lady has just been discovered in her garret, sequestered by her unnatural children for twenty-nine years. It appears that it is unprecedented. Public opinion is aroused.

20 March. El Guebbas' army is still camped facing Raissouli's. It is preparing to fight a great battle. In these conditions, it is generally considered that it would be undiplomatic to have the Franco-Spanish troops intervene.

---

[29] Raissouli was the name attributed in French newspapers to a Moroccan "brigand," who would probably have regarded himself as a rebel against French rule, His activities were an issue at a conference held in Algeciras in January-April 1906, to which various foreign powers sent delegates. He was pursued by a local militia supervised the commissioner Mohammed Guebbas

14 April. Parliament has just voted to pass the seventh law on the separation of Church and State; the Panthéon, disaffected for a long time, has been declared open once again for worship. Such conditions seem intolerable to the Church, and everyone is agreed in saying that religious war is inevitable. Today is Sunday and my neighbor has just departed for Saint-Sulpice; she is going to her persecution, as usual. How black the future is!

22 May. The second Duma, in Russia, has just been dissolved. The Stolypine ministry has fallen and has been replaced by a Golypine ministry. Furthermore, the League of Russian Peoples has just been substituted for the League of Slavic Peoples; it is impossible to foresee the consequences of such a great upheaval.

Today's newspapers inform us that the Emperor of Germany, addressing the soldiers of his guard, has said that they must serve him blindly, as much against internal enemies as those without. That language, entirely new in his mouth, is very worrying.

30 May. El Guebbas' troops have advanced ten kilometers, and Raissouli's have retreated by the same distance. A great battle is expected. In these conditions, it is generally considered that it would be undiplomatic to disembark the Franco-Spanish troops.

13 June. Two bands of apaches have fought a pitched battle with knives and revolvers on the Boulevard Ornano. It appears that it is unprecedented. Public opinion is aroused, and all the newspapers, no matter what opinion they hold, are complaining about the increase in criminality.

It is very hot. At the end of a session in the Chambre, a socialist député slapped a center député. Such aggression is unusual in parliamentary affairs. Where are we headed?

In Italy, the Bonmartini trial has just recommenced.[30]

7 July. Parliament has just voted to pass its fifteenth law on the separation of Church and State. An immense cathedral is to be constructed on the amphitheater of the Champ-de-Mars. Such rigor, of course, renders any kind of accommodation impossible. Today is Sunday, eleven o'clock. My neighbor has just departed for Saint-Sulpice; she is going to her persecution.

A cadaver has been discovered in the Rue de Belzunce of a woman cut into pieces. The police are completely baffled by the novelty and unexpectedness of the method employed by the ingenious criminal to multiply the traces of his crime; everything points to the belief that the guilty party will never be found.

29 July. Automobile accidents have killed this week: at Trouville and Deauville, eighteen people; a Étretat, nine; at Dieppe, seven; on the other highways of France, nine hundred and forty. No one understands it at all; no one has ever thought that automobiles driven at a hundred kilometers an hour could present such a danger. One is inclined to believe that these accidents are due in large measure to the elevation of the temperature and are nothing to do with the automobiles themselves.

15 August. The Emperor, finding himself aboard his yacht, the Hohenzollern on Sunday, has fulfilled the function of pastor and addressed a homily to the sailors of his crew. He

---

[30] The 1905 trial of five people accused of conspiracy to murder of Count Francesco Bonmartini of Bologna in 1902, including his wife, Countess Teodolinda Bonmartini, her alleged lover, Dr Secchi, and her brother Tullio Murri (one of the actual murderers), was one of the most sensational of the era, and the affair dragged on for years, proving the newspapers of Europe and America with abundant copy.

told them that they must serve him blindly, as much against internal enemies as those outside. The novelty of that manifestation is surprising; people are wondering, for the first time, whether the Triple Alliance is not beginning to come unstuck.

In the Austro-Hungarian parliament, the Czech, Polish, anti-Semitic, Magyar, Croat, Rumanian and Pan-Germanic parties have had sword-fights, with the aid of their paper-knives. Never before, it is affirmed, have those weapons been employed.

12 September. El Guebbas' troops have resumed their former positions, but Raissouli's have drawn nearer. They are going to fight, that is certain. In these conditions, everyone is agreed in recognizing that it would be undiplomatic to have the Franco-Spanish cohort advance by a single step. The committee of the Dames de France has made a gift to the latter of three English billiard tables and a large number of sets of dominoes.

The North-South line of the Paris Métropolitain is completed for the Rue de Rennes and the Boulevard Saint-Germain, but it appears that all the water-pipes had been forgotten, so a big hole has been dug alongside the Métropolitain. It is only seven years since the work began; the inhabitants of the quarter, who are reactionaries, affirm that they are waiting, in order for it to be completed, for the return of the legitimate monarchy. Thus, for Republicans, there is no urgency.

18 October. A provincial scientist has just demonstrated that by treating particles of tellurium sesquitannate with nitric acid in a saline solution, one can obtain amoeboid cells that behave like living beings and reproduce by seissiparity. A Parisian scientist has proved, on the other hand, that the experiment in question signifies absolutely nothing, but that it had already been carried out by Berzelius in 1806. Extraordinarily, the public, generally so intelligent, does not understand it at all.

4 November. In the Chambre, the budget is under discussion. Monsieur Joseph Reinach[31] has made a eloquent speech on the inconvenience of functionarism in France. He revealed that since last year, the number of employees in the Ministry of the Interior has been augmented by seventeen units, while that of England's Rome Office has diminished by twenty-eight. Monsieur Reinach was applauded on all the benches of the Chambre.

5 November. Monsieur Jules Coutant, député d'Ivry,[32] has requested the creation of a new corps of inspectors of labor, charged with unifying the capacity of hogsheads in France. The Tourangelles hold two hundred and fifty liters, but the Bordelaises only two hundred and twenty-eight. That whimsy on the part of hogsheads is shocking in a free country. All barrels will therefore be unified at two hundred and twenty-five liters, and everyone will gain by it: the barrel-makers, who will have less material to work with; the wine-merchants, who will sell less merchandise at the same price; and the twenty-two inspectors, who will each receive six thousand francs a year. Only the consumers and the taxpayers will find something to say about it, which is of no importance. Monsieur Jules Coutant's motion was passed unanimously.

15 December. Two large-scale strikes have broken out, one in Toulon, the other in Santander; the Franco-Spanish corps has been recalled to Europe in order to maintain order. Simultaneously, El Guebbas' troops have returned to their hearths. That conclusion has astonished everyone; we had thought that a great battle was inevitable.

---

[31] Joseph Reinach (1856-1921), a prominent supporter of Alfred Dreyfus and a prolific polemicist.
[32] Jules Coutant (1854-1913), who began styling himself Coutant-d'Ivry, was a militant socialist firebrand.

22 December. The French Parliament has just voted to pass the twenty-fourth law on the separation of Church and State. The venerables of all the Masonic lodges in France will go to make honorable amends at Notre Dame in chemises, with ropes around their necks, and the Eiffel Tower will be dressed in crepe as a sign of mourning. But the masculine energy of that attitude has not made Rome recoil, and the religious war is continuing with the same ferocity. Today is Sunday and my neighbor has just departed for Saint-Sulpice; she is going to her persecution.

31 December. Statistics have just been published from which it emerges that this year, 1907, the same number of people have been born in France, and the same number have died, as last year; that the public treasury has been augmented in the usual proportion; that the number of suicides, marriages and separations in Paris is, as usual, neither greater nor fewer; and that Paris, still finding itself on the same meridian, has received very nearly the same quantity of rain and sunlight. How curious that is!

Originally published in Le Temps, *28 Mars, 1907.*

Pierre Mille: *In Passing:* Conte de Fées

This is a story for little children, and I beg grown-up people not to read it.

The events that I am going to relate happened in the year 1910. Don't be astonished that I'm already so well-informed, for I'm a prophet.

So, learn that in 1910—and scarcely three years now separate us from that blessed year—all the trade unions went on strike successively, each of them several times over, to augment their salaries, to increase the figure of their members' retirement pensions with money derived not from the members but by taxpayers, and in order no longer no work on Saturday. For, all the shops, thanks to the cares of the General Confederation of Labor, being closed on Sunday, that tutelary confederation decided that workers must keep their Saturday completely free, in order to make their purchases in the aforesaid shops. And as a large number of valiant workers continued, having joyful souls and respect for traditions, to celebrate Monday, France rested for three days a week. It was truly a fine spectacle, which was well worth what it cost.

In truth, it cost very dear. Obliged to recover the expense that the augmentation of salaries and the diminution of the number of their trading days, the shops increased their prices—and not only those shops in which clothing was found, or those that sold objects made of iron, sheet metal, zinc or wood, but even bakers, butchers and shops from which fish and vegetables were obtained. They strove thus to attain the same receipts as in the past, but many did not succeed. As for the workers, they had obtained increases in salary but were astonished, without understanding it at all, to be no more fortunate than before, because everything had become dearer. As for the peasants. who could not sell their wine and wheat any better than before—it was only in the cities that the pries increased, and they did not profit from it at all—their misery was painful to behold, and was only equaled by that of unfortunate employees in shops and offices whose salaries had not increased; they had diminished instead, for times were hard, because of all the fine reforms.

It was one of those poor employees who, almost in spite of himself, took the initiative of the resolution that changed the face of things. His name was Innocent Malifait, and he had the custom of only having himself shaved once a week, on Sunday, as an economy measure, by a petty barber in the Rue de Dragon. And the latter, who employed two assistants during the week, worked all alone on the Lord's Day in order to obey the law.

"And," that philosopher sometimes said, passing a brilliant steel blade back and forth over a rather coarse leather strap, "it's a veritably healthy and moralistic law, for to pay the rent of their shop, the income tax, the tax of capital which came afterwards, and in order to pay for workers' retirement pensions, it's the employers who now toil all alone, while their employees go for walks, and for six thousand years it was the other way round. I suppose, therefore, that in order to reestablish equilibrium, Providence wants it to be the turn of the bosses to be as unfortunate as the stones in the road for six thousand years, after which the ingenious mind of a general confederation of employers will perhaps find something less stupid. But I won't be here any longer. Let's not think about it, and just shave any client who comes along."

One Sunday morning, while that modest artiste was shaving Innocent Malifait, a labor inspector passed by.

"What are you doing?" asked the functionary.

"You can see very well," he replied. "At your service."

"What about your workers?"

"They're resting. But it's necessary that I toil to pay the rent, the income tax and the tax on capital,"

"That's good," said the inspector, "but be careful. You're working on Sunday while your workers are out for a walk. They might take that for a provocation."

The following Sunday, in fact, as Innocent, with a napkin round his neck and his face covered in shaving soap, stretched himself out in the operating chair, a large stone broke the shop window. The barber's employees, or a few of their friends, were striving to prove to him in that way that it was necessary not to spoil the métier. Innocent Malifait received a few shards of glass, which cut his skin without shaving him.

"It's nothing," said the philosophical barber, "I assure you. It's what's known as direct action."

Having wiped his face, Innocent Malifait departed with his week-old beard and a few scratches. The following Sunday he perceived that the cuts had healed and that, his beard having grown, he was a little less ugly than before.

After all, he said to himself, *I'd be very stupid to touch it. Why, while I'm at it, don't I let my hair grow?*

His friends did not fail to notice the change in his appearance. They asked him the reason for it.

"Barbers bore me," that ingenuous sage replied, simply.

When he had explained why they bored him, they found that he was right, and imitated him. A single shrewd Englishman had once put an end to the fashion for powdered hair by covering with powder not only his lackeys but also his dogs and his horses. Innocent Malifait's decision was soon the cause of there being not a single Frenchman who did not wear his beard and his hair long. When they were too long they clipped them with scissors themselves. Even people who had the habit of shaving themselves did not shave any longer, for it is only polite to do what everyone else does.

And that was a great and profitable lesson when the electricians went on strike for the twenty-seventh time. They had already obtained, in addition to the advantage of being nourished and lodged at the expense of the State, the same salary as députés and senators and free entry into the subsidized theaters. Now they demanded that the President of the Municipal

Council render a deferential visit to their syndical offices once a week in order to present him with a bouquet of roses as a sign of homage. The Municipal Council gave in immediately; but when the electricity began to flow through the wires again it was in vain; no one in Paris and the whole of France consented any longer to turn a commutator.

"The beard!" said the consumers, wanted to recall by that single word the heroic initiative of Innocent Malifait. They illuminated themselves tranquilly with oil lamps, acetylene lamps and candles. Numerous portraits were sold in the street of Monsieur Chevreul,[33] the inventor of stearin and a benefactor of humankind. The General Confederation of Labor, by contrast, burned that portrait with great ceremony; but that was the only response they could find, and the electricians remained with idle hands.

It was the same for the cafés, the restaurants, the grocers and even the bakers, who raised their prices continually because of the demands of their staff. No one went any longer to the café or the restaurant; they bought conserves and biscuits, stoically.

The employers pointed out then that they were being ruined.

"It's necessary," responded the consumers, "that we go on strike, since you haven't had the courage to do it yourselves. So much the worse for you."

In any case, that struggle did not last long. The barbers' assistants were the first to abandon the confederation. The other corporations soon followed that example. The Labor

---

[33] The physicist and chemist Michel-Eugène Chevreul (1786-1889), whose work on animal fats and oils elucidated the nature of soap and identified its crucial ingredient, stearin, as well as improving the manufacture of candles. He also did research in gerontology, aided by becoming the last living person in France born before the Revolution.

Exchange was neglected. The religion of Monsignor Vilatte[34] attempted to establish itself there, but not many people came...

---

[34] René Vilatte (1854-1929) was an itinerant priest who associated himself with various different denominations in various parts of the world in order to obtain titular advancements, eventually becoming an archbishop of sorts, and founding new cults in profusion.

Originally published in Le Journal, *10 mai 1907*

Pierre Mille: *The Sirens*

There is a man who has lived with the sirens. It's at Zeilah that one can see him now. He buys coffee from the caravans that come from Abyssinia and gives them in exchange old Maria-Theresa thalers, empty cartridge-cases, loaded cartridges and rapid-fire rifles that serve to kill Europeans. But many years ago he was the keeper of a lighthouse in the Farsan isles in the Red Sea, and that's how he saw the sirens.

He isn't mad. I assure you that I don't think he's in the least mad. Only he no longer speaks English very well because he spends most of his time, for his commerce, talking with the indigenes in Arabic or Galla, or Amharic, which is the language of the true Abyssinians, those of the mountains. And then, when he consents to relate his marvelous adventure, he sometimes interrupts himself for a long time, such a long time that one goes away without having the patience to wait for the end.

I don't know why he stops. Perhaps it's when he sees the sirens again more clearly...and for other motives, very mixed: because, for entire days, he did nothing but sleep or dream with them, on the rocks and in the hollow pools of warm water, and then, of those days when he was so happy, he retains the taste, because they were delectable, but he doesn't find anything to say, because they were empty, absolutely empty of action, while his heart was full; because he has secrets, also, things that he doesn't want to say, out of modesty, or for fear of not being believed; finally, out of jealous suspicion, because he's afraid that someone might go where he knows they are. I'll try, however, to recover his story in my memory. But you won't have, like me, the vision of his bright, moist, unfathomable eyes, the eyes that made me think of the abysms over which he claims to have floated for months.

He said:

You don't know what it's like to be the keeper of a beacon in the Farsan Isles. There's no sea more badly made than the Red Sea. People think that it's wide, but that's only an appearance and an illusion. There's only one channel in the middle, deep but rather narrow, where one can pass through. The rest is full of banks of coral or extinct volcanoes, planted in the middle of the channel, the sole utility of which is to serve as reference points for mariners. The big ships head straight toward the volcanoes like moths attracted by a gas jet. The gas jet is the lighthouse. They call that reconnoitering.

And they come, one after another, screwing their twin propellers in waters warmed by the sun, stuffed with living things: jellyfish; starfish armored with stony lace; microscopic algae; and when they've seen, in daylight. The points of those arid pebbles, or, in the great night full of the even and dry wind from the deserts, with fires lit on the shores, they give a little turn of the wheel and go away very quickly, seeming to say: "Is that you? We know now that we're on the right route, but you aren't pretty to look at, so good night!" Such is the ingratitude of those great machines.

It's never fun being a lighthouse keeper. But supposing that there are lighthouses in Hell, confided to the most compromised of the damned, those damned can't be much more unfortunate than the poor devils who nourish the red fires of the Red Sea. A cistern-boat came every month to bring me water and provisions; and when the crew detachment disembarked I started to laugh like a savage: "Men! Men! How oddly made men are!" Then they went away, and I remained alone with my matelot, a Danakil incapable of pronouncing three words of English.

There wasn't a single blade of grass or plaque of moss on that rock; nothing but old hardened cinders, pumice stones with veins of green and red lava; and the terrain, which sounded hollow under foot, was so hot that I sometimes said to the captain of the cistern-boat: "What if the volcano were to rea-waken?"

He replied: "It's the sun, imbecile, that burns this pebble. The volcano is dead, quite dead!"

But the Danakil made grimaces in order to change the subject; all Danakils know that talking about things makes them come, and he was scared of the volcano.

One night—it was just after the boat had left—I seemed to respire an unexpected and yet familiar odor, an odor of chlorine, as rough as the one that catches you in the throat in big laundries. I dreamed, imagining that I was seeing the big vats full of lye, and the women leaning over the pale water, beaters in hand, their breasts gleaming with sweat over their open bodices. That gave me pleasure.

The Danakil, who was on watch at the lamp, came to take me by the hand in a fearful fashion. I opened the little window in my room and the same odor of chlorine nearly made me fall backwards. The entire island was fuming. Columns of noxious vapor were coming out of the ground in hundreds. They came out in gusts, gasps and hiccups, as thin as the clear thread of a lit cigarette, rising in enormous jets like the escape valve of a steamboat's engine. I went downstairs, I wanted to run—I was as naked as a worm because of the heat—toward one of those fumaroles.

The Danakil shook his head and said to me: "The water! The boiling water! It's eating the land."

I put my foot on the soil and pulled it back swiftly. The islet was dissolving under the subterranean pressure of acrid springs charged with chemical poisons, and boiling. It was dissolving like a sugar-lump; it was turning to mud, into stinking dirt, morsels of rock that were cascading down softened slopes, into bubbles full of gas that went "pop" when they burst, dirty abscesses in that dirty ground. And the lighthouse started swaying like a tree, because it was being eaten away at the base, and now it could no more stand upright than a match in a pot of molten pitch.

I shouted to the Danakil: "To the sea, to the sea right away!"

I scalded my feet in that mud, which was burning and decomposing; I felt the bite of flames over my skin—black flames, if I can put it like that, for I never saw a spark in that stifling darkness—but finally, I reached the hospitable sea, the calm, fresh, maternal, welcoming water. She took me on her back.

The Danakil? I never saw him again.

It was when I came round that I saw the sirens, on another islet, further to the south, where they had doubtless taken me while I was unconscious. My head, out of the water, was resting on a cushion of wrack, and I was very frightened before those shifting bodies, larger than humans, brown and lustrous, all streaming. I imagined at first that they were sea-lions or manatees, and that currents had thrown me by chance on to a beach they frequented. But as I extended my arm I perceived, leaning over my head, at the slight sound I made, a head scarcely rounder than a man's, with hair—very long black hair divided in the middle by a parting, and eyes more tender than those of the most tender of women, which were speaking to me.

For it's necessary to say before anything else that for as long as I lived with the sirens, I always understood what was happening in their brains by virtue of the kind of silent language that was spoken not only by their profound eyes but I know not what emanation coming from their entire bodies. They also understood me, although less well. That's because I only thought by reasoning, and they scarcely had reason, but sentiments as numerous, as varied, and as nuanced as my logic.

I say "*elles*" for the sirens, as one does for swallows, seamews and gazelles, but they're a species, they reproduce, they have males and females. The first one that approached me wasn't a male, and when I thought, in a semi-delirium: *I'm alive! I'm alive! Is someone going to do me harm, now that I've recommenced living?* I understood that the being who was

142

there—an animal, a fay, or a particular species of savage human?—replied to me: "There's no need to be afraid; you're with us."

I felt her breath on my forehead and her two round breasts like those of a woman, posing on my chest, out of amity. It was only later that I perceived that my friend only had stumps of arms, terminating in flippers, and two other similar stumps instead of legs. She was only happy and lively in the light water; her rump bounded there like that of a mare in long grass.

I astonished the sirens more than they astonished me. My repugnance at nourishing myself on the fish they brought me, and my preference for shellfish, even though the pulp was as raw as that of the fish, appeared risible to them I disconcerted them again when I refused to drink sea water, but they took me to a spring that emerged at the level of the waves under a cliff, and when I drank from the hollow of my hand they admired me; my hands were always marvelous things for them.

I made them necklaces of seashells, coral and nacre, garlands of algae as yellow as gold—and the enormous moustached males with the air of warriors, covered in scars, wore them with as much pride as the siren-women. Often, when they were all ornamented, they held a ball in my honor. Oh, their backs, their rude and long tresses, the straight breasts of the women under their upright necks, the quivering of their bodies under the green water! They took me into their tournament; I was afraid and I screamed; but they carried me away like a child, with cares so gentle, in spite of their velocity, that I felt nothing but a bitter pleasure, a vertiginous sensuality.

One evening, they all sang.

Until then, I had only known them to use the mute language that I mentioned. Their song didn't have any words either, but every note said more than a long human discourse. That isn't a figure of speech; I distinguished the meaning of their lament as clearly as if it had been written on paper. They sang; there were dolorous cries, harmonious and slow, so sad

143

and so clear in the mouths of the siren-women, so grave and somberly desperate in the profound throats of the males!

They sang about the antiquity of the race of sirens, and its decadence. It had appeared almost in the first ages of the world, when the sea covered the whole surface of the globe, and the sirens had been the first attempt of Nature to realize, in the womb of the universal ocean, a being that was not a pure brute, to create an organism that truly had a brain and a heart. And then the land had emerged from the waves, and Nature had abandoned that marine sketch. She had left it there, imperfect, even degrading in the course of the centuries, and the sirens have the sentiment of their ruinous grandeur and their decadence. We humans suffer eternally from being almost similar to God, of whom we have an idea; the sirens suffer from being almost similar to humans and not having conquered human intelligence.

They ought to have been monarchs of the ocean, as humans reign over the fields, the woods and the mountains, but Nature had forgotten to perfect them, and the sharks will soon have devoured the last of the sirens. That is why they once followed the hollow boats, drowning sailors put to sleep by their charms; it was out of jealousy. But now the race is going to die. There are only a few tribes of sirens in the Red Sea and on the other side of the world, on the edge of the Malay archipelago, and, far from drowning me, my sirens had saved my life in order to enjoy the melancholy pleasure of seeing a human at close range, a specimen of the species to which hazard or who knows what mysterious design has given the empire, while inflicting humiliation, defeat and agony on them.

It is thus that the race of sirens contemplates its fatal destiny, remaining full of mildness, generosity and also futile vigor, when it's necessary to fight against the monsters of the abyss; and, far better than humans, they know and savor beauty: the beauty of the sky, the air and the waters, the mysterious rhythms of the blood in the arteries and the quivering organs. But for the rest, they're animals.

Thus, the moment has come to tell you one more thing. Being animals, so long as the amorous season hasn't arrived, the male and female sirens live as chastely as children. They form innocent couples; they live two by two, playing, fishing, and going to the gardens of the sea to look at splendid mollusks, living and flowery anemones and luminous fish that brush steamers of seaweed. Their instinctive souls penetrate one another and are only one. My siren friend had adopted me in that fashion, and when she drew me over the waves, with my arm on her shoulder, I felt happy, purely and delectably, as I had never been with a woman. Her entire body quivered under my caressant hand; but when I wanted more, she didn't understand.

I didn't imagine what would happen at the moment of amours. I said to myself *Then, she'll love me as one loves on land.* I was mistaken. When the great season comes, the couples disunite. I don't like to recall it; I'm horrified! I'm not a prude, but I'm horrified because I'm suffering. When they experience the frenzy of desire, the siren-women are no longer anything but animals, and the males become roaring brutes. They no longer chose. Everyone went with anyone. I saw them bounding, stuck together, in the foam, their monstrous stumps writhing to enlace or for battles; the sharp teeth of males—never the same male—bit the nape of my friend's neck, and her eyes, her brown eyes, whose grace and caress I loved, no longer gazed at me.

When her great amorous fury was somewhat appeased, then she swam toward me.

She said: "What's the matter?"

I replied; "I hate you!"

And with all her body and with all her senses she asked me the cause of my hatred; she explained to me that she needed all those males, one for his strength, another for his prudence, and the young ones, all the young ones, for their dash and their courage. And it was necessary that it was thus. I went to hide my head in the rocks.

"Ah!" she said to me, finally, weeping, "You're a human and I'm a siren. You want all of me, but I can't belong to anyone. You want me to be yours alone, when I no longer belong to myself, but to the god of my race. We were wrong to keep you with us... O my friend, put your hand on my shoulder once more!"

I obeyed her, and we cleaved through the sea more rapidly than we had ever done. We swam all through one night and half a day, to arrive at a flat beach, below a mountain where eagles were flying.

"Here," she said, "you'll find men similar to you and women as you desire them; adieu!"

But I knew, before her departure, what the love of a siren is; I knew her! The sand was warm under our bodies, the color of the sky filled my eyes. I still have in my mouth the salty taste of hers. I shall always have it. One evening, perhaps, she'll come back. Or I'll go to her.

Such was the adventure of Elias Whitney, who now buys coffee from caravans

Originally published in Le Journal, *25 July 1907.*

Pierre Mille: *The Victory Song*

The Journal of a Parisian in 1920

Tomorrow will be the seventeenth of July. That day, the anniversary of the death of Bonaventure Espérandieu, has become that of the new national festival. There will be flowers, songs, and women who go about the streets brightly clad and happy, saying: "Our sons will no longer be killed." And all the speech-makers—because they are necessary—in the smallest villages, in more or less inflated or naïve phrases, will celebrate the memory of Bonaventure, while in the academies and the amphitheaters of the Sorbonne, all the scientific palaces in France, essays will be written about the great scientist who is no more; the fatherland that gave him birth will be glorified; people will say that at the moment when everything here seemed to be dissolving—laws, mores, faith in the future and even the race—one worship remained, that of science, and it was by means of science that it was finally saved. But no one will dare to tell the whole truth, no one will dare to speak sincerely about the true Bonaventure Espérandieu, such as I knew him: devoured by genius and burned by alcohol; dazzling, crapulous, sublime, ragged and enthusiastic; full of virtues that people around him were avid to destroy and vices for which hypocrites scorned him; as simple as a child, dazed by laughter, delirium and intoxication.

Everyone remembers the day when war broke out. It broke out in spite of all the prayers, all the climb-downs, all the kneeling. It broke out because there had been too much talk of peace, too much adoration of peace, too much preaching of it, at the same time as the war between classes and the role of war between peoples—as if those people out there

147

were not, they too, of another class, since they had another ideal! The imbeciles who had sung those ballads, the insensate individuals who had stirred up those hatreds, woke up one morning before the threat of a defeat and the evidence that the defeat in question would signify the material ruination of millions of people, on whom the victor would impose conditions such that it would be impossible for them henceforth to earn their bread. For it is no longer to steal land that people fight today, but to take possession of labor, to be alone in being able to work and to make gold.

Oh, all that disarray, all those cowardly politicians who recriminate against one another, and all of whom are right, alas, to recriminate, and those futile madmen who demand *the lives of the guilty*...! I still blush with shame when I think about it. One pulls oneself together quickly, however. Everyone knows that it is not only a question of honor or territory, that one is going to fight in order not to be condemned to die of hunger. And the men departed, grave and resolute, through the mute streets.

Only the face of Bonaventure was bursting with joy, when he came to find me.

"You've never been to my attic," he said. "The moment has come. And then, you can help me. I need money. You'll give me the money, won't you?"

I perceived that for several months he must have been drinking even more than usual. The features were swollen in his pale face and his hands were trembling. I accompanied him without confidence, almost without curiosity, glad nevertheless of a step in which I found distraction from a horrible anguish; only a few days separated us from the great battle, and after that...I shuddered in thinking about it.

As we went past an armorer's shop Bonaventure asked me to buy some cartridges for his hunting rifle. Afterwards we went up to his lodgings. It was worse than an attic: a hovel. In a corner were the dirty and unkempt sheets of a wretched bed. In the middle of the room, a trestle table bore broken instruments of physics. Nothing but disorder, and in me, the dolorous impression that I was dealing with a madman who was living a vulgar dream, maintained by debauchery. He started to laugh like a child.

"It doesn't seem very engaging to you," he said. "Bah! Le Bon[35] made his experiments on the corner of a table, with cardboard boxes. But look, here's the lyre!"

It was, in fact, a lyre, or rather a kind of cithara, which was distinguished from ordinary instruments by a few strings of singular aspect, some of enormous length and others extremely short.

"But you're not very strong," said Bonaventure. "With you it's necessary to commence with the demonstration for beginners."

He extended a catgut string over a bridge, which he plucked with his fingernail. It rendered a clear sound, which died away slowly.

"It gives the A," Bonaventure continued, "the A of the third octave."

While speaking, he dusted the string with a yellow powder.

"Now," he said, "I take a violin...the fiddle of a mad gypsy, isn't it?...and I make it yield the same A of the third octave."

He had seized the bow in a hand that was curiously expert in spite of its tremor. The note sang in the calm air, and at

---

[35] Gustave Le Bon (1841-1931) was a polymath nowadays chiefly remembered for his work in social psychology, but better known at the time for his experiments in physics, which won him a Nobel Prize in 1903, and the speculations to which they gave rise, summarized in *L'Évolution de la matière* (1905) and *L'Évolution des forces* (1907). Having hypothesized the equivalence of mass and energy before Einstein, he proposed that the discovery of a method of dissociating matter rapidly would be able to create enormous explosions—a notion appropriated by numerous items of *roman scientifique*.

the same moment, a slight explosion responded from the string extended over the bridge.

"You've understood?"

"No," I said.

"It's a classic experiment performed before schoolboys," said Bonaventure. "The vibrations of the violin are communicated to the string stretched over the bridge. It vibrates in sympathy. It only vibrates to the vibrations of the note that it would render if it were touched, you understand. And at that moment, the fulminate of mercury with which it is dusted, a very sensitive explosive, is detonated.."

"And thus," I asked, "a cartridge, or a shell?"

"A cartridge or a shell would only explode if their detonator were in contact with a taut string, in sympathy itself with a powerful musical instrument. I could play all the tunes in the world without making the cartridges that you have in your pocket explode."

I had forgotten the cartridges. I threw them on the table with a certain anxiety. Bonaventure laughed again

"Except," he said, "that it's here that I intervene. I've found it. I'm sure that I've found it. I won't give you my exact formula, for two reasons. Either you're scientifically ignorant, in which case you wouldn't understand, or you could assimilate the formulae, and then my authorial rights would be at risk. But I'll employ a comparison. Do you like someone to carve a stopper, a cork stopper, within range of your ears?"

I shivered.

"Bonaventure," I cried, you know full well that I can't bear it. Merely the allusion that you've just made to it shakes my nerves. I get aggravated nerves and gooseflesh."

"Good," said Bonaventure. "And yet it's a little sound, a very little sound, that of a pen-knife on a cork. But it's precisely because it's a little sound. Know that beyond the sounds you can hear other notes exist, too high or too low to be perceived by the ear. Their vibrations are multiples or submultiples of those that reach you, and they have particular properties. The ones that the knife biting into cork produce are almost of that kind; they attack your nerve cells. Prolonged or better chosen, they'd decompose them. Well, I've discovered the number of sonic vibrations necessary to decompose and detonate all known explosives, and I can produce those vibrations."

"So?" I asked, not daring to comprehend yet.

"So I can make those cartridges in front of you, on that table, blow up. Don't be afraid, all hunters know that a cartridge that explodes in the open air only scatters the lead that it contains for a few centimeters around. In any case, we're only going to keep two of those you've bought, and wet the powder of the others...that's done. Now watch."

He approached he lyre with a sort of bizarre bow.

"It's very high-pitched vibrations that we need. Brace yourself, interesting nervous person!"

The bow eased over the strings. They resonated, full, forceful and harmonious; in ever-rising octaves. Then there was silence. How shall I put it? A silence filled with a sound that was inaudible. A silence that devastated al my nerves, which nearly made me scream. And Bonaventure stated trembling in all his limbs himself, paler and more decomposed than me, because his nerves were in a poorer state, because of the alcohol.

"*Floc!*"

A slight flash, a dull sound, and the room filled with smoke: the cartridges lay on the table, disemboweled, their cardboard burning slowly, like tinder.

"*Voilà!*" said Bonaventure, simply.

Scarcely a few hours after that experiment we departed eastwards, toward the terrible Orient, already in flames and bloody. Bonaventure took another instrument, incomparably more powerful than the model in his workshop, capable of communicating the mysterious vibrations over a long distance. That instrument was already finished. Bonaventure needed money purely to pay the industrialist who had constructed it to his plans, and that was why he had asked for my help, poor fellow! I paid, and an automobile carried us away.

Oh, France invaded, people in flight along the roads, poor carts full of wretched women and famished children, the farms pillaged by the fugitives themselves, all the horrors of panic! I've seen those things, I've seen them. But they will never be seen again; the world is liberated from those terrors today.

I was driving the automobile. Bonaventure continually applied his lips to a bottle full of an alcohol that stimulated him without getting him drunk; he no longer knew, and had not known for a long time, the possibility of drunkenness, but he was going mad.

And I said to myself: *He's rendered me mad too. None of this is true—nothing! We're traveling toward ridicule, as well as toward captivity or death.* But he kept repeating, perpetually, with frightful laughter:

"And to think that Amphion built cities to the sounds of the lyre! We others..."[36]

The he touched with his foot the great iron lyre extended in front of us. It rendered formidable lamentations, a terrible cry, immense and somber. And Bonaventure stood up, his arms in a cross, still sniggering...

How we arrived at nightfall, in the vicinity of Neucharmes, where the enemy army was concentrated for its great forward movement; how we succeeded in installing ourselves at the summit of the Nauve, the hill in the Ardennes where we overlooked league after league of country, I no longer know. We were maddened by the imminence of the action, we were moving like sleepwalkers, but penetrated by the harassing anguish that all those know who have attempted

---

[36] Amphion features, along with his twin demigod Zethus, in a myth of the foundation of the city of Thebes, in which stones moved by the song of Amphion's lyre moved to form the walls of the citadel spontaneously.

something great. "We're sure, mathematically certain, of success, and yet..."

Bonaventure planted the lyre on a slab of red sandstone.

"This is it," he said, "Our troops are far behind, out of range of the vibrations. This is it!"

As far as the eye could see, camp fires were burning in the shadow. Sometimes, from a village more brightly illuminated, the songs of drunken soldiers rose toward us. Beneath our feet a rider passed, doubtless carrying an order, and the resonance of four horseshoes, launched at the gallop, made us wince.

"Let's hurry!" said Bonaventure. "Suppose someone comes!"

But when he had picked up his great bow, he cried, in spite of our fears: "Something is necessary, something first. Hurrah! Eureka! *La Victoire en chantant nous ouvre la barrière...*"[37]

The tall lyre sounded the first notes of its heroic song. They were slow, grave, and powerful. A sad black crow took flight, moaning. Above our heads, the fir-tees agitated. They spread terror. The soldiers who were singing in the distance, fell silent, astonished, already vaguely troubled, inclined beneath the menace and the mystery.

"And now," said Bonaventure, "now...!"

There was then, as in his attic, a frightful silence, a strident silence full of mordant waves, but a thousand times stronger, a perfidious charge through the nocturnal air of un-

---

[37] This is the first line of *Le Chant du depart*, a Revolutionary song composed in 1794 by Étienne-Nicolas Méhut with words by Marie-Joseph Chénier, first sung in response to the battle of Fleurus but then taken up by the Committee of Public Safety to celebrate the anniversary of the capture of the Bastille. Mille could not know in 1907, of course, that it would be taken up again by soldiers departing for the front in the Great War of 1914-18, when France was invaded for real and Bonaventure's lyre was, alas, nowhere to be found.

precedented vibrations, multiplied by millions, wild and omnipotent, the mute surge of death precipitating upon its goal.

"Oh! Enough!" I cried. "Don't you see, wretch, that we're going to die too?"

Within us there was a decomposition of nervous cells, a mortal shock, the dissolution of being. He hadn't thought of that. Yes, we were going to die. I saw Bonaventure fall first. I had just time thereafter to perceive a giant conflagration, the eruption of a volcano, the sound of ten thousand ammunition trucks exploding at the same time, the dry successive crackle of millions of cartridges, like that of a dactylograph maneuvered by a gigantic hand. A bell-tower in the form of a bubble, of which there are many in the East, opened up like the lid of a vast cooking-pot before falling to the ground. The scream of three thousand dolors and a hundred thousand agonies responded to the lyre. I lost consciousness.

When I came round, a man as putting an ice-water compress on my head.

"Bonaventure?" I demanded. "My friend?"

There was no reply; but I saw a poor, wretched form lying at my feet. His nerves had not resisted. The grim music of the lyre had been too strong for his cells, tremulous and burned by alcohol.

But the enemy? There was no more enemy. There was nothing but bloody debris, hundreds of thousands of wounded, an unspeakable, unprecedented rout, which would never be repeated, because there would be no more war: no one would dare any longer.

La Victoire en chantant...

Oh, that terrible night!

Albert Keim (1876-1947) was a prolific writer of popular bi-ographies, many of which were translated into English; his subjects included Honoré de Balzac, Charles Dickens, Louis Pasteur and Richard Wagner. His laconically surreal short fiction was relatively sparse and largely unappreciated. "The New Race" *was originally published in* La Lanterne—Le Supplément, *21 janvier 1908.*

Albert Keim: *The New Race*

It was a warm evening in the year 2006. Rapid aviators were crossing paths in the air. Enormous electric globes were beginning to illuminate the city, which was calming down under the mild gleams of the dusk.

The astronomer Le Cartier, after having swallowed a pill containing the synthesis of the nutritive elements necessary to his organism, took his place before megistocope number one and started to read the sky with as much patience as intoxication.

He was interrogating the familiar constellations, passing from Sirius to Orion, when an immense bolide of sorts appeared, alternately dark and luminous. It was a pointed mass. It did not resemble a dirigible. No aircraft could, in any case, have ventured so far into space.

Although habituated to lunar reveries, the savant Le Cartier rubbed his eyes. The phenomenon seemed decidedly strange to him.

He quit the instrument and blew into an acoustic tube. A few moment later, the engineer Goury, who lived down below on the fourth floor, came into the vast observatory.

Together, they examined the thing, obscure and then shiny, which appeared to be coming from the astral region, coldly and scientifically. They tried to define it, in vain. How-ever, in accordance with the essential appearances, observing that the movement was subject to variations, they diagnosed a thought and a will directing that movement.

From then on, it was no longer a matter of a sidereal perturbation. The two men were shaken by a frisson.

As they were exchanging opinions in loud voices, Mademoiselle Sidonie Le Cartier, unleashing melodious and pathetic chords from her organola, came to join them and to share their surprise.

"It's a veritable machine, with a triangular face," the astronomer finally pronounced. "Red and violet flames are escaping from it."

And the machine in question was visible, clearly visible. One might have thought that it was a sort of gigantic flying pyramid.

The sky became dark; night was now passing floods of ink over the ether. The stars, large diamonds of the darkness, were no longer anything but timid glow-worms.

The scientist projected scintillating beams of light toward the mysterious moving object.

Sidonie uttered an exclamation of surprise: "One would think that it's about to crash on top of us."

Blonde and frail, the young woman had gone pale. She was trembling. Her father and Monsieur Goury tried to joke.

A rumor rose up from the enormous city, which was going to sleep. The scientist applied himself to his apparatus again, and thanks to his powerful searchlights, succeeded in following the reasoned and steadily decelerating fall of the moving object.

"Where does it come from?" he wondered. "From what star? It's stopping; someone's trying to steer it...Someone! With what precision, what surety...it's coming down..."

"Toward us!" howled the engineer. And abruptly, he extinguished the six globes and the colossal lamps neighboring the megistocope.

The giant pyramid from space described several curves, and slowly, majestically, floated about four hundred meters above Le Cartier's glazed hall, at the height of the Tower erected by the illustrious Fravison at the center of the universal exposition in 2000.

Afterwards, with extreme prudence, it resumed its descent. It traveled in a zigzag, following its plan in complicity with the nocturnal expanse.

Avidly, with a curiosity that dominated her vague and terrible anguish, Sidonie was unable to turn her gaze away from the huge black object that was approaching, very real in the penumbra.

"Wait," vociferated the engineer. "I shall know."

"What are you going to do? Don't tempt God," begged Sidonie.

Goury was her childhood friend. She knew that her father was thinking of marrying her to the bold and valiant young man.

"I'm going," he said. "God is on Earth as well as on the other planets. I'll take my armored airship."

He escaped. Le Cartier was breathless.

The sinister vehicle accentuated its descent, with a sort of solemnity. A ray of moonlight had pierced the scattered battalions of clouds and cast its peaceful light over the fantastic delta.

Suddenly, Goury's airship rise up, fragile and pointed, and climbed...

A jet of phosphorescent vapor emerged from the moving object, enveloped the poor aerial skiff and precipitated it to the darkness.

Then there was a loud grating sound outside the observatory. In the night, a radiance and a shower of sparks sprang from the black delta

Le Cartier had rushed to the iron screens, but an immense, agile, hairy being seemed to emerge from the air. It leapt upon him and knocked him down.

Endowed with Will and Intelligence, it seized the astronomer, opened a door and threw him on to the floor, like a thing, in a trice.

Sidonie had turned the electric button. She tried to flee, groping her way. A blue light filled the vast room. The unfortunate woman saw that she was doomed, for it was there, beside her, gigantic, with a luminous gaze and a fantastic mane.

At first, it was as if Sidonie were paralyzed; then she threw herself upon a dainty revolver that was hanging next to the lens cupboard, took aim and fired. The weapon fell from her hand.

The THING uttered a kind of cluck.

The bullets had skimmed over its bushy and scintillating yellow hair.

She would have liked to annihilate it. A supreme curiosity preserved her consciousness.

The being grabbed her dress with a savage and triumphant clamor; and suddenly recumbent, under the flamboyant gaze and the monstrous breath, she felt an ardent skin against her own.

A sharp, horrible pain tore her flesh. Then an abrupt, marvelous sensuality traversed her. It was like a light penetrating her, like a new and sublime heat that lavished over her terrestrial body all the illuminations of the sky, and made it radiate splendidly, like a star, in vertigo and domination, and in the beyond.

Finally, she fainted.

Simon Le Cartier strove to believe that it was a collective hallucination. However, he had found his daughter naked, overwhelmed by a leaden slumber. Goury, who had been lucky enough to fall, with his airship, into the Port de la Concorde, from which he emerged safe and sound, no longer knew what to think.

Sidonie remained profoundly thoughtful, shivering. Soon, she experienced disturbances, those of pregnancy. She, so slim and so petite, swelled up.

After a wait of sixteen months, she gave birth very laboriously to a long hairy child with a forehead garnished with a tuft of yellow hair, and a surprised, triumphant and resplendent gaze.

Originally published in Le Journal, *26 September 1911.*

Edmond Haraucourt: *Memoirs of an Ephemeron*

4.50 a.m. Dawn is about to break. A pale whiteness is quivering at the base of the sky on the horizon of the world; the original pond is still all blue in its girdle of motionless reeds, but already a plaque of light is extending at the limit of the water, and the instinct of our race informs me that that light is the promise of life. Time has revolved, the future is announced. Once again, the saved universe is about to emerge from the chaos of shadows and resuscitate. For the law that regulates space determines that the earth is engulfed in the obscurity of death for an entire cycle, and that life triumphs in its turn in the cycle that follows, one being called Night and the other Day; and we have a cycle to live. I await mine. It inflates and stirs. I sense it trembling in my innermost depths as it rises over the mists of the Orient. O gods, how long it is! How long it is! Rise, sun!

5.08. I'm still only a larva; I'm still waiting. Throughout the cycle of the Night I have waited, and also during other diurnal cycles which have passed of which I don't remember the count; swimming, crawling or hoisting myself up toward a leaf sticky with mud, I was interminably a damp, slow creature displacing itself with effort; toward the elastic regions of the air, still forbidden to my flight, vainly, I lifted the double silk of my antennae, and, soft, curbed and fat, I dragged myself through the mud—me, whom a sublime destiny invites to ride the sunbeams! I've slept, I've eaten and the time was so long... Are all those of my race racked by an identical impatience, or am I an elect, dissimilar to others, richer in strength and more haunted by hopes?

5.20. The bleak litany of the seasons unfurls monotonously. But the term is approaching. The warm orange color is invading the azure and deploying there; a fine cloud, charged with prophecies, is scaling the sky in order to command the stars to go out and make way for the ephemerae whose reign is about to begin. Under the pressure of the wind, which aids the sun, the celestial fleece extends; it floats, it extends its wings; lying on its belly, which becomes pink, it advances, and its back is lilac. A golden plume lights up at the tip of its wing! Two resplendent darts have sprung forth and wounded it; it is bleeding! Rise, sun, that I might live!

6.35. The sun is warming me. But how many events already in the last season! I'm a nymph; my wings are stuck to my back in a double roof; they still refuse to obey me, and I go, I seek, I hope...I also remember! Without the power to distract my thoughts, I think about the old one and what he said to me. I found him, quivering, on a reed leaf that he was climbing in order to receive the reanimating rays; he watched me coming, and only when I was nearby did I know that he was of our race; he only had one wing, and his entire body was wrinkled by age. While I contemplated that lamentable debris of a performance toward which I aspire, he spoke to me.

"O nymph," he said to me, "keep your pity; it has no other reason for being than your ignorance of things. Instead of scorning my fate, rather envy it, for you will not attain the wisdom that has earned my deformity. Thanks to it, I have lived or eight cycles, and thanks to it, my soul soars while my body crawled. From the place where I dwell, I have flown higher than all of you, and I know the secret of the world."

And the old one also said to me:

"Eight alternate cycles of day and night have rotated over me. I have seen generations born and die; I have observed the dream of your childhoods, the ambition of your youths, the flight of your maturities, and four times I have seen you sink into oblivion. Certainly, your existence is long, since it endures as long as a sun, but how much further it might be prolonged if you drew from your souls the strength to escape the trap that the gods extend for you!"

The old one added:

"Thus I have done, and I have survived all of you."

This time, he said nothing more, and I drew away from him; but his words haunted me, with the desire to know.

What, then, is the mortal trap that the hatred of the gods sets for the people of ephemerae in order to abridge their life? If I learned that before opening my wings, I too could be the master of time, and the generations would also pass before me, one after another.

Often, I came back to the old one; I surrounded him with care and respect. He rejected me at first, by virtue of the habitude of being alone and rendering rancor to those who crush him with their disdain. Gradually, however, he has tolerated my presence, and the timid amity of an impotent and a nymph. He will speak and I shall know! Before the sun is high I shall know the secret of the gods.

8.10. Drunk on light, the old one shook his unique wing in the air; he has spoken! I know! He has spoken, and the skies have trembled with anger or fear. At the moment when I provoked his confidence, heavy clouds scaled space to assault the sun. Rumbles of thunder growled in the distance. A warm vapor weighed over the pond; in that fecund oven, germs stirred in the mud and in the scum that floats on the water; in thousands of thousands, around me, hatchings are in preparation, the work of the storm, which is my work; and the gods know that I know!

9.00. In gaps between the clouds the sun is shining, half way to the zenith. All that eight cycles of meditation have taught the old one I have weighed, examined and judged. Unique among those of my race, I hold the secret of life, the key to the enigma, which the pitiless gods hide from us. My studious childhood has wanted that conquest, and my genius has obtained it. I am the exceptional being, the annunciator of verities, the immortal ephemeron! I shall dominate innumerable peoples, I shall found an empire and institute a dogma. The predestined individual who must bring the liberating word to the palingeneses is me. The formula that saves, the word of science that will render us similar to the gods and as durable as them, I have, and I can offer it to all! I shall be the prophet and the leader, the king of duration, the pastor of the myriads who do not want to return to the oblivion of the green waters! I am the universal benefactor, the one whose memory ought never to perish, the founder of the dream! The cruel law that the gods imposed upon us at the dawn of time will be abolished by mine. Gods of forces, the time has come for you to die, since the ephemerae of whom you are so afraid will know henceforth by means of what prestige you impel them to be the artisans of their own death. I am the voice of the avenged race, and I am rising!

9.30. Not yet, not yet. It's necessary that my adolescence, which is coming to an end, should pass through the ordeal of dolor and tear its turn. I'm suffering. My wings are soft, hanging over my flanks. A veil covers my eyes; my entire body, from the head to the abdomen, is wrapped in bandages, my feet are clenched under the embrace; I'm cracking; I'm choking. Am I going to die, and my dream with me?

10.00. I've struggled; I'm victorious. But that long illness has exhausted my strength. Under the energetic tension of my young muscles, I've torn the membrane that imprisoned me; I've freed my brilliant back, my head and my folded feet; the false wings of my nymph and its flaccid remains are lying beneath me like a carpet, and above the detritus I'm stretching my wings in the sunlight. O youth, illusions! This, then, is what remains of my presumptuous past? I believed that I existed once, but those nascent wings, of which I was so proud, were only a vain image. Before having tried their flight, they have fallen beside me and I have made litter of them now!

Adieu, defunct things, naiveties of yore, verified lies, I no longer know you! I have my true wings now, those which bear, those which can. I am Me, I shall be Myself! Adieu, chimeras! But of the age of enthusiasm, when you abused me with hopes, I have at least retained the memory, for it was while agitating in place those deceptive wings that I conceived the dream with which my life will be strong!

10.10. I have had a good rest. My convalescence is over. My tarsi are gripping the leaf solidly. My wings are erect, vertical and vibrant. The silks of my tail extend behind me. With my free feet I have cleaned my head and my antennae. I'm ready. I'm mature. I'm setting forth.

10.25. In order to try my wings I have explored the world. In my vertical flight I have danced over the infinite waters of the pond; and then I launched myself all the way to the region of the clouds: two and ten times higher than the tempestuous layer where the summits of the reeds oscillate, I rose up amid the vertigo, without trembling, and joyful. I have seen how vast the world is. I have seen what the old one will never know: the immensity of the deserts that undulate beyond the oak tree, and the unsuspected ponds, where races similar to ours might perhaps live. It is there that I shall extend my conquest and impel my people; to the extreme limits of unknown countries, where only the advanced gaze of the clouds penetrated before mine, I shall extend the glory of my name and the benefit of my doctrine.

11.00. From the direction of the occidental inferno where they hide in darkness, I can hear the gods growling; their thunder makes my wings vibrate, and the electric storm excites the hatching of your germs. Irritate yourselves, powers of the heavens! It's for me that you are working, by multiplying my armies; your anger aids them to be born. From all parts I see ours welling up, like a white snow that the pond is launching toward the sky. To me, myriads! Listen to me, palingeneses! This is the time when the bearer of the good news has awakened among you!

Noon. Relentlessly, I have flown indefatigably over the groups and over the couples, and I have seen death working in the full joy of life. The old one had not lied; ephemerae kill one another by virtue of the furious appetite of amour; the white wings only serve them to rush to aerial couplings; the males launch themselves from one female to another, clasping the backs of their prey, and the rounds of coupled dancers whirl madly in amorous clouds, until their exhaustion allows them to fall back on to the glaucous mirror where the devourers swim. Their sin kills them! For excess is sin, and the punishment that follows is proof of the fault. Without that frenzy, our existence would be prolonged for cycles. Through the crowds I have preached the religion of chastity. I have promised duration to those who heed me. At first they laughed at me and the lovers insulted me, but a horde has followed me and we are flying toward the heights.

1 p.m. I have launched my disciples toward the four horizons. They are going everywhere, crying: "Come to the vanquisher of death, and never forget his lesson or his example!"

5 p.m. Triumph! My glory is worldwide. For half a cycle those who were propagating the dogma have repeated my words and proclaimed the law. It is founded. The sun of the cycle will die alone; the sun of this cycle, reentering into night, will not go to tell the gods that they can rest in peace and that the ephemerae are destroyed. They were thousands, those who did not want to listen to me, and the demons of the water have closed their voracious mouths upon them. But millions have obeyed me and are only waiting for my order to launch themselves forth to conquer the universe.

5.30. I have given the order. My emissaries have carried it. Clouds of palingeneses are rising up toward me and rallying behind the imperial escort. The people are saying: "Where is he?" But in the whirlwind of leaders who are rising and descending around my sacred person, I remain invisible, the one who is revered but whom one does not accede. Approaching me is forbidden to females over an extent of five reeds and my guard of ascetics is vigilant.

5.40. The horde is on the march. Thousands of millions hasten in my wake; the atmosphere is darkened by them. We are advancing westwards, chasing the sun before us, which is running away.

6.00. I have conquered five ponds, thirty puddles and a stream. I have recruited their peoples, which are swelling my army. Now we have reached the edge of the world. I have crossed the barrier of fabulous willows of which our legends speak. I can see the poplars, and the Waterless Land, which desolates the arid crops, and where the green clouds of forests crawl. Incredible giants, monstrous and wingless, which move over the ground with the aid of two or four feet, and which might be the gods, dwell there. Before the agony of the sun, we shall enter their territory.

6.15. I have led my armies into the land of the god-giants. Their heads raised toward us, they gazed at the opaque cloud of our hordes, and were immobilized by terror, in the evident anguish of thinking what their destiny will be if the ephemerae will no longer consent to the intoxicating suicide.

6.20. The reports of my police are disquieting; I tried at first to attenuate the peril, and perhaps my agents have only revealed a part of the truth to me. The real fact, henceforth indisputable, is that defections are multiplying in the army excessively. I the last quarter of a cycle, infractions of the law of chastity, which were only individual and clandestine, have become frequent and public. Amorous couples no longer deign to hide; their cynicism is provoking contagion; since the decline of the sun, the evil has taken on an endemic character. The fall of the agonizing no longer frightens anyone, and one might even think, on the contrary, that their death excites desire. Under a rain of falling males, who fall, exhausted, their wings hanging, one sees other males hastening to decease; the spectacle of death animates then to lust, just as the spectacle of lust invites them to death. Is it, then, a fatal law that those two forces work for one another, and that they are truly two sisters, so powerful by virtue of their union that my moral power is bound to crumble before theirs? O Palingeneses, O my brothers, who do not want to be saved, an infinite sadness is entering into the soul of the prophet!

6.40. The solar globe is red in the occident. The horizon has bitten it. I have returned to the army. Horror! Behind us, the plain traversed is white with cadavers, like snow, and the oblique radiance of the cycle that is setting is making my people a pink shroud. What is the point of struggling further? What is the point of denying it to myself? I no longer have hope, I no longer believe. I have wanted the impossible, since no one has listened to me. What remains of my former ambition, of my former glory? I no longer even regret them. It is in myself, now, that I see the void, and when I contemplate the interminable succession of efforts that were my life, a pity takes hold of me, and it resembles disgust.

6.50. I sense that my soul is very old. I no longer even tell myself that the gods have vanquished me; I no longer believe in the gods. My innumerable army is reduced to an escort of the faithful, who persist in fluttering around me. A swarm of late-born virgins recruited at the last pond has penetrated the supreme cohort; they are dancing and making graces, requesting the lessons of the Master; in order to show us their strong wings, which can bear the weight of a male, they spring forth before us, and with the wind of their flight they shake ours, as if inadvertently, as they flee... If my soul has grown old, my body is still young, and rich in its reserves...

Get away, female! What does your virginity matter to me? I am the Prophet, the Unique... She has replied, assuring me of her respect and her piety, and has requested the favor of serving me as a slave... Forward! Ever forward! Since I have decided, and although I no longer believe, since it is necessary for me to play the comedy of my role to the end, forward!

7.00. The sun of my cycle is dead, and I survive. Here is the region of Lamps, illusory suns that promise us the illusion of perpetuated joys... Don't come any closer, female! Get away from my antennae! Don't slide your brilliant back under the feet of the Prophet! I don't want to feel the warmth of your fine down, into which my silky feet would sink. Stop—they're looking at us!

7.10 The shadow...I can no longer see the others... No one can see me any longer... You want to draw me toward he false sun of that Lamp, Sister? They've all abandoned me, except you. The storm is rumbling in the distance, and making the alert blood of my heart flow faster. The beating of your white wings is enveloping me with a frisson.

My sister, my sister...

"Adrien Vély" was the pseudonym of Adrien Lévy (1864-1935), a prolific author of vaudevilles and café-concert songs. "The Ruination..." was originally published in Le Matin, *28 July 1912.*

Adrien Vély: *The Ruination of the Anthropogenic Institute*

Paris was the first city in the world that could be proud of having founded a Carrel Institute.[38] Soon, all the great cities in France had established branches, which did not take long to become flourishing, and in which young scientists supplemented, in their audacious endeavors the admirable discoveries of the inventor of human grafting, the illustrious physician who had died a quarter of a century before, rich in years and honors.

Our fine country had thus become the exclusive supplier to the whole world of arms. legs, fingers, eyes, spleens, pancreases, kneecaps, ileocaecal valves and, in general, every kind of piece detached from the human body. The infirm, the wounded and amputees flocked to us from the four cardinal points, for they knew that we alone could submit to them such a varied choice of impeccable viable anatomical items. At the time of the end-of-season sales, in particular, the Carrel Institutes were visited by an innumerable host of buyers. Some had

---

[38] The Nobel prize-winning biologist Alexis Carrel (1873-1944) remains famous as the great pioneer of organ transplantation, then more often called "human grafting," in association with Charles Lindbergh, after emigrating to America. Frenchmen continued to claim him as one of their own, although he claimed to have been forced into exile by the French scientific establishment after providing testimony in support of one of the alleged miracles at Lourdes.

preferred to wait in order to benefit from the advertised discounts. Others, seduced by an opportunity, took away with them, although they had no need of them, a spare nose or ear, just in case, as a precaution. One never knows what might happen, and, all things considered, two carotids are better than one.

While continuing to devote themselves to that intensive culture of human grafts, the scientists of our Carrel Institutes took their research further. Had nor Doctors Loëb[39] and Gustave Le Bon, two celebrated contemporaries of the great Carrel, affirmed that nothing opposed, theoretically, the possibility that one might eventually succeed in creating living beings? It was in that direction that our scientists directed their investigations.

They ended up being crowned by success. One day, people learned that the Carrel Institute in Paris had succeeded in creating a man.

In France, in Paris, there was a true delirium. The newspapers giving details of the newborn, publishing his portrait and recording his progress were snapped up every day.

The day when it was learned that the spontaneous child, devoid of antecedents, had said "Papa" and "Mama" for the first time, the delight reached its peak. Enthusiastic delegations wet to deposit wreaths and bouquets at the feet of statues of Carrel, Loëb and Gustave Le Bon.

The next day, in the Chambre des députés, the President of the Council mounted the podium and made a brief speech:

"Messieurs, I have the honor of depositing in the bureau of the Chambre a request for the opening of a credit of two hundred millions for the creation in Paris of an Anthropogenic

---

[39] Jacques Loëb (1859-1924) worked alongside Carrel in New York, and achieved a slightly surprising fame by means of his experiments in artificially-induced parthenogenesis in marine invertebrates, which prompted Mark Twain to write a polemical essay in defense of open-mindedness and scientific progress.

Institute. Thanks to the genius of our scientists, the question of depopulation is resolved. In twenty years time we shall have at our disposal all the armed corps necessary for us to attain or enemies and discourage our rivals. We have only to command the elements today."

A thunder of applause greeted those words, and the credit requested was voted unanimously. A year later, the Anthropogenic Institute was inaugurated, in great pomp. Then, in the silence of the laboratories, unbridled biologists prepared the future generations. At the same time, our diplomacy commenced employing a language that, if not dignified, was at least firm.

Unfortunately, it is always difficult to keep the secret of great inventions. Our adversaries had an exceedingly powerful interest in penetrating the one that permitted us to conceive the hope of splendid reparations. They succeeded in stealing it from us, and it was soon learned they were also founding an Anthropogenic Institute.

We had only one means of conserving our advantage, and that was to increase our production. That is what we did. But our neighbors immediately followed us in that path. On the other hand, the other European nations, concerned about equilibrium, devoted themselves in their turn to the fabrication of men. And a great peril menaced humankind!

This far, peoples had buckled under the burden of excessive armaments. Now they were about to be stifled by their own density. Not only was it necessary relentlessly to arm the ever-increasing populations, but it was also necessary to think about nourishing them. The solution of that double problem was unrealizable.

Philanthropists demanded that the great powers limit the number of their citizens themselves. Negotiations were engaged between chancelleries. The governments recognized that the imitation was desirable, that it was even necessary, but none volunteered to take the initiative, fearing to be alone in attempting a trial that might be fatal to their country and deliver them as prey to less scrupulous neighbors, more numerous and stronger. And the Anthropogenic Institutes continued to pour out over the earth millions of men for whom it was impossible henceforth to provide subsistence, and who would have no other resource than to kill one another.

Naturally, at the same time as the populations increased, criminality was augmented. Frightful abominations were committed in France.

One bandit, redoubtable among them all, imagined stealing aircraft from their owners; and, armed with murderous machines, he furrowed the air, sowing death everywhere. He killed more than three thousand people in a week. The police learned that he was hidden in a house in the environs of Paris. An expedition was immediately organized in order to capture him. The prefect of police received the mission to take him alive, no matter what the cost, so he decided that the imposing forces put at his disposal would be completely unarmed.

Agents and soldiers went to lay siege to the house in which the wretch was barricaded. Thousand of curiosity-seekers joined them. The countryside and the highways were black with people.

When all the dispositions were made, the prefect of police ordered the attack. From his lair, the bandit slew fifty agents, thirty soldiers and a hundred onlookers. When the door of the room that was his last refuge was broken down and the prefect of police penetrated it courageously at the head of his men, the wild beast felled him with a revolver shot fired at point blank range at his chest.

As he fell, the prefect cried: "Above all, take him alive!"

They fell upon the bandit, disarmed him and tied him up. The prefect, who was in his death-throes, asked to be lifted up, and in a voice that was continually growing weaker, he said: "My friend, you have killed a thousand citizens, fifty agents, thirty soldiers, a hundred and twenty bystanders, and me. You have been a great credit to the fatherland. The government of the Republic has charged me to award you the gold medal of mutuality…"

Having said that, he rendered his soul. There was a violent stir in the crowd. Then, in a rush, it precipitated itself upon the Anthropogenic Institute and set fire to it, with great cries of joy.

Probably the writer Louis Champeaux born in 1888 who was killed in action during the Great War; one source listing such deaths alleges that the name was a pseudonym employed by Georges Babet. "The Master of Death" *was originally published in* Le Mercure de France, *16 septembre 1912.*

Louis Champeaux: *The Master of Death*

Extracted from the notes of Professor Alfred Barbier

To the great shade of Edgar Allan Poe, in all humility.
L.C.

Scientific milieux were greatly intrigued a few years ago by the abrupt retreat in which Dr. Alfred Barbier, chevalier of the Légion d'honneur and independent professor of physiology, enclosed himself, at the height of his reputation. The eminent scientist, in the wake of a terrible experience of which he never wanted to give precise details, abandoned completely the studies that had earned him such just renown and cloistered himself in an almost-vegetative existence. His prostration became such that his close friends experienced for a while the gravest fears for his sanity. The professor, it will be remembered, died after eighteen months without anyone being able to explain the mystery of the sudden modification that had intervened in the career of one of our most esteemed scholars.

Some time after that decease, the following lines were discovered among the doctor's handwritten notes. Their publication will provide the key to that resounding enigma.

18 October 19**. For the first time, in many long years, since I have been making these notes regularly; I am obeying in writing them an inexplicable feverish haste.

Fifteen years ago—I was, in consequence, twenty-four—I recognized once and for all the necessity of a methodical record of my daily reflections, quintessentially preserving, in a few brief words, of the salient facts of my observations and the progress of my experiments of every order.

I saw in this work a reliable calming, a kind of decantation that would clarify the seething, sometimes troubled flood of my ideas, as well as a means of passing again at a later date through each of the emotions of my scientific life.

But this evening, it is no longer a matter of exposing tranquil observations. And since this preamble, drafted carefully in the insensate hope of appeasing myself, leaves me in the same fever, in the same terrified agitation, it's necessary that I arrive at writing what has become of me...

Yesterday...it was yesterday!...when I returned from *out there*, and when, with my gesture still quivering with horror—and weak, so weak—I had sent away my colleague Dr. Danglade, I collapsed again in the armchair and I went to sleep. That I was still able to sleep confounds me, and yet, I slept heavily, like a brute, dreamlessly...dreamlessly, thank God!

Today, Danglade came to see me. He is anxious about my health. But when he tried to interrogate me about what had happened, I begged him, tremulously, never to talk to me about that again—absolutely never. And he shut up.

He shut up, but what is in me did not shut up. It isn't in my power to prevent *That* from having been... I'd like to doubt it but I cannot. And it's necessary that I tell *That*, like the rest, with the same pen—O derision!

I remember everything, in the slightest details, with a frightful lucidity. But can I find words to relate the superhuman adventure? Do words exist that can retrace it?

Let's try, though.

The Human Machine

Yesterday afternoon, at about four o'clock, I was in my work-room, on this very spot, in conference with Danglade.

I don't know how the discussion had begun, but we were arguing passionately, as always.

It's extraordinary, I thought, *that a science like physiology can serve as an aliment for mentalities as dissimilar as ours. It would seem, however, that parallel research in the same field of action ought fatally to lead minds to analogous conclusions. Now, Dr. Danglade's theories and mine are essentially divergent—which does not prevent us, however, from being good friends, and perhaps it even consolidates our amity: an amity, furthermore that is purely intellectual, in which we seek one another out mutually, while often resisting the desire to strangle one another.*

With the same materials, we edify two opposite theories, and reflecting on that sometimes throws me into mute indignation.

Is it possible that a man as learned as my colleague, who has paled over our illustrious modern physiologists, can still hold to the doctrines of Buffon and Cuvier, still admitting I know not what obscure quid divinum *in the constitution, and above all in the functioning, or the human organism?*

Has not our corporeal machine been analyzed and dismantled in its slightest mechanisms by geniuses named Magendie and Claude Bernard, and their successors[40] Has not

---

[40] François Magendie (1783-1858) was the great pioneer in France of experimental physiology, and held the Chair of Medicine at the Collège de France from 1830 to 1855, somewhat controversially because of his great fondness for experimental and demonstrative vivisection. He was succeeded in that post by Claude Bernard (1813-1878), previously his assistant, who carried forward his research, and becoming a notable exponent of rigorous scientific method in biological research.

the famous materialism, so criticized and denigrated, succeeded in imposing itself victoriously, and has not experimental science, going back from effects to causes, clarified the mysteries that were once most the unfathomable? Has it not dazzled with its precise evidence the intelligences still asleep in the vague and the inexplicable?

And yet, people of value claim not to understand, and declare themselves unsatisfied. What proofs do they need, then, for what prodigies are they waiting, in order to yield to reason?

Those reflections were mine yesterday, and I find them again, perfectly clear, arranged in good order in my brain, even now.

The passionate experiments reported by Claude Bernard on the action of poisons, considered as agents of physiological analysis, returned to my mind then, and I overwhelmed my obstinate colleague with that sheaf of luminous observations.

"How long," I asked him, "Will you be obstinate in seeing in human life the intervention of some mysterious power? Can the hypothesis of our phantasmal soul, a living principle of the organism, resist for an instant the facts cited by our great discoverer? Has he not proven superabundantly that life is a phenomenon of an entirely material order, caused by the normal functioning of the organs? Since it is permissible for humans to provoke and prevent death, I do not see what can subsist, for you, of the supernatural."

"The fact of causing death at will is not sufficient to prove its uniquely material character," said Danglade, in a peevish voice.

"And the fact of suspending that death, of extinguishing and reigniting life like a torch—does that prove nothing?"

"What are you saying?"

"The exact truth. Doubtless you remember the experiment of Watterton and Brodie in 1815?[41] I can cite that one among a hundred others. I won't remind you about the effects of poisoning by curare, that terrible American toxin; you know everything that Claude Bernard has been able to extract from that agent of death. Well, when Watterton and his colleague, after having inoculated an adult she-donkey with the poison, saw the animal's muscles paralyzed progressively, the action of the lungs gradually stopping, the heart ceasing to beat—in brief, death becoming manifest in all is symptoms—it was sufficient for them to provoke an artificial respiration with an *ad hoc* bellows to make each organ resume its suspended function. They prolonged the insufflation long enough to permit the elimination of the poison. When the effect of that disappeared, the animal resumed its normal life. An hour before it was well and truly dead, as dead as can be. What do you say to that?"

"I say that you're choosing a special case. Curare, in sum, only induces torpor..."

"And I say that you're a man of bad faith. Curare is a deadly poison, which leads in ten minutes to the death of any being subjected to its action. But what demonstrates that the human machine is only a machine like any other is that it is sufficient, when no lesion or decomposition of the tissue intervenes—which is the case for curare, which causes death uniquely by the paralysis of all the motor nerves, including those of respiration—to supply the absent impulsion in order to reactivate the whole ensemble.

"It's the same for a clockwork mechanism whose spring is relaxed: everything is motionless. If the pressure of your finger replaces the pressure of the spring, all the parts will resume their movement."

---

[41] Charles Waterton, or Watterton (1789-1869) and Benjamin Collins Brodie (!783-1862) made an intensive study of the effects of curare, including the experiment cited.

"I'll grant you," Danglade conceded, "that surprising examples of resurrection have been observed. But in sum, operations have only ever been carried out on animals; and without wanting to fall into the doctrines of Malebranche and the like, one can admit that death offers in animals a character less mysterious—more material, if you prefer that word, than in humans."

"Where are you going with that, my friend? Humans are only animals like others, absolutely like the others. They possess a larger proportion of cerebral matter, that's all. We're merely two mammals of the order of primates, my dear. And if you see in humans some sacred being to which the other laws of the species don't apply, you're nothing but a backward mind, unworthy of the science you profess.

The Specter

"Has the experiment that you're talking about," said Danglade, without flinching before my furious assault, been carried out on a human being?"

"Not so far as I know; but it can be, whenever you wish."

"Hmm—possibly! I'd be curious to see it, though."

"Well, I sustain that if a subject could be procured, I'd take charge of killing him—killing him incontestably enough for you, as a physician, not to hesitate to recognize the decease—and, once that death is established, to reanimate the cadaver, first artificially, and then definitively."

"Get away! All that's theory."

"I'm ready to put it into practice."

"You know full well that you'll never find a subject. One doesn't play with a human life. Remember William Patterson..."

Those words sounded lugubriously. The memory thus abruptly evoked by my colleague plunged me into a discontented silence. What a specter Danglade had just caused to emerge from forgetfulness! Three years had passed since that sad affair, conducted by me so methodically, but terminated in such a frightful fashion. How far away from me it already was! Under the incessant flux of my scientific preoccupations, it had been completely effaced from my memory…but then I remembered with a tragic intensity young Lord Patterson, a frail debilitated millionaire, not hesitating to let me carry out on his person, thanks to the interested devotion of a poor vigorous fellow, an audacious attempt at animal grafting: the fitting of a new stomach. In spite of all my cares, the operation, which I believed to have succeeded, terminated in a drama. The double death that closed the experiment brutally placed me—me, Barbier, the severe physiologist—under the coup of a criminal investigation.

I had been acquitted by the law and public opinion, and my conscience did not reproach me. However, a vague timidity remained in me, which my colleague's remark had resuscitated. Danglade was right: one cannot toy with a human life.

While I was thinking that, and my head was bowed, my interlocutor thought he had confounded me, and the timorous individual rejoiced in the defeat of the audacious one.

But I raised my head again. An idea had just occurred to me, fulgurantly.

"You're right, my friend. One can't yet dispose of the life of another, as I have unfortunately observed. But what prevents me disposing of my own?"

It was Danglade's turn to fall silent. A stupor was legible in his eyes.

"To prove to you," I said, "how certain I am of such a resurrection, this is what I propose: I'll lend myself, personally, to the experiment in question, and it's you, Danglade who are going to carry it out. You'll follow my instructions, and when you've observed my death, you'll resuscitate me. You can see that I must be confident."

"You're mad," he said, shrugging his shoulders. Your great fault, Barbier, is making the craziest decisions with impetuosity, at the slightest contradiction. I won't lend myself to such an attempt."

But his voice trembled as he said that, and I sensed a hesitation in his refusal. I persisted: "What fear is holding you back? Do you dread that your personal theories might founder before the victorious reality, or are you recoiling before the danger?"

"I can't kill you," said his dull voice.

"Kill me? Get away! You're frightened of the mystery, trembling to help me vanquish death. Danglade, a scientist doesn't have the right to be a coward."

"No, I can't. It would be a crime..."

However, a vertigo was growing in my friend's eyes. He fixed me with a gaze in which I distinguished, simultaneously, fear, hatred—yes hatred—and above all, an excited curiosity, which ended up dominating him. The appetite of the seeker reawakened. Danglade's protestations became gradually weaker. Then, as I objurgated him vehemently is a resolute tone, he lowered his head and murmured a weary consent.

"After all, too bad. It's you who will have wanted it..."

Preparations

I had extracted Danglade's acquiescence, but perhaps that timid mind would soon regret his sudden decision. It was necessary for me to take advantage of his temporary good will and, as the vulgar saying has it, strike while the iron was hot.

As, on the other hand, I had no doubt as to the success of our experiment, it did not matter to me whether it took place one day rather than another. I even put a sort of interior bravado into not wanting to think about the eventual consequences, and not taking the most elementary precaution. To make the slightest preparation in view of a hypothetical death would have been to admit the possibility of that death. I set aside the ideas of that possibility completely.

So, when Danglade, after having yielded to my insistence, let himself fall into the big armchair in my study, I hastened to get up, affecting a mental liberty that I was far from possessing.

"Well, my dear friend, we're going to verify the matter without delay. I have everything necessary. Don't worry, you role will be very simple."

Don't worry... I, the benevolent victim, was the one tranquilizing my operator. That reversal of roles made me smile while I prepared the necessary compounds and apparatus unhurriedly.

I took a phial of dissolved curare—my entire provision, enough to kill thirty men—and a minuscule Pravaz syringe. I fitted a leather bellows, brand new and carefully sterilized to one of the flexible tubes that served me for pulmonary inhalations. Then I returned to my study.

Danglade had not budged and seemed to be plunged in a profound reverie.

"This is what will soon replace the Creator's breath," I said, jovially. "Perhaps the apparatus is slightly primitive, but the lesson will be all the more striking for that. Doubtless one could imagine a pump with an alternating movement more appropriate to the usage; that's something to look for...bah! War is war. You'll be reduced to aerating me manually, like a furnace. I hope you won't let the fire go out..."

"Barbier," my colleague said then, with a fearful slowness, as if he had not heard any of what I had said, "we're going to accomplish a terrible endeavor."

"I'm counting on it, my friend, I'm counting on it." I tapped him on the shoulder in a comradely fashion. "Come on, Danglade, don't be childish. "You've practiced surgery, damn it. The operation itself has nothing that can alarm you. Am I afraid? It seems to me though, that I have more to fear in the adventure than you do."

"I don't know," he said, gravely.

In my turn I was shaken by a frisson, and I tried to read the meaning of those enigmatic words in his eyes; but his gaze remained impenetrable. By means of an abrupt effort of will, Danglade seemed to have recovered all his self-control."

"Come on," I said, chasing away the painful impression that had just gripped me. We'll commence immediately, if you don't mind."

"Let's begin. Where are you going to put yourself?"

"In this armchair, quite simply. The curare, in paralyzing all my muscles, will keep me immobile as effectively as the most complete bondage. I'll inject myself with the required dose of the poison."

So saying, I half-filled the syringe and carefully sealed the bottle.

"After ten or twelve minutes—I don't know my own strength of resistance—I'll be completely inanimate. Then you'll introduce the extremity of the tube into my tracheal conduit. You'll wait until all the symptoms of death are manifest: first the total cessation of respiration, the fixity of the gaze, then the stopping of the heart. Then you'll let a delay of ten seconds go by, no more; that will suffice for you to establish the appearances of death fully. When the ten seconds are over you'll activate the prepared bellows, alternating the insufflations and exhalations; my lungs, full of air, will be able to aliment my blood with oxygen again; the heart will recommence beating and the entire organism will resume its normal operation.

"It's at that moment, my friend, that you'll need patience. You understand that the life thus provoked will only be an artificial life of sorts. It's necessary to give the curare time to be progressively eliminated from the organism by the intermediary of the kidneys, which will require about an hour.

"You'll be able to test the progress of the resurrection by suspending the respiratory maneuver momentarily. At a given moment the entire machine of my body will continue to function of its own accord when you stop. That will mark the complete return to life for you. Then, my dear, we'll truly be able to say that we have vanquished death."

"That's not certain," said Danglade, between his teeth.

"You have pencils and paper here," I went on, without appearing to have heard him. "I'm counting on you to make all the useful notes. Try to replace me in that role. Believe that I regret keenly not being able to be both the subject and the observer. The passive role is scarcely amusing."

"I was speaking with a slightly forced joviality, to try to rebuild my colleague's morale. But when I fell silent he fixed me with a suppliant gaze.

"Barbier, I beg you, renounce this experiment."

"Never in this life," I said. "It's much too interesting."

And I lay down on the armchair. I rolled up my left sleeve and inserted the needle into the flesh of the forearm. The pain died away very quickly; the curare was already deadening the vicinity of the puncture. I placed the syringe on the table and abandoned myself to the padding of the chair.

"Now, my dear," I said to Danglade, "I'm mortally poisoned. If you want to save me, you have only to follow my instructions. My life is in your hands."

I Sense Myself Becoming a Cadaver

We did not say anything for a moment. Danglade seemed to have recovered from his emotion and remained standing beside the armchair with a grave expression. In front of me, on the wall, my clock displayed its large enamel dial. I consulted it: five twenty-two.

"My friend," I said, "I can still talk to you for a few minutes, so let's take advantage of that faculty. You know that language is one of the functions that is paralyzed more rapidly. When my speech is annihilated, you can still interrogate me; I have reason to believe that the sense of hearing persists almost until the end. I'll respond to you by my blinking my eyelids; the muscles of the eye are among the last to become torpid."

Without responding, my colleague reflected. His attitude, so different from mine when I become excited by a problem that is on the point of being resolved, struck me disagreeably. What austere meditation was absorbing him, then, for me not to see awakening in Danglade the alert curiosity almost obligatory in an experimenter at his post? I flexed my fingers.

"My phalanges are still functioning. The poison, injected into the tissues, has to travel through the venous system as far as the heart, and then return to the extremities by way of the arteries."

As I was speaking, I suddenly felt my left hand cease to obey my will, and fall back, flaccid, on to the arm of the chair.

"Note, Danglade," I said, "the beginning of the paralysis—three minutes. The progress will be more rapid henceforth."

To my great astonishment, I saw that my companion was not making any note. He was looking at me with the same grave expression that had surprised me so much.

"Do you know, Barbier, that you're a frightening man? You can preserve your composure in such a circumstance; that reveals you to be even more terrible than I could have imagined. Is it possible that before the death that is threatening you, which is already gripping you, you don't experience a revolt of your entire being? But if you're capable of sacrificing yourself in this way, what terrible ferocity are you not summoned to show to others? What crime will you commit tomorrow?"

"Oh, my dear," I interrupted, "is it a sermon you're preaching to me? You've chosen a singular moment..."

"Perhaps. You see, I'm afraid now of what might happen. What if you don't wake up? I'm thinking about the monster that you are, Barbier, and wondering whether it might not be better if you didn't wake up..."

His voice chokes as he says that, and I doubt that I have heard him correctly.

Danglade is one of those physicians of the old school, imbued with prejudices, who only admits science that offers an immediate utility, and is scandalized by any audacity. Satisfied with his humble role as a "officer of health," he had often declared to me that I was "a dangerous individual." Why dangerous? Those are simply hollow words.

At any rate, he detests me and is scornful of me; I've known that for a long time, and yet I hadn't hesitated to entrust my life to him. I sense a vague unexpected danger before

184

me; but my companion's calmness reassures me. Is my intelligence weakening already? I glance at the clock: five twenty-seven. My entire left arm is numb; my right hand is paralyzed in its turn.

"Danglade," I say, in a voice that is beginning to thicken, "A truce on odious reflections, I beg you. In five minutes, I'll be a cadaver. This is the moment to be scientific. Do your duty."

Then he looks at me with a wild expression, and pronounces a single word: "Which?"

From that moment on my ideas and my impressions become precipitate. An unknown phenomenon accelerates my cerebral activity, and refines my senses to the point of exasperation. I can now distinguish the progress of the curare along my limbs. A deathly cold chills my muscles. I observe that my feet are no longer obedient. Then I raise my eyes toward the clock-face: scarcely twelve seconds have elapsed since Danglade proffered the word whose memory returns to me like a flood:

"Which?"

And a mad terror is shaking me now. What absurdity have I committed in entrusting such a role to my colleague? Is he not a man to suffer some terrible vertigo? What if, by virtue of carelessness or malevolence, he does not reanimate me?

That fear suddenly becomes a frightful certainty. I sense that I am going to die; and all my living flesh quivers; my back arches; I make a desperate effort to sit up I my armchair, I order to shake off the torpor that is gripping me.

Then, even more rapidly, the fear vanishes. A flood of hope and tranquility inundates my soul, in spite of the chill of paralysis that is traveling bizarrely along my shoulder. My legs are dead. My thighs are dead.

What are those clicks that are resounding at such interminable intervals? I search, and I suddenly understand that the ticking of the clock, amplified by my exacerbated hearing, is dragging out for me—for me, who is dying—the seconds of eternity.

I am able to experience my voice one last time.

"Danglade, note that..."

But it is in vain at I attempt to articulate. My tongue, devoid of force, remains immobile. Only a hoarse groan resonates in the depths of my throat and shakes my whole head. Danglade leans toward me. I divine by his attitude that something is finally interesting him.

"You can't talk any longer? Can you still hear me?"

My eyelids respond: "Yes." And I observe: five thirty. I have scarcely two or three minutes to live. But I fear being mistaken and I recommence the calculation. It is eight minutes since the injection. Then I think about my foolish terror: what childishness! Danglade is incontestably as passionate as me in regard to the problem And I want to know what death is. A sentiment made of ecstasy and horror germinates with me, without my curiosity diminishing. And I raise my eyes toward the clock-face. Five thirty again.

Oh, it's impossible. Either I'm going mad or the clock has stopped. My mind hesitates momentarily. But the tick-tock is still audible, slower than a knell. My last seconds are stretching indefinitely.

My entire being is becoming inert and insensible. Do I still have a body? My limbs seem to be an enormous distance away from me, from the *me* constituted by my head and my breast, in which my heart, slowly, ever more slowly, is resonating like a nightmare drumbeat...

The Great Vertigo

And still my thoughts are racing, vertiginously. It seems to me that my brain is functioning at top speed, like a mechanism going mad before breaking down. But the alternatives of dread, confidence and long meditations with the duration of a lightning-flash are all affirmed clearly in my consciousness and imprinted in my memory, where I sense that I will find them again, *if I return from out there.*

From out there...

Where am I going? Toward what terrible destiny is my determination of a little while ago precipitating me? I seek to evoke within me the idea of death. I try to repeat the word: *death*; but I cannot recover its familiar significance, the significance to which, a minute before, I was clinging. Desperately, I invoke words: *the human machine... cessation of the vital functions... intervention of an artificial action...* But all of that no longer signifies anything for me.

I have the dolorous sentiment of an intellectual impotence. However, my critical sense does not appear to be enfeebled. My attention, which is concentrated within me, is fixed on the outside. The clock-face is still shining on the wall: five thirty-two...

Ten minutes, already...nothing any longer exists for me but that extent of wallpaper with an enamel clock-face and its black hands, and the great muted, profound, lugubrious strokes, which are the beats of my heart. That vague whistling that arrives from the immediate vicinity of my brain must be my respiration...ten minutes, and I'm still breathing. I shall last longer than I foresaw.

Danglade leans toward me and speaks to me. His voice reaches me, but so faintly, so faintly, a very small distant voice:

"Have no fear, Barbier; I...*zz...zzz...zzzz...*"

I haven't been able to understand the end. His lips are moving, but my eardrum no longer perceives anything but a shrill hum, drawn out like the song of a mosquito. Now I'm becoming deaf.

I have the impression that my entire body has just abandoned me and that I'm floating, weightless, in an imponderable ether. At first that sensation is blissful; then, without transition, it becomes a frightful hindrance, which increases to the point of torture.

I know, by virtue of my memory, which subsists, that my head is thinking, that my throat, where I sense a dryness, and my eyes whose eyelids are still fluttering, are supported by a neck that connects my head to my trunk. I know that, but the neck in question no longer belongs to me. An infinite, lamentable desire, claws me: to turn my head, to sense that bundle of muscles obeying me one more time. I would give my life—what remains of my life—to act, to react against the paralysis that is separating my being from its substance. But I can't, because I'm imprisoned in a cadaver.

That cadaver ought to be me; and yet I sense that we are two, the cadaver and I. I renounce explaining that prodigy; I sense it, that's all.

At that moment, a new idea surges forth, imposes itself and chases away all others. Death is there, very close, and I am not going to have thought everything. It seems to me that I still have years and years of intelligence to live, that I have the right to think all that, and that my due is going to be snatched away. By whom? Myself.

My perception of death becomes more precise, and magnifies. There is a gulf before me into which I am falling. What is it, that gulf, which my reason does not admit? I want to make one last appeal to it, to that reason...but I observe that it is no longer in me.

It's finished; my human thoughts are no longer following one another. Just now, I was afraid; I divined that Danglade was going to let me die. That no longer has anything to say now, since I'm already almost dead; and I sense that I'm no longer afraid.

Just now, I had hope; I was clinging to the idea of my imminent resurrection. Now, I perceive mysteriously that hope is no longer possible, that hope no longer exists. I have just passed though I know not what portal, which hope cannot pass through.

Meanwhile, I am still observing, contemplating untiringly everything that my eyes, which I can sense becoming numb, can still see: the wall, on which the motifs of the wallpaper are blurring, enlacing my ideas immaterially, becoming confused; and, more than anything else, the pale round eye of the clock. But I suddenly perceive that although I can make out the hands, I no longer comprehend the hour. I see a black angle, and that angle no longer signifies anything.

It really is the end; I am falling further and further into the gulf. The last shreds of the tangible world are drawing away from me; I am tumbling frightfully toward I know not what void. I don't know whether I have closed my eyes, but no image any longer pierces the great red sheet that has replaced my sight.

Nothing reaches me any longer: no sound, no vision, no tactile impression. I'm alone, in a solitude unknown to humans, a solitude that I divine to be infinite, and the cadaver no longer has anything of me.

Nevertheless, if I can no longer sense myself, one last sensation traverses he cadaver, a sensation that I register. What force has just parted the teeth, what rattle is scraping the palate and extending into the back of the throat? The cadaver does not know, and the self no longer knows, either...

...

The insufficiency of human words!

I am floating in the absolute void, in the eternal nothing; and I am only a particle of that nothing...for centuries, it seems, forever...I no longer exist...

And suddenly, that void opens, I am inundated by a flood of light. My being becomes more precise and fixed. I exist again, and yet the cadaver is no longer there...

It seems to me that I get up and walk, but a walk that is no longer that of the Earth...an enormous mystery surrounds me and welcomes me...and the tide of light streams over me more and more...it penetrates me; I understand that my substance is dissolving in it...and my soul is no longer anything but an infinite eye that can see *the absolute*...

Resurrection

Suddenly, a frightful silent din destroys everything that was about to be...

A heavy veil, the color of blood, envelops me with its folds. A new fall rolls me and drags me way, but a thousand times more frightful now...*and I understand that the fall in question is descending...*

Abruptly, in a shock that makes something howl within me, one of the dead sensations is reestablished...and that sensation, which no earthly word is able to define, appears monstrous with reality. It is monstrous because it is real...

And I understand that life—what we call life—has just seized me again.

It is a heavy wave that courses through the interior of my being, an embryonic memory that only expresses the inexpressible, and which effaces the ineffable light of a little while ago. I divine that I have rejoined the cadaver and that I only form one with it again...

Oh for a language, a more subtle language, in order to express that! How difficult and inappropriate our terrestrial phrases are! If ever I go mad, it will not be because of those extrahuman sensations, but the hallucinant disproportion that subsists between my words and my ideas.

I sense that Existence is gradually conquering me. At first it is a flood of abolished memories that surges forth and wounds my brain, as an abrupt daylight wounds an obscure retina; I know that I exist, and where I am. I know that I am struggling against death and that someone—I do not know who as yet—must be there, beside me, to aid me to struggle.

And again my mental functions are amplified, enriched. Here come all my fears and here are my hopes; and here come material sensations—so familiar and so good. I sense that my heart is beating, and joy inundates me, an animal joy.

Something is caught in my throat, so I know that I have a throat; my lungs are filling with air, so I have lungs, and air still exists.

I remember, I remember everything. I am Alfred Barbier, I am lying in my padded armchair, and it is Danglade, the excellent Danglade, who has just recalled me to life.

Successively, the red fog reappears before my eyes and then splits, and I see the section of wallpaper and the pale roundel of the clock. I can't make out the time as yet, I'm so weak, but I know that I shall be able to do it soon...

My sensations become more precise; I perceive the pressure of the flexible tube on my tongue and the gentle and regular breath that is raising my breast. Suddenly, I have a frisson in the shoulders, and for the first time since...since my death, I experience the action of one of my muscles.

I shudder, and that is a joy; I can hear, and that is a delirious joy. I hear Danglade murmuring in my ear:

"Barbier, my friend...Barbier..."

I can't talk, but my eyes blink hectically to show that the voice, that dear voice, is reaching me.

"You're alive, really alive. God be praised!" it says. "Be glad; you've triumphed. But I was afraid...it won't fatigue you if I talk?"

No, says my head, faintly, for it is beginning to obey me.

"You see," Danglade continues, "I followed your instructions to the letter. For ten minutes I've been blowing you up like a balloon."

I look at the clock: five forty-eight.

How many centuries have gone by in those twenty-six anguishing minutes! In my now-clarified brain, I observed my colleague's surprising good humor. What impression can I read in his eyes? One might think it a mild and proud satisfaction. Has the fact of having triumphed over death sufficed, or is not rather the trace of a silent triumph over himself? I don't know; I never shall know.

Danglade jokes: "If you wish, Barbier, I can recommence the experiment. Do you want me to stop the bellows? You know what awaits you."

This time, I make a sterile effort to speak, In spite of the rubber tube that is obstructing my larynx, and I succeed in uttering a hoarse grunt, which signifies: "I don't want to..."

"Aha! Return of speech, twenty-seven minutes. Very good, I'll continue. We have only to wait for the progressive elimination of the curare."

But now, although my limbs are still numb, I sense that all my internal organs are alive. I close my eyes and I wait. I'm exhausted, and no longer thinking about anything, except life, the good and sweet life that I had lost and have found again."

A long time goes by; we remain silent; I have no consciousness of duration. Then Danglade extracts me from my torpor.

"Come on, Barbier, that ought to be sufficient. An hour of insufflations...the curare ought to have been entirely eliminated by the kidneys. You can 'live alone' now."

And, in fact, when the tube is removed, my lungs continue to function normally. I try to move me arms, and my arms obey me; but my legs buckle beneath me.

"How exhausted you are!" Danglade says. "Where have you returned from, then?"

Those simple words shake me terribly.

Where have you returned from, then? For an hour, I have been bogged down in an entirely animal slumber, and now the evocation abruptly surges forth of what I have just experienced. Where, in fact, had I come from? From what abyss, from what mystery?"

And while Danglade goes on, serenely: "You were really dead, you know; a few moments after I had introduced the apparatus into your throat your heart stopped and your eyes were revulsed; then I waited for ten seconds, as you had prescribed, and then commenced to inject the air...oh, I confess that I had no great hope; decidedly, I'm convinced, and you're a prodigious man..."

I realize what has happened.

I understand that those ten seconds of physical death were for me—for the Me that was separated from the cadaver—the entrance to a new state of being, into some beyond, of which I had not even glimpsed the possibility.

192

Is that death, then, the death that I had braved, something other than a simple cessation of the organism? I sense my theories collapsing lugubriously within me. What is there, then, on the other side, what is there that I was about to know when life, the mysterious life so crudely resuscitated, came to snatch me away from it? I don't know; I can't know, but I'm certain now that there is something...for merely having brushed the immense enigma, I have retained—and forever, forever—the certainty that had bowled me over. I shudder and humiliate myself before the dazzling light that has now vanished for me...

And while Danglade, with his eyes full of respect, says to me in his grave voice: "Barbier, I must incline before your audacity' you truly are the master of death...," I clamor, desperately:

"Insensate! My person will never vanquish death. I have just entered its domain; I have just accomplished the terrible voyage. And now I am broken by the Unnamable, annihilated before something incomprehensible, something that it will be necessary, however, to end up knowing... Me, the master of death! Oh, insensate, insensate!"

And as he looked at me, trembling, believing that my reason had fled, I sent him away. I sent him away in order to remain alone, to remain alone with my memories...

I slept all night; how, I don't know. And since this morning I have been coming and going in this severe and calm room, which saw my death-throes and my resurrection.

All day long, I have paced back and forth in this room like a wild beast in a cage. And I pressed my forehead, my indefatigable and tortured forehead, with my fists...

And I'm exhausted this evening, before my desk; for hours I have been writing, writing feverishly, heaping up the pieces of paper in which I have traced my terrible Adventure...

No one will ever read these lines; and yet, it's necessary that I write them, it's necessary that all this remains...why, I don't know, but it's necessary...

If I were to die tomorrow...

Originally published in La Lanterne—Le Supplément, *14 décembre 1912.*

Albert Keim: *The Last Idyll*

There had been a vast and disastrous collapse, powerful shocks, and on the desert of ice, through the empire of shadow and silence, a formidable winter reigned.

The terminus of evolution was announced by the universal catastrophe. Life, movement and order had been vanquished by death, stagnation and chaos.

The omnipotent will of nature remained obscurely implacable. Living beings were gradually assimilated to matter. Borne away by ice-sheets bristling with giant stalagmites, they had lost the pride of existence. Henceforth, they ceased to participate in joy or suffering under the splendor of the sun.

A pale star no longer illuminated anything but ruins, confused images and the despair of things.

Amid the debris and the shreds, in the depths of a grotto with menacing vaults, haunted by blue gleams, a human being, bruised, livid and emaciated, making a supreme effort, overcame somnolence and torpor.

He was the last king of creation. A sublime intelligence enlightened his gaze, illuminating his weakness before the brutality and triumph of external forces.

His reason protested against the incomprehensible destruction. Prey to the atrocity of suffering and solitude, he gave impetus to his thought in order to conceive and even to resolve the strange problem of destiny.

Hunger, thirst and the horror of being an infimal spectator amid the rigid and glacial rubble, the frantic, vertiginous mourning of the human species has not defeated the majesty of that wretched but noble creature, that dispossessed monarch of the end of cycles and the world.

Avid to interpret so many unusual phenomena before disappearing in his turn into the abyss in which the hierarchies and generations of the living had fallen, he seized his electric lamp. He had conserved it in spite of the frantic vehemence of the cataclysm, in the depths of his quadruple overcoat, as well as a phial of concentrated regenerative nutriment.

He contemplated the blue shadow or, in places, the whiteness with flashes of violet-tinted light. Then, endowed with a bitter energy, he nourished his humble and pitiful body. And the last man rediscovered, intact in his mind, the accumulated treasures of human science. The entire experience of races extended under his skull, which still summarized, in terror and in decadence, the marvelous effort of civilizations.

So, audaciously, he confronted the milieu of anguish and lividity in which the absolute victory of the Cold had destroyed millions of seeds, extinguished respirations, and solidified in enormous and shapeless masses the innumerable individuals absorbed into the bleak unity of the ensemble.

Blocks of ice creaked. The man perceived radiance. A din resounded. The man feared the engulfment of his shelter. The sun shifted. But again the silence reigned. A raw light invaded the grotto. The man closed his eyes.

Then, a groan reached him, a kind of murmur, not far away, very monotonous and very melancholy.

The man emerged victoriously from his semi-slumber. He stood up, lucid and vigorous, ready for some sovereign struggle to preserve his superior pride against fatality.

Was he not—he above all—a predestined being? A miracle had given him that cavern as a refuge, in the invasion of the Supreme Cold. Might not other miracles in his favor still be possible?

For a second, he had the intoxication of his frightful, and yet quasi-divine, solitude.

A murmur—the same murmur, but more intense—suddenly snatched him from his meditation.

Through the glacial rocks he went. At intervals he perceived a terrible daylight, but he fled those vast widows on the motionless universe, because they welcomed the mortal breath of the invincible winter.

In a lair visited by the azure radiance, under an extended vault of giant stalactites, like fantastic stone tears, before the drama of cosmic annihilation, the man distinguished a recumbent form.

He knelt down before a creature, human like him. He recognized in her, with a great dolorous piety, the last woman in creation.

Saved like him, by virtue of the same prodigy, almost in the same place, scarcely injured, she was breathing.

It was her plaint that he had perceived.

With delicate precautions, he drew that fragile and magnificent Eve toward him. In his desperate mercy, he communicated his warmth and strength to her. He built her a wall of rock, a bed of sand and fabrics.

She finally escaped her torpor.

Hr plaint became more distinct.

Her eyes also opened very wide before the eyes of the man. A kind of paradisal vision must have visited her, for she smiled at the man who was there, in the white, blue and violet shadow, and who was protecting her.

When he took out his phial, he observed that the ardent desire to live, even in the heart of the rubble, was flourishing in that supreme petty goddess of the earth.

He spoke to her in a low voice, and she responded suavely.

All the age-old aspirations had taken refuge in that privileged couple. A universe of ideas and sentiments was alive in them, in spite of the end of everything, in spite of the oppression, in spite of the shocks, in spite of the victorious cold, in spite of the annihilation.

He pressed that innocent victim tenderly against his heart. He wanted to defend her, to save her, to prolong the miracle, and because of her, he was no longer able to resign himself.

Meanwhile, he experienced the enchantment of her charm, of her music, of her perfumes. Their shared poverty had a splendor, a sumptuousness that no one could have suspected before them.

At the ultimate limits of space and time, they lavished unique caresses, and thus they dominated still the upheaval and the chaos.

There had been an immense collapse. An opaque and dusty night invaded the cavern.

The movement of the sun accelerated.

Glaciers surged forth, on the march, and slid down the slopes.

The last things were confounded with the abyss.

Now enlaced, the man and the woman were borne away in their bed of rocks, under the ephemeral protection of the ancient vaults.

Rapid fulgurations magnified their embraces. For they sought one another, penetrated one another, discovered supraterrestrial forgetfulness in their kisses, in their amorous friction.

Their flesh was united, like their ardent thoughts, in the face of the inexorable rigor of the unleashed elements.

They were buried in the sacred frenzy; they were attached; they were riveted together, ambitious for a harmony more beautiful than the disorder.

The infinity of the dreams and desires of all epochs and all living beings was divinized them.

And the last human gesture was to be a gesture of hope and defiance.

Originally published in Le Temps, *21 decembre 1915.*

Pierre Mille: *In Passing: Among the Tchouktchis*

Around the year 3000 of our era—eleven hundred years, in consequence, beyond the agitated era in which we are living—after having traversed the whole extent of Siberia from the west, a voyaging citizen of the Empire of America reached the extremity of the Asiatic continent on the shores of the Gulf of Anadyr, a land inhabited by the indigenous Tchouktchis.

I perceive here that I ought to explain two things. In the year 3000, when Europe had become a vast democracy, America formed a rigorously autocratic empire destined to provide a counterweight to that of China, governed by the descendants of Yuan Chi Kai;[42] history has kept the memory for us of a large number of those exchanges But you might be a little more astonished to learn that I know what happened in the year 3000. I will respond that it is thanks to the time machine imagined by the ingenious H. G. Wells, of which I make frequent usage.

That is how I am even able to reproduce a rather curious passage from the journal of that voyager, whose name was J. B. W. Tylor, of the eighteenth province, once known as the state of Kentucky.

After having noted that the chief of a small Tchouktchi tribe was very useful to him in extracting an antediluvian mammoth carcass from the sand and congealed mud that enclosed it, J. B. W. Tylor added:

---

[42] Yuan Shikai (1859-1916) was a military leader who came to power at the end of the Qing dynasty and tried to preserve it by means of a number of modernization projects, prior to the abdication of the last monarch of the dynasty in 1912; he then became the first president of the Republic of China.

"That chief, although he showed himself at first to be rather rapacious and not inclined to do anything for nothing, became quite communicative by custom, and relatively intelligent. He demanded of his subjects great external marks of respect, and, in response to one question that I asked him, told me that he had the right to the title of Emperor, like the sovereign of America himself. 'And thus,' he concluded, 'we are no more than three: the Emperor of America, the Emperor of China, and me. I am also called Kézer, which is the same thing.'

"The sonorities of that last title having awakened vague recollections in my memory, I pursued my investigations, remaining in the territory of his tribe much longer than I had initially intended, in the sole hope of penetrating that mystery. For in truth, otherwise, there were no very new observations to be made there. The mores of the Tchouktchis and their chief have remained much the same as they were a thousand years ago, according to ancient explorers; they eat the flesh of reindeer and seals, of which they make their habitual nourishment, either raw or cooked; they light fires with the aid of a 'firestick,' which they rub rapidly on a piece of wood that is not as hard; they wear impermeable garments of fish-skin for fishing, which are very comfortable; finally, the old men among them continue to commit suicide with great pomp, either in order not to be a burden to the community, or in order to be surer, quitting existence thus in full possession of their faculties, their *mana*, before being resuscitated in the body of a newborn. But you will judge, like me, given that depiction, that it is even odder that the poor fellow who commands those few hundred poor people can command the title of Emperor, ornamenting himself with it with an uncomfortable dignity and giving his wife, whose sex it is difficult to distinguish at a distance, that of Empress.

"This is what he eventually explained to me, one day when I was chatting to him in the tent of hide in which he lives in summer. 'My ancestors,' he said, 'have never been qualified otherwise, and that goes back to an epoch of which men have lost the memory. Nevertheless, there is a well-established tradition in my family that one of my ancestors, more than a thousand years ago, was already the Emperor of a great people who lived in the distant west, far away from here, in the middle of Europe. He commanded immense armies equipped with firearms, possessed a great treasure and enjoyed an agreeable existence; it even appears, although it is difficult to believe, that in his land winter only lasted four or five months.

"'Unfortunately, he had the whim of declaring war on all the people surrounding him—all the people, without exception, who touched his limits, even the Nippons, who still inhabit today, as you know, islands off the coast where the sun rises. He did that because he was very strong, even stronger than the Emperor of China or your Emperor. He was a superlatively strong man, our traditions affirm. He therefore won great victories in the west, in the east, to the right, to the left, facing him and behind. But his enemies said: *So what?* They were like overly numerous sea-lions, which do not feel harpoons through their blubber. And when they had said *so what*, shrugging their shoulders, they added: *Why are you doing this, fellow? What's the point?* And he replied: *I want peace; I assure you that I only want peace; give me peace.* But the others replied, without understanding: *Peace? What kind of thing is that? It's merchandise that we don't possess in our land. We don't know it. Go further away; perhaps it's there.*

"'Then, in order to go further away, he made the decision to head westwards. At first, he marched straight ahead, thinking: *It's there, very close.* But when he stopped, he hadn't found it. Then he turned southwards and camped in the ancient city of Roums, dominated by a Mongol tribe that is distinctly related to us, because we're Eskimos, but crossed with Mongols. He looked around, very attentively, and looked at his enemies, but he didn't find what he was looking for; he set forth again.

"'He crossed Mount Ararat, therefore, where it's said that there had once been a been a ship that landed there as on an island. It was high, that place, very high; it seemed to him that he was overlooking the world and that nothing could escape his sight—and yet, he couldn't discover anything.

"'That's why he kept going, ever further, always eastwards. He began to feel fatigued, and his soldiers were even more so, but he kept going. He traversed another land, which I believe you call Persia; a Russ, who came here to sell iron cooking-pots, which are very useful, and also to exchange glass for ambergris, swore it to me, and it accords with our traditions. He cried: *It's there! Isn't it there, you others?* But he heard nothing except the echo of his own words. He thought: *Are they mad or is it me?* And he resumed his route, his soul black but always keeping a stiff neck; for my ancestor was proud, and we are all proud. He knew a part of China, he knew Mongolia, but he didn't see anything, except hares— except that the hares were white, whereas before they had been yellow. He rubbed his eyes, but only saw white hares, all white. He rubbed his eyes, as I said, and shouted: *Let's march, peace is somewhere!* And it was by always marching that he arrived here, before the frozen sea.

"'Peace wasn't there. He said: *I'll cross the frozen sea. It's gray and sad, but solid. One last effort, my soldiers!* But his soldiers didn't say anything. He turned round, and didn't see anyone. He no longer had any soldiers; they were all dead. He didn't want to admit that he was beaten. He cried: *I'll buy men! I've already bought .the land of the Roums.* So he offered his coffers, but they were empty. All the gold had flowed away through the gaps.

"'We don't find that the land is bad. There are reindeer, there are seals, and even dwarf birches to make fire. Merchants come here in summer, merchant from the lands of Russ, and the Chinese. He could no longer turn back. He stayed.

"'The chief of our tribe adopted him, because he continued to say noble things and make gestures at the stars. He married one of our daughters. He put his hand on her shoulder and said: *You shall be the Empress*. So she was the Empress; she engendered a lineage; I am her descendant, and the Emperor. But she was submissive to him, as she ought to be, and sewed his garments of hide, making them supple with grease. It's said that at times, he sighed, as if astonished—but he got used to drinking fish-oil.

"'What do you expect?'"

Originally published in Le Journal, *7 avril 1919.*

Pierre Mille: *A Futurist Story*

In that epoch, Madame Juliette Leblanc considering her husband, Monsieur Leblanc, with all the external signs of a passionate affection, said to him tenderly:

"You'll still love me, won't you?"

"Yes, of course, yes!" affirmed Monsieur Leblanc.

"But forever? For ever and ever?"

"Oh," he said, "you exaggerate. Forever, I don't say no, but for ever and ever is perhaps too much, in sum."

With that, Madame Juliette Leblanc, her soul filled with the bitterest and most legitimate despair, went to fetch her revolver. Applying that improved weapon to Monsieur Leblanc's right ear, she blew his brains out in less time than it takes to write it. I am speaking here, you understand, in the literary language of the charge sheet.

For Madame Leblanc passed before the Court of Assizes: a simple formality, as one might think. She was acquitted without the defense having any great difficulty, the jury having only affected for form's sake to retire in order to deliberate; its conviction was formed before the opening of the debates. If any hesitation had, impossibly, been manifest among some of its members, an irrefutable document produced by the accused's advocate would have sufficed to dissipate it. That document was nothing other than an authentic copy of the marriage certificate, supported by the contract signed before Maître Pommier-Laprune, notary of Paris. Madame Leblanc really was the legitimate wife of Monsieur Leblanc; no doubt could persist in that regard. No more was required to enlighten the religion of a few jurors, rare in any case, who still attached some importance to the obsolete formality of legal marriage; Madame Leblanc was the authentic spouse of the man whose brains she had blown out, and therefore had the inalienable right to kill him.

But it happened that the unexpected death of Monsieur Leblanc cast into the greatest disarray the heart of Madame Legris, who had had generosities for him. She felt offended in her rights as well as in her affection. Without contesting the decision made by the jury, since it was a matter of a crime of passion, Madame Legris considered that her first duty was to kill Madame Leblanc, who had wounded her in her sentiments. That is why Madame Leblanc died, as decency demanded, by the hand of Madame Legris.

The noble and disinterested motive of that execution was evident. It was, therefore, with a tranquility at least equal to that previously manifested by her victim, that Madame Legris presented herself before the Court of Assizes. Nevertheless, one juror, in the course of the deliberations that followed the debates, raised an objection: "The personal right of the accused to follow the impulsions of her generous heart," he said, "is incontestable; but is it permissible to forget that the person who was the object of her just vengeance had been previously acquitted by a jury? And was there not, consequently, in her action, an outrage to the majesty of that institution—an outrage that merits punishment?"

The question thus posed appeared delicate. However, the foreman of the jury having risen up with vigor against a condemnation that might have been thought to be dictated by motives of personal rancor, Madame Legris was acquitted in her turn.

She had some difficulty fleeing the crowd of her admirers, but when she reached the threshold of her domicile, a young man whose manner marked melancholy and decision accosted her very courteously.

"I do not have the honor of being known to you, Madame," he said, "but the fact is that I nurtured a profound sentiment in regard to Madame Leblanc, which was, I believe, shared. You will understand, therefore, what it remains for me to do: all my apologies."

So saying, he plunged no her left breast an appropriately sharpened dagger, and Madame Legris collapsed, without even uttering a sigh.

"May your manes rest in peace, my angel!" cried the young man. "This dagger is worth more than the blunted blade of the Law!"

He allowed himself to be arrested without resistance and taken to the cells of the prefecture. Before the twelve fellow citizens who judged him, his attitude was simultaneously masculine and disenchanted. He requested death with loud cries, saying that existence no longer meant anything to him, since he had lost the object of his unique amour, stolen forever from his embrace by the inconsiderate woman that he had been obliged to punish.

That maladroit attitude having cast disorder into the minds of the jurors, he had the surprise of hearing himself sentenced to a few years of forced labor. Then he protested, very justly, affirming that it was perfectly idiotic, and, moreover, immoral, to send to prison, where one lived very badly, a man who no longer wanted to live at all. The jurors, gripped by remorse, immediately signed his plea for mercy and the government hastened, understandably, to satisfy such a natural desire as soon as possible.

But things, as could already have been foreseen, did not stop there. As it was permissible to expect, the young man was executed at the exit from the Santé by the legitimate spouse of Madame Legris, inconsolable at both the death of his wife and having been deceived by that vile seducer. Then the latter succumbed himself, under the repeated blows of the father of the last victim, who felled him very adequately with the aid of a lead-reinforced cane.

Then France entire divided into two equally-convinced and equally-incensed camps; one remained persuaded that the jury had every reason to acquit, always to acquit; the other declared that it was beginning to be little over the top to see the jury acquitting perpetually. That was the inevitable motive for a large number of other murders, committed, like the first, in the heat of the most sincere passion, and which were, as was only to be expected, the object of further acquittals.

And as the acquitted individuals were not long delayed in being assassinated in their turn, those generous and legitimate massacres spread throughout France, and in the meantime, juries continued to acquit, and to acquit untiringly, in their sublime fidelity to the dogma of acquittal, which is the duty, the initial principle, and the very honor of that institution.

However, everything has a term. One day, there only any longer remained, throughout the bloody and devastated territory of France, exactly twelve jurors. And one of them, being unable to accustom himself to the silence of his house, and to the henceforth-perpetual idleness of the court, hanged himself in his grain-loft. The others looked at one another, surprised and shocked; it was necessary for them to dissolve because they no longer had a quorum.

It was in that fashion that the practically-complete disappearance of the population in the ancient territory of Gaul was explained to his audience by Monsieur Omaho, a gentleman of Maori origin, professor of social sciences at the University of Honolulu, in Hawaii.

"Some have wanted to attribute that disappearance," the eminent specialist said, "to the Great War that devastated the region in question in the early years of the twentieth century and the insufficiency of births among the inhabitants, but the investigation I have made on the spot, as well as the authentic documents reported by me, leave me no hesitation as to the cause of the phenomenon; it is such as I have just told you. Nevertheless, the territory appears to me to be destined to be repopulated slowly by a mixed race composed by the immigration of Italians, Spaniards, Germans and the natives of the Republic of Andorra."

René Morot (1864-1939) was a journalist who edited La Vie de famille, journal hebdomadaire illustré *in 1891; he became an art expert who compiled many catalogues for auction sales of paintings, sculptures, ceramics and furniture, including Gustave Flaubert's collection when it was resold in 1931, and might have related to the painter Aimé Morot.* "Drosera Cannibalis" *was originally published in* Le Mercure de France, *15 décembre 1921.*

René Morot: Drosera Cannibalis

I do not know why people are trying to cast doubt on the death of the celebrated Professor Hartenstatter; I am particularly qualified to establish the truth: the great botanist has not simply disappeared; he really is dead; I saw him die and I was one of the two witnesses who signed his death certificate while I was mobilized in November 1918.

No doubt can exist about his final disappearance. The word *final* is necessary, in application to an eccentric who had been said to be died several times, when he had only disappeared; those mysterious disappearances for two or three years were customary to him, during which he lived lost in the virgin forests of Africa or South America, searching for unknown plants, the discovery and classification of which had made him the greatest contemporary botanist.

The drama in which he lost his life was so abominable that the censor had forbidden the newspapers even to print Hartenstatter's name; it was necessary not to publish any information capable of overexciting the emotionality of the public, already hypertensive.

You will remember that Hartenstatter was passionate about the study of carnivorous plants, and that he had succeeded in giving some of them a monstrous development.

In the huge greenhouse twelve meters high that he had constructed near his villa at Rothmunster, which no one, even his domestic, had the right to enter, his *Drosera longifolia*,[43] in particular, attained heights of nearly thirty feet, and the illustrious professor claimed to be able to a further increase of more than half in less than two years.

In the notebook in which Hartenstatter summarized his daily observations, I have found absolutely fantastic notes, written with the unconsciousness of a researcher leaning over his scalpel; one senses the he was uniquely preoccupied, outside of any considerations of pity, humanity and morality, with extracting a secret from Nature, like a master executioner torturing his patient in order to obtain a confession.

Hartenstatter notes all the actions and gestures of droseras, which are endowed, as everyone knows, with the faculty of seizing the flies and other insects that settle on their leaves; those plants close upon their victims, immediately glued, and digest them in a matter of hours thanks to the secretion of an extremely active pepsin, absorbing them without any trace or debris subsisting.

For a long time Hartenstatter had applied himself to stimulating and developing particularly the appetite of a giant drosera, specially trained, which had become a tree with enormous stems, capable progressively of devouring grasshoppers, guinea-pigs, mice, rabbits and lambs.

There are descriptions in Hartenstatter's notebook made, one senses, with an almost sadistic joy, of that slow and complete absorption of animals by those monstrous vegetables—perhaps cruel, since their provider notes that they devour living beings with a greater appetite—his own term—than dead ones.

What a triumph it was when the scientist found proof that the plants in question are endowed with the faculty of sight.

---

[43] *Drosera longifolia* is a designation, now obsolete, once applied to the English sundew, *Drosera anglica* and closely related species (sundews appear to have been subjected to considerable natural hybridization).

Yes, he demonstrated that the plants could see. Death did not leave him the time to discover where the organs of vision are and how they function, but he related an experiment that he made several times, of placing a mouse or a guinea-pig under a crystal bell behind a screen; the drosera had not budged; no instinct or divination had revealed to it the existence of a prey within each of its tentacles, but they agitated and extended slowly toward it as soon as the screen was removed and the organs of vision had been stimulated.

Plants, as many people have remarked, extend their branches in the direction of light; they appreciate it, they love it; but Hartenstatter demonstrated with his drosera that they *look*—and, furthermore, that they cannot see in the dark, for the same experiment repeated at night did not have the gift of moving them.

I have the proof, he wrote in his notebook, *that plants look and see and I have demonstrated it as clearly as Sir Jagadis Chunder Bosc[44] has demonstrated in Calcutta, thanks to his ingenious crescograph, which multiplies the slightest movement by ten million, that a plant is an impressionable little person agitated by various and incessant movements. Sir Jagadis Chunder Bosc has demonstrated with the needle of his apparatus that plants are not the same by day as by night, that they have various positions, that they settle down to sleep; I have confirmed his discoveries saying: plants can see in daylight, but no longer see at night; plants are sensitive; yes, they have senses; we have known for a long timed that they have a sex.*

---

[44] It is not obvious whether the author has deliberately altered the name of the great Bengali scientist Sir Jagadish Chandra Bose (1858-1937), or whether the *Mercure*'s typesetter simply could not read his handwriting. Bose's invention of the crescograph for measuring plant growth and movement followed important pioneering work in wireless communication technology.

That general activity demonstrates the link that unites vegetables with animals, and confirms the brilliant thesis of Claude Bernard, who proclaimed the community of all living things.

While noting that his drosera seem to prefer devouring living beings to dead ones, Hartenstatter adds that the victims do not appear to suffer until the moment that life abandons them; they do not even seem to take account of their situation, even though their absorption has already commenced.

And each engulfment by the monster, which seems insatiable, leads in two or three days to an augmentation in the circumference of the trunk and the length and sturdiness of the branches and leaves.

One day, Hartenstatter decides to orientate his research in a new direction, and, from the military hospital where he renders his medical service every morning, he carries away the hand of a wounded man, which he has just amputated and cleverly hidden in the tub of surgical debris destined for the crematory oven.

And the notebook records that his *Drosera gigantis* has absorbed that hand completely in five hours forty-eight minutes.

Whereas a triple weight of nourishment furnished by the corpse of a rabbit the previous week had only augmented the trunk of the drosera by half a millimeter, the human flesh develops it this time by two-thirds of a millimeter. Doctor Hartenstatter is triumphant; he has discovered an anthropophagous plat, the *Drosera cannibalis!*

From that day on the horrible doctor employs all his cunning in procuring human flesh, and his functions render that provision only too easily.

But a preoccupation appears in a note in the notebook: since the drosera prefers living animals and obtains a more considerable profit from them, would it not be the same with living human flesh?

Horror! On the date of the second of January 1917, Hartenstatter brings home a baby two months old, which he has stolen in the vicinity. The notebook records that the drosera glued its "nourishment" more rapidly than usual; Hartenstatter did not dare write "the child," but there is no doubt, for he describes the gag that he put over the mouth of his victim, who does not appear to suffer, and who, five hours after having his legs seized by the vegetal monster, still has enough appetite for life to suck the teat of the feeding-bottle that the abominable scientist puts in his mouth, in order to prolong the life of the patient and the duration of the scientists' observations.

Magnifying glass in hand, Hartenstatter follows all the phases of the informal repast; they are noted every fifteen minutes.

Unfortunately, several pages are missing from the notebook, which I recovered, saved by chance from the ruins of his habitation, sacked and burned by a furious populace when his frightful experiments and his thefts of children were discovered. But the pages that subsist are terrible, as well as full of bold, crazy observations, which might be confirmed one day and declared to be brilliant.

Can one read without shuddering a confession as cynical as this:

12 May 1918. The imbeciles who are repelled by vivisection! Well, what is the disappearance of nine brats (*he had reached that point sixteen months after his first crime*) when one wants to extract such a secret from Nature? Is Nature not pitiless herself, our mother, our wicked stepmother?

My experiments, devoid of suffering are less cruel, fundamentally than that of Sir Jagadis Chunder Bosc, who asphyxiates flowers; his description of the slow agony of a mimosa by chloroform under his bell is crueler than the slow and unconscious assimilation of all these human embryos.

No more than the others, this one does not denote any suffering or any malaise, and yet a third of the body has already disappeared, and now the tentacles are gripping the shoulders; only the head emerges freely; as with the others, it is when a tentacle grips the vital node the psychic life disappears.

It is more beautiful and neater than the engulfment of a living being by a boa constrictor or a squid.

21 November 1918, seven o'clock. My experiment today is magnificently revealing; the children of a few months that my *Drosera cannibalis* has absorbed previously were human flesh devoid of intelligence, but this one, which is surely more than three years old, must understand that he is being absorbed, that he is disappearing; his eyes do not translate any fear, he does not utter a plaint; it is not resignation, nor anesthesia, since he felt the prick of the pin that I tested on his neck a little while ago; there is no agony.

I can conclude that the assimilation to "vegetatism" is a normal phase, albeit in a form unknown until today, but which supports my thesis of the ultimate subjugation of the animal kingdom to the vegetal kingdom. The former might be annihilated on our planet tomorrow, and Life would continue, at least for a time; it is almost infantile to observe, once more, that if the vegetal kingdom were to disappear, the animal kingdom would die a few days later.

I believe that a perfectly conscious destiny directs the ideal of vegetal life toward the end, full of a mysterious abnegation, of becoming, by way of transformation, the necessary elements of animal life. Humans, who think themselves sovereigns of Nature, are only one of the principal slaves of Vegetatism, nothing but more or less laborious workers. The vegetables, the trees, dominate them, and their immovability does not prevent them from guiding and inspiring them.

The veritable animator in the vegetal realm, the roots of which go to collect under the ground not only purely chemical agents but emanations, radiations, inspirations, vibrations and waves, which, by their activity, draw from the great mysterious reservoir, about which we know nothing as yet, the psychic substance that aliments our brains; it does not dwell in the air, in the atmosphere, where it only resides temporarily in

212

suspense; it is into the Earth that the vegetables go in order to extract it.

And in the appeasement of nights, during the numbing of the brain by sleep, the vegetal realm, the conscious dominator or caretaker, insufflates into the animal realm, particularly to humankind, the great currents of thought that gradually change the face of the world, which ferment to as greater or lesser degree in each brain, ravaging our free will at their whim; via the vegetal realm our minds receive the ideas that open to us the paradise of enthusiasms or plunge us into the darkness of anxiety or pessimism.

If great currents of ideas did not exist, how could the wind of folly be explained that has led to the war, that reasoned absurdity?

With their appearance of protectors, the great trees are tyrants, despots who play with our destinies.

If Doctor Boernstein[45] has demonstrated that the Earth respires, absorbing the air for ten or eleven hours and returning it during the thirteen or fourteen hours of daylight, I have demonstrated that the vegetables go in search, much further than their roots, of the elements of the material envelope of our planet, for the atmosphere certainly contains a substance other than a fluid, which is renewed, not from the exterior but coming from the depths of the earth.

It is by way of the vegetal realm, which dominates us with all its impassivity, that the renewal of the vital milieu is operated. It is the vegetal realm that enables the earth to respire.

And, I repeat, it is not in the air that the psychic substance forms with which our brains make thoughts; it is in the earth that the vegetables go to extract it, which put it into circulation, where more or less powerful cerebral antennae seize it.

---

[45] Probably the physicist Richard Börnstein (1852-1913), a professor at the Agricultural University of Berlin.

Tomorrow, researchers will reveal to us the real and not inert life of minerals, for already, Becquerel and Curie have surprised the secret of some, such as uranium, barium and radium, which engender, or restore, electricity, heat and light.

The duration of matter, if it is not immortal, is incalculable; and in admitting that it has, with its transformations, immortality, Weissmann[46] has only seen a part of the truth; yes, our envelope, *soma*, is promptly perishable, but if, according to him, our *germen* is immortal, it is because it is a function of the vegetal realm.

21 November 1918, seventeen twenty. The gaze of the infant seems to be changing expression; it's unfortunate that I don't understand his words; he must be the child of Flemish refugees.

It's strange that, after having wept for the two hours of my return journey by automobile, he has been tranquilized to this point since he has been in the power of the drosera.

22 November 1918, four forty. I must have gone to sleep briefly, after twenty-seven hours of uninterrupted wakefulness, for a stem of the drosera is presently devouring the left eye, which was still out of range a little while ago.

Resistance to sleep has its limits, and Hartenstatter must have made the dangerous experiment; for, charged with a mission of requisition, I penetrated alone at midday into his great hothouse, in spite of the opposition of his fearful staff. I found Doctor Hartenstatter with his head caught, as if in a vice, by three enormous stems of his drosera; the vegetal monster had also slid two tentacles under his shirt, which were gripping and doubtless "assimilating" the shoulders of the scientist,

---

[46] The evolutionary biologist August Weissmann (1834-1914), the pioneer of the theory of the germ plasm, which differentiated reproductive cells (egs and sperm) from somatic cells.

evidently surprised in his sleep; he was still awake, lucid and fully conscious of the danger that menaced him.

I perceived at the same time what remained of the cadaver of the poor child, scarcely half of an exsanguinated face, and, knowing about the numerous disappearances of children in the region, I understood at a stroke the atrocious drama of which the scientist was the author, and then the victim.

So, when the doctor begged me to hasten to cut the stems of the drosera with my saber, my indignation told me to allow the punishment to follow its course.

Faithful to military orders, which are to make a report of everything, I wrote down what I had discovered and left, taking away the key of the door, closed by my care, in order to go and refer it to my superiors.

Unfortunately, during the short time in which I was taking that step, a domestic more curious and less disciplined than the others, had entered the hothouse; I don't know by what means. He had called for help and a furious population had killed the scientist, held in the monster's vice, with blows of clubs, and then sacked the hothouse, doused it with gasoline and burned the *Drosera cannibalis* alive.

In the debris I found a few pages of the torn notebook, unfortunately three-quarters consumed, for reading it in its entirety would have been passionately interesting.

Who, then, at present, could put in doubt the death of Professor Hartenstatter?

Maurice Renard (1875-1939) was one of the most important writers of roman scientifique, who attempted to popularize the importance of a Wellsian literature of the "merveilleux scientifique," in opposition to the more conservative species of Vernian romance. Black Coat Press issued a set of his major works in the genre in 2010, in five volumes: Doctor Lerne,[47] A Man Among the Microbes;[48] The Blue Peril,[49] The Doctored Man,[50] *and* The Master of Light.[51] *He wrote copious short fiction in various genres for newspaper slots, prolonging that practice long after the format has been subjected to a marked decline in its fashionability.* "Suzannah" *was originally published in* L'Intransigeant, *21 November 1925.*

Maurice Renard: *Suzannah*

Suzannah the last giraffe in the world, was about to die. In her hall in the Zoological Gardens—her well-heated hall, at equatorial temperature—she lay on a thick litter. Blankets enveloped her huge body, deformed and yet graceful. Her elongated neck, devoid of strength, stretched out as if to move the delicate horned head out of the way, and her vast dark eyes, full of sadness and mildness, were tarnished gradually at ground level.

With her, an entire species was dying; millions of giraffes had died before her nut it seemed that they would die definitively with the death of Suzannah, the last of all.

There were bottles and bowls on the ground. The warm air of the hall reeked of turpentine. Three men were there: the warden, the veterinary surgeon and Barthe, the naturalist.

---

[47] ISBN 978-1-935558-15-6.

[48] ISBN 978-1-935558-16-3.

[49] ISBN 978-1-935558-17-0.

[50] ISBN 978-1-935558-18-7.

[51] ISBN 978-1-935558-19-4.

When he had understood that all effort was vain, Barthe had the blankets removed, and for a few minutes, passionately, he gazed at what no man would ever see alive again—never, never, never.

Since the death of Jenny, it had been known that Suzannah, her sister, was the last giraffe in the world. It was known for certain that no others remained, either in the forests of mimosas where the lions and the explorers had destroyed them, or in the farms of the Cape, where an attempt had been made, in the name of science, to breed the survivors. So the curious crowds had filed before the railings of the hall in order to contemplate that ultimate living specimen...

And tomorrow the hall would be empty. Tomorrow, it would be the Museum to which it was necessary to go, to know what the animals of old named giraffes had been. They would be a far from us as the mammoths, and their baroque skeletons would rise up in the livid light of the galleries— skeletons almost as paleontological as those of the iguanodon or the diplodocus.

Barthe could not defend himself against the emotion that gripped him. He perceived marvelously the immense under-side of the individual drama. A superior, privileged race was being extinguished in front of him, as others had been extinguished in the course of the ages, from millennium to millennium—a race whose origin was lost, like all of them, in the primitive night. Suzannah was about to die. And eyes similar to hers would never again open upon things: those gigantic gazelle eyes, those magnificent eyes, with those long beloved lashes... Nature had not wanted that bizarre, uneven, truly archaic being to subsist, which seemed to be the work of a novice god...

Outside, it was snowing, for December was coming to an end. The animals of the zoo were living in their winter palace. Nothing could be heard in the neighboring halls but the rhinoceros rubbing its thick armor against the wall and the hippopotamus gazing in its pool. They too were condemned. Their brethren could be counted.

A feeble convulsion shook the dying giraffe

How simple and seemingly ordinary everything was in that hour, nevertheless so profound. At first nothing could be distinguished but an animal, dying after so many other animals. Yes, but that was on the planet what the extinction of a star was in the heavens. Soon, when that creature ceased to live, the earth would have aged, at a stroke, by virtue of an entire long past suddenly closed. That poor gasping beast was marking, in the history of the universe, a capital date, and her death was more important than that of Caesar. The curtain was falling on a multisecular spectacle that human eyes had not seen commence, and their ear was able to surprise, for once, by chance, the slow tick-tock of eternity.

Its pendulum beats the centuries as ours beats the seconds.

Suzannah extended her four limbs to the point of stiffness. Her side was panting beneath the beautiful spotted pelt, the ocelli of which, at a distance, resemble the interlacement of branches. Then the breath, transmitted by the ancestors, stopped...and that was all. No one heard the solemn hour sound, when it sounded—except Barthe.

He went home sadly, and tried to work.

But his thoughts were wandering in the fields of knowledge.

And suddenly, he experienced the imperious need to go out, to mingle with crowds, to lose himself in the multitude of his fellows...

An entire people was circulating in the monstrous city; and other people were living at the same time on the rotundity of the globe; Barthe sensed all round him the innumerable presence of human beings—and that was singularly agreeable, in truth, after having seen Suzannah die.

Originally published in Le Matin, *13 July 1927.*

Maurice Renard: *The Future*

The engineer Francel occupied a splendid apartment on the fifth floor of a rather old house situated in the heart of Paris, in a grandiose quarter where the commune of Boulogne had once extended.

At eight o'clock, as it did every morning, the elevator took Francel up to the twenty-third floor, on to the spacious terrace. His wife accompanied him. Every day, affectionately, she followed him that far and watched his departure. The scientist's laboratories were installed in the suburbs, in Reims. He went there every day by helicopter. Thirty minutes sufficed for that short journey of a hundred and fifty kilometers—just time to listen to the day's news on the cabin wireless.

The aerial apparatus was ready, as were several others disseminated in front of the garages on the terrace. Large numbers of aircraft, fixed-wing or helicopters, could be seen flying in the blue sky—which, from that height, seemed immense. A vast hum made the space sing.

Francel and his wife embraced, tenderly but rapidly.

"I'll be home early," he said, with an expressive smile.

"Oh, you haven't forgotten! I'm glad!"

"Forget! Forget the fifth of July! Our anniversary! Oh, Gloria!"

We confess that we do not know what anniversary was in question. Why did the engineer never let the fifth of July pass without offering a rose to Madame Francel? That is confided to the imagination of the reader. For ourselves, we think that there was some basis to it, like a first kiss, but that really has nothing to do with the story.

Madame Francel, so opportunely named Gloria, watched the helicopter fly away above Paris, at the altitude required by the police regulations for vehicles heading east—there were as

219

many altitudes and directions, in order to avoid collisions. When it had disappeared, she remained there for a moment in order to contemplate the formidable panorama of the capital and to feel the wind of the summits lifting up her short hair.

A loudspeaker of the Illustrated Radio Gazette growled like vocal thunder:

"Attention! Here is the great meeting in Prague."

And immediately in the void above the city, the gigantic image appeared of a human crowd acclaiming an orator surrounded by radiophonic loudhailers. But it was many years since the discovery of artificial mirages had been industrialized. When Gloria had come into the world several companies were already exploiting the patent permitting the projection over distance of the reproduction of a spectacle, exactly as nature does in the desert on her own account. Madame Francel, therefore, only darted an indifferent glance at the monstrous vision by which the sky was illustrated, having become the page of a enormous magazine for a few minutes. She returned to the elevator and descended softly to the threshold of her home.

What followed that re-entry is of no importance for the story either, and in any case, we do not know what Gloria Francel was doing until eleven o'clock. At the most, we can suppose that she was occupied with the children, along with the nurse, the only servant who could not be replaced by mechanical devices. Perhaps the young and charming Gloria had the leisure to start up the perfume organ, or rather the televisor—for she loved to put herself in optical communication with distant countries and thus give herself the pleasure of perceiving, in the depths of the televisor tube, night in the middle of the day: night on the other side of the globe, with its constellations invisible from this one.

The historical fact is that, at eleven o'clock precisely, the bell of the official loudspeaker made its three warning strokes audible.

The window was open on the radiant morning. Madame Francel listened to that voice, similar to that of the tempest.

"A great discovery has just been made. We shall make you party to it in a few moments. Pay attention everyone!"

But Gloria however curious she was, then had to run to the telephone—the wireless telephone, naturally—the harmonious appeal of which resounded

"Hello, Gloria!"

At the same time, in the depths of the televisor tube, without being in the least surprised by that daily miracle, Madame Francel distinguished her husband, out there in Reims. The ancient cathedral was visible through the window behind him. He was speaking into his telephone and holding a superb crimson rose in his hand.

Madame Francel was struck by his happy, triumphant expression.

"Look, Gloria!" said the telephone, while the lips of the little living portrait moved. "Look at this rose..."

"I can see it," said Madame Francel, slightly astonished.

"Very good. Now look at the planchette hidden behind the curtain near you. Move the curtain aside, Gloria..."

A bizarre little shelf was there, quite unexpected, liked to two electric piles by supple conductive wires.

"Look, Gloria!" the engineer repeated.

Then there was a sudden condensation on the shelf. A mist was designed there, which became pink and green, and solidified, red and green...

A magnificent crimson rose had just surged forth, and from the depths of the tube, Francel, laughing, was no longer holding anything but a passably complicated apparatus.

It was four minutes and six seconds past eleven.

The official loudspeaker thundered: "Pay attention! The engineer Francel, already celebrated for his studies of the dissociation and recomposition of matter, has found the means to transmit substance through the atmosphere. Radiotransmission has been discovered. A rose has just been sent from Reims to Paris via the airwaves."

An unimaginable rumor rose from the city. Madame Francel felt her heart beating faster and her face going pale.

Timidly, she picked up the embalmed voyager, and pressed the illustrious flower to her quivering lips...

And this happened in distant future times.

Originally published in Le Temps, *17 décembre 1928.*

Pierre Mille: *In Passing: Interview With the Pole Star*

Scientific information or deformation: An astronomer has just announced that, according to his calculations and observations, the pole star has changed position.

Star suspended over the green hill
From the mantle of sad night with silver thread,
Who gaze from a distance at the ship that sails
While the others, in the sky, are all in flight.

Incomparable star, the only one motionless
Lovely golden nail fixed in the northern night,
While your sisters, in their eternal futile orbit
Wander from one horizon to another,

Is it true that, in your turn, attained by dementia,
You want to flee, at last, to go who knows where?
And, still as beautiful, in the silent hour,
To go gallivanting in the unknown ether?

Of everything that remains, O sublime symbol.
You, whose appeasing and mild clarity,
Reborn each night, consoles celestially
An endless wanderlust of mad humanity,

Always in the same place over our haggard heads,
Unique in the firmament, pale and delightful,
Sage star, pure star, stop, then, stop!
Star of repose, don't budge in the heavens!

That pastiche of de Musset was, to begin with, all that the abovementioned information inspired. I was not overly discontented with them, firstly, doubtless, out of authorial vanity, but also—and, I believe, principally—because some of its rhymes were as feeble and irregular as my model.[52] Soon, however, reflecting that contemporary poets make many others, no longer rhyming at all, or have recommenced, imitating an illustrious precedent making *misericorde* rhyme with *hallebarde*, I conceived some doubt about the originality and value of the fragment.

As often happiness, it was only in that moment of discouragement that my mind labored, causing meditation to be succeeded by reveries of my sensibility. It appeared to me that the pole star not only served to suggest chimeras and images to poets, or to those who believe themselves to be such, and that, until the present day, it had been considered, by reason of a habitude that it seemed due to conserve until the consummation of centuries, destined to mark the north. Since the discovery of the compass, and, in recent times, the invention of William Lauth, which permits ships to navigate without a pilot, mariners scarcely envisage the pole star any longer as anything but a slightly outdated heavenly body, but it is not the same for sergeants and adjutants charged with informing recruits of the mysteries of service on campaign.

If one is no longer authorized to put one's confidence in that little star in the constellation of the Little Bear, only the compass remains henceforth with which to steer—an instrument with which simple soldiers are not normally equipped—and, for want of a compass, the moss on trees, which, the

---

[52] I have translated the poem literally, thus destroying the rhymes in the original. Had I improvised a rhyming version, it would have been direly difficult to reproduce the false rhymes hast the author lists in parentheses: *camp* and *argent*; *septentrion* and *horizon*; *têtes* in the plural and *arête*, and there would be little point in poking fun at Alfred de Musset here and now.

manuals affirm, grows more abundantly on the side of the bark exposed to the wind and perpetual shadow of the north. But in order there to be moss, there has to be trees; in order there to be trees there has to be a wood, or at least a grove. What can one do, then, if one is in the Sahara? No one is unaware of the interest that my patriotism directs toward military matters the deficiency of the pole star was therefore of a nature to inspire some anxiety in me.

I am not only a poet, a philosopher and—as you can see—a strategist; I am also a journalist. I resolved to go and interview the pole star, which had become erratic. My profession imposed that duty upon me. A few years ago the enterprise would have seemed impossible, but everyone knows that Monsieur Robert Esnault-Pelterie,[53] thanks to the judicious employment of rockets replacing obsolete kerosene, has succeeded in obtaining heavier-than-air propulsion in the stellar void.

Parenthetically, that will became a cause of political and economic ruination for the United States and England, which share control of the exploitation of fuel oil and the states that produce it, because rockets only utilize nitrogen-based explosives, and increasingly, that nitrogen tends to be extracted from the atmosphere. That puts the whole world on the same footing. But when there is no longer any nitrogen in the air that we breathe—nothing but oxygen and helium—the whole world, overly excited by the unique inhalation of those excessively stimulating gases, will go mad—which, moreover, we are already beginning to perceive.

Our voyage, which I accomplished with Monsieur Robert Esnault-Pelterie himself, was quite short: only forty days, thanks to the incredible speed, far superior to that of light, that our rocket-ship acquired in the void. I shall not reveal the details, which are reserved for the more authorized pens of the

---

[53] Robert Esnault-Pelterie (1881-1957), the aircraft designer and propagandist for the employment of rockets in space travel.

specialist scientists who accompanied us. I shall mention nevertheless that we saw Mars and Venus in passing. They seemed to me to be rather sad lands, useless for colonization. The climate of Mars varies, in accordance with latitude, between that of Greenland and that of the interior of Australia. It is only habited by degenerate species reminiscent of crabs and lobsters, which are not, but rather insects that resemble those crustaceans externally. Venus presents analogies with Mount Pelé in eruption; that planet is entirely devoid of living beings, except for bacteria and trilobites. The atmosphere there is almost irrespirable because of the excess of carbon dioxide.

Finally, we arrived at the pole star. I was able to chat with her, albeit at a distance, for she is a very hot star—which might astonish certain persons, inclined to imagine falsely that everything found in the north is cold. She has a good voice, though, and with the aid of our wireless apparatus she was able to hear me.

"Me!" she cried. "Displace myself relative to the Earth? Are you all idiots, you terrestrial journalists? I displace myself, to be sure, but like all the other stars, including your solar system. According to your astronomers, we are heading with a common accord toward the constellation Taurus. But that's a joke, or at least an appearance, given that the constellation in question is behaving like all the others, and we'll never catch up with it. The truth is that we don't know where we're going; that's the only resemblance we have with human beings."

"But in sum, how it is that we think that we have observed it?"

"If your colleagues and you had the slightest capacity for reflection in your brains, you would have realized that it isn't me who is changing location but your own north pole: the Earth, in sum, or the Sun. Personally, I don't know; I'm too far away and I don't care. However, I'm inclined to believe that it's the Earth. You humans have a deplorable influence on her. You spend your time turning everything upside down, all the time. Although I'm even further away than the most distant nebula, in spite of my total indifference to everything that might be happening out there, I can take account of it without even looking, without needing to move. It leaps to the eyes. You're frightful crackpots! You want to go quickly, ever more quickly. You always want to change location. How do you expect the genius of the Earth not to be influenced by that? It makes her spin on her axis—uselessly, moreover, like a dog trying to catch its tail. It's a ridiculous operation, which the entire society of stars is in accord in regarding with irony, compassion and disdain. But it's not entirely the fault of the genius of the Earth, who is rather conservative, and would like things to remain as they have always been. Unfortunately, she can't do anything about it; it's a question of weight."

"A question of weight?"

"Evidently. How many people were there in the Americas, for example, four centuries ago? A few hundred thousand. Today there are a hundred and twenty millions in the United States alone. Not only do they have weight, they have volume. Add to that forty millions in Brazil, and I don't know how many in the rest of the continent—which you call new, I don't know why, since it's as old as the others, but you humans relate everything to yourselves, as if you were something great and proper!—in sum, that makes two hundred million individuals of your strange and insupportable species in a space where there were almost nothing before. A rupture of equilibrium! One would think that you'd perceive that yourselves with regard to questions of production, competition and a heap of stories that don't concern us and about which we don't care, like the death of your moon. But do you think they don't weigh anything, those two hundred million people? And that's not all: the Chinese and Hindus are multiplying more and more, while you're depopulating. That augments the relative weight of some parts of the globe at the expense of others. It changes the possibilities of the Earth's balance"

"But what do you expect us to do about it?"

"Nothing at all. That's the way it is. You see, at the distance we are away from you, these little modifications of your insignificant planet are all the same to us. If it continues..."

"If it continues…?"

"Well, anything might happen. A change of orbit, or the equator moving to the poles and the poles to the equator, which would inconvenience the negroes without any advantage to white people. Or you might fall on to the sun…"

"No!"

"Yes. Why not? It's getting cooler, your old sun. We contemplate it with pity. The fall of the Earth would warm it up again. It would become more luminous. We stars of light like light. We'd be quite content."

"But tell me, do planets exist in other solar systems where there are also human beings, as on our Earth?"

"I don't know everything," the pole star, "but none to my knowledge. It's your pride and your lack of imagination that lead you to suppose that the same forms are invariably produced throughout the universe, ultimately to end in beings similar to you. I'm inclined to believe that, fortunately, it's nothing of the sort."

Originally published in Le Matin, *3 décembre 1929.*

Maurice Renard: *Gardner and the Invisible*

Gardner was now living in a pretty house in Nogent, on the bank of the Marne. I went to see him at the beginning of my sojourn in Paris. Our last encounter had been two years before. He received me with an enthusiasm in which I detected a hint of feverishness. That surprised me, for I had always known Gardner to be the most phlegmatic of chemists.

Aged? Changed, rather. Gardner was now a jerky individual, agitated and almost talkative, with eyes that shone with a distracted ardor, giving the impression of being occupied with something else—to such an extent that my first words were:

"At least I'm not disturbing you, Gardner?"

He took my hands. "You, my dear Krauss? Such a thought? I swear to you that your visit is the thing that I could wish for most in all the world, you hear?"

"Too polite!" I said, smiling.

"Don't reply like that. I'm not saying that out of banal politeness, Krauss..."

He held me by the shoulders and plunged his gaze into my eyes. Then, separating from me abruptly, he started pacing in all directions, biting his fingernails rubbing his face compulsively, and sometimes stopping in front of the large bay window overlooking the river and its magnificent trees,

He came to a standstill suddenly and fixed me with his eyes, which always seemed to be looking at you in an accessory fashion.

"Krauss, you're the best man I've encountered in my life, the surest friend. It's necessary that someone knows what I'm doing; it will be you."

I didn't make any reply, and strove to adopt a grave and dignified attitude. He reflected for a further three or four minutes—which is a long time, in reality—and he came to a decision, making another nervous gesture.

"Oh, too bad! You see, Krauss, I hesitated over the fashion in which to confide my secret to you. Ought I to talk to you in a loud voice, or write, or employ some other procedure? The more I thought about it the more I thought that it's pointless to reflect, since I don't know anything about them, nothing about their senses or their knowledge, while perhaps they can read all my thoughts in my head."

"Hmm!" I said. "What are you talking about, Gardner?"

"Come, Krauss."

He took me through his laboratory, which offered an admirable and incomprehensible spectacle. It was a vast luminous room filled with inconceivable things, mysterious apparatus, crystalline reflections, red lights, little sounds of bubbling, emissions of gas and disquieting odors. Then, by a narrow ascending stairway Gardner took me into a chamber that was even more spacious, and he illuminated it by means of a powerful arc lamp, because it was as obscure as a cellar.

With a brief gesture and a glance of extreme vivacity, he indicated to me a series of pipes fitted with taps emerging from the wall, spaced at regular intervals. The pipes seemed to be designed to furnish gas to heating apparatus. Gardner told me rapidly that they communicated with the laboratory.

I was increasingly astonished, and even impressed, by the instability of his gaze; he never ceased looking up and down, and from right to left, like a sick person subject to hallucinations integrating the void with the dread that phantoms might form there. An intense preoccupation had gripped Gardner again. For the third time he made an abrupt gesture of uncertainty and anxiety, and it was in a low voice, his mouth close to my ear, that he explained the strange concept of his enterprise.

"After all, Krauss, I'll tell you about it as quickly as possible; it's more prudent. Listen, Krauss; it's here that the invisible world ought to appear for the first time to human eyes.

"The invisible world?" I murmured, stupefied.

He shook his head impatiently. "Come on," he said, "You know very well that our five senses are impotent to enable us to perceive everything that exists. It would probably require thousands of senses to have a complete perception of the world. We are, therefore, surrounded by a quantity of things and beings that we can't see, which we can't hear, and can't sense in any manner, because they're invisible, silent, impalpable, etc. That's the mystery in the midst of which we live, and which is undeniable. In the last hundred years, science has discovered enough things and enough beings previously unsuspected for us to be certain of not being as alone on earth as we appear to be. Invisible companions surround us. They cross our path silently, perhaps traversing us; they mingle with our existence without our suspecting it. Their presence is doubtless not without effect on ours. Without them, we wouldn't be what we are, in the same way that, without microbes and radiations, we'd have an entirely different way of life. What a terrible possibility it would be if, among those invisible beings, there were some who are our masters..."

"What!"

"Yes, Krauss. We believe ourselves to be free. Are we? Might not the actions that we accomplish, with the certainty of only obeying our will, be the result of pressures, suggestions or tyrannical orders emanating from ungraspable despots? Perhaps we're dealing with despots much more powerful than us, and more intelligent. Perhaps humankind is only their livestock—a livestock on which they nourish themselves. When we suffer, when we're ill, why should they not have determined it, in order to extract energy from us, a fluid or I know not what, to repair their own physiological losses? When we die, is it them who kill us?"

"That's terrifying!" I stammered.

"Now," he continued, "I've found the means to render visible momentarily everything that is normally not. In this sealed room, which I shall have invaded by a gaseous mixture, everything that is invisible will appear to me. I shall see, Krauss, as I can see you, what no man has ever seen before:

the beings that are beyond our senses, their bodies and their movements. It might be the commencement of an immense struggle, and in any case, an era of unlimited observation. When I say that I've found it...no, I need another week, and everything will be ready. What a triumph, then! Unless..."

"Go on! What do you fear?"

"You know very well, Krauss, or you wouldn't be so pale..." He went on, more coldly: "Are you very busy in Paris? Would it be possible for you to come and see me every day? I'd be very grateful to you, my friend. It's not a long journey by automobile."

"That's agreed. But tell me, Gardner, these beings— these monsters, in sum—what aspect do you think they have?"

"Shh!" he said. "We shouldn't talk too much. If our mute thoughts are sealed to them but they understand our language, what I've just told you has betrayed me."

I looked at him as I had never looked at anyone before. I experienced the vibrant pride of finding myself confronted by prodigious superman. But then, without transition, his constantly watchful face troubled me...

I quit him under an impression of perplexity.

The next day, and the day after, I went to see him again. He did not breathe a word about his research, but we were both impassioned by it and the gazes we exchanged said a great deal.

The following day he received me while pronouncing a single word in a tremulous tone: "Found. It will be tomorrow."

But at dawn, Gardner was dead, struck down by apoplexy.

Chance? Overwork? Execution? Dead, that much is certain.

In a sealed envelope, with a letter in which the scientist envisaged the eventuality of his end, he delivered to me the complicated formula that was to enable everything hat nature has hidden from us thus far to surge forth for him, and he gave me practical instructions so minutely detailed that I decided to attempt the same extraordinary experiment myself.

It's possible that I haven't taken all the precautions necessary for the manipulation of the chemical substances. It's possible that I haven't protected myself from the emanations, vapors and radiations appropriately. At any rate, since the day before yesterday, my eyes have been giving me trouble and my sight is declining rapidly. The oculist I consulted remains indecisive regarding the cause of the troubles, but he hasn't hidden the fact that, if they persist, I might be blind in a matter of hours.

Forgive me, my poor Gardner. The unknown frightens me. I'm giving up.

Originally published in Le Matin, *3 octobre 1931.*

Maurice Renard: *An Adventure in the Forest*

When they perceived the Dionaea[54] in the process of de-vouring a hummingbird it was exactly eight days since they had plunged into the forest, and it was exactly nine days since they had murdered the Dutchman, in order to obtain a profit of only eighty florins, and the stupidity of traversing three hundred kilometers of virgin forest, for fear of the gallows. I don't believe that I'm mistaken in affirming that they would have to march for three or four more weeks, at the lowest estimate, before reaching the northern edge and finding themselves in security.

Excuse me: *they* were three good-for-nothings. But is it my fault if adventures don't happen exclusively to gentlemen?

Harris, Wilbur and Morton: those were their names, as they were reported to me. I was also told that Harris was very tall and red-haired; Wilbur was short but curiously massive, with eyebrows as black as coal and the nose of a boxer, all crushed; as for Morton, it appear that he was something extraordinary, with regard to his muscles, his ugliness and his stupidity. I don't know anything more on the subject of their physique, for which you'll excuse me, but I dare to suppose that a demoiselle wouldn't have liked to encounter them in that forest, during the eight days that they were fraying a passage, at a forced march, through the thickness of lianas, branches and everything that you can imagine. You can see their bristling beards and torn clothing from here, not to mention the situation, which gave them, I assume, an appearance even more damned than usual.

---

[54] *Dionée* [Dionaea] is the conventional French rendering of the name of the plant known in English the Venus fly-trap.

In the beginning, they had traveled at a furious speed, not stopping by day or night, eating fruits and a few tinned goods, forbidding themselves to hunt because of the rifle shots, which might have betrayed them. Now they were more tranquil, sleeping during the siesta, traveling less rapidly, and cooking the pieces of game that they brought down.

As for the Dionaea, it was Harris who spotted it first, for the reason that he was leading the march at that moment. And it was the cries—the very faint cries—of the hummingbird that attracted his attention.

Do you know what a Dionaea is? No? Well, it's a plant: a carnivorous plant. It has leaves that are mouths, and those mouths are also stomachs, you understand? Imagine as many jaws, the lips of which are bordered by lashes, like eyelids. No teeth no thorns that make fangs. Those jaws don't chew, but they catch their prey by closing on it, and imprisoning it, and they digest it conscientiously.

Harris showed the plant to his companions, and they looked at it curiously Dionaeas were familiar to them. They had already seen them in the country and in the forest, but those had been Dionaeas of restricted dimensions, which nourished themselves on insects and flies, and they hadn't known that the larger species devoured little birds and other small creatures; they were interested in that vegetal ferocity, which had just captured a hummingbird. The charming winged creature was struggling as best it could, but the strange maw tightened its vice, and furthermore, glued the poor little bird with a viscous liquid.

Wilbur pointed out the noxious odor that the plant gave off. Then they continued on their way, indifferent to the fate of the hummingbird, no longer thinking about that scene of savage life.

You might say to me that they had other preoccupations. That's true. And that evening, a panther dropped from a branch on Wilbur and only just missed him. It was killed by a bullet fired by Morton. The three adventurers, perfectly calm, remained insensible to that aggression.

The next day, after a night resonant with howls and con-stellated by eyes that reflected the light of the camp fire, they resumed the northerly direction without emotion, having slept well, while one of them placidly watched over the sleep of the others.

And nothing notable occurred, that day or the next. Noth-ing: the forest simply became more imposing as they penetrat-ed further. The trees offered no specimen of any new kind, but their growth was remarkable. Harris, Wilbur and Morton had a confused impression of having shrunk. It was not a mystery for them that the forest, in its depths, took on unusual propor-tions; certain explorers, without having ventured into the heart of its darkness, had spoken of its gigantic character, after hav-ing reached the edge of the zone where the three men were now advancing, without surprise or apprehension.

Then, on the following day, at about four o'clock, as they were following a path through long grass and brushwood cleared by I know not what pachyderm, they encountered an-other Dionaea. It was sensibly more developed and vigorous than the first, and when they saw it, the dirty beast of a plant was only making a mouthful of a squirrel.

Morton started to laugh, like the brute he was, but Harris remarked that the pestilential scent acted upon them like a stupefying gas, and before the squirrel had been swallowed he had used his hatchet to smash the green hydra and its dozen drooling maws, which bore a disagreeable resemblance to vast empty bloodshot eyes. The operation, moreover, was not ac-complished so easily; the flesh of the stems and the frightful leaves opposed a serious resistance; its destruction required force; Harris spared no expense of it, and he struck the debris with a bizarre rage until he had flattened it on the ground into a nauseating pulp.

Afterwards, the same day, there was the bear: a huge an-imal that gave them a lot of trouble. Finally, though, they got out of it, after a veritable battle, the effect of which was to rejoice them powerfully in the pride of their bestiality.

However, Harris and Wilbur, followed by Morton, now maintained a new prudence under the higher vault of foliage. They sometimes stopped, sniffing the breeze, and if a fetid odor reached them, they hastened their pace, hatchets in hand, scrutinizing the mass of plants with a keen gaze.

Thus, always heading north, they arrived in an impressive region in which the trees were certainly the most formidable on earth. Their monumental trunks extended to vertiginous heights; and beneath them there was another forest made of enormous bushes, in which shrubs attained the stature of common oaks.

They were engaged in the tangle of an interior jungle. They would never have been able to carve a corridor through it; they continued to follow animal trails. I can assure you that they did so diligently. However, the slightest suspect odor suddenly immobilized Harris and Wilbur, although the bewildered Morton did not understand their attentive faces, their dilated nostrils and their searching eyes.

You'll excuse me; this isn't a tale, and it's necessary to put oneself in their place, isn't it?

Finally, one evening, when Morton had gone to collect dead wood with which to make the fire. Harris and Wilbur heard a kind of stifled scream, half-moan and half cry for help. And then...nothing more.

Yes, something arrived: the odor, violent and formidable, proportionate to the giant forest.

For a moment, they didn't move, gripped by fear, paler than corpses. They were lost in the depths of the worst solitude; lost at the feet of immense trees; lost in a nameless horror.

"Let's get away!" murmured Wilbur. "Let's go back. I'd rather risk the gallows. I'd prefer no matter what."

"Me too," Harris stammered. He was struggling against fear himself. What fear? The most terrible, that of the unknown; that of the monster. I haven't said that their bravery was proof against anything. I've told you that they were murderers; true courage was not for them.

Harris, however, overcame it.

"It's necessary to go and see," he said. "Let's go."

So they went, but side by side, their hatchets raised.

Well, what they discovered wasn't what they feared.

I swear to you, though, that no spectacle in the world is more frightful than that of a python finishing crushing a man in order to feed on him. And that's what they saw.

But having said that, it was *normal*.

The reptile didn't have the leisure to follow up its preparations. Harris dispatched it with a well-placed bullet, too late for Morton, who paid in that fashion for his part in the murder of the Dutchman.

Where did the odor come from? Would you like to know?

Not far from there, in a clump, medium-sized Dionaeas were yawning with all their carnivorous mouths.

Harris and Wilbur considered them in a satisfied manner.

"Thank God," said Wilbur. "Numerous, but small. Quite small…"

"There aren't any large ones," Harris confirmed. "That would be known, you see."

At daybreak, they set forth again, heading north.

Originally published in Le Matin, *26 mars 1932.*

Maurice Renard: *The Dinornis Egg*

"Mesdemoiselles, Messieurs, my dear comrades..."

Fortier, who had pronounced those preliminary words in a loud voice, waited for silence to fall. In the room, situated on the entresol of a café in the Latin quarter, about fifty young people of both sexes were not depriving themselves of the pleasure of making a joyous racket.

When the noise had ceased, Fortier went on cheerfully: "My dear comrades, you have decided to confide to me the mission of seeking, and finding, a gift worthy of being offered by us to our dear and venerated master, Monsieur Dubois-Dontonfet, Professor of Paleontology, in the occasion of his fifty years of service. I want to announce to you immediately that my research has been crowned by a unhoped-for success.

"Your subscriptions added up to the jolly sum of four thousand and twenty-five francs; I am happy to inform you that, for that price, a man whose name is known to all of you, the scientist Beffroi-Saint-Gilbert, who has returned from a scientific mission to Madagascar, has consented to cede to us, in favor of his eminent colleague, one of the most precious curiosities that he has brought back from out there. You desired that our present would be of a nature to rejoice the scientific mind of our respected master. Most of you, I know, expected to see me appear before this assembly bearing some bronze art-work symbolizing science or recalling the vanished ages that are the objective of our dear paleontology. Well, I believe that I have put my hand on a treasure—yes, a treasure!—that will fill Monsieur Dubois-Dontonfet with joy and enrich his collection of fossils superbly. This treasure is...

"...The egg of a dinornis, the giant bird, the monstrous cassowary that, as you know, attained a height of nearly three meters. The egg that I have been able to acquire is one of the finest that has ever reached our days, being seven times more voluminous than the egg of a vulgar ostrich. Anyway, judge for yourselves. Here it is!"

And Fortier lifted in his pious hands the enormous while rotundity of which a formidable egg-layer had unburdened herself in the night of time.

At that sight, a concert of bravos and applause saluted Fortier's egg.

"I request to speak!" shouted Mademoiselle Lauriot, who was a charming brunette. "Easter is approaching. I propose to fix for that very day the banquet that we want to give in honor of Monsieur Dubois-Dontonfet. And thus the dinornis egg..."

"Will be an Easter egg!" concluded Fortier, enthusiastically. "An excellent and gracious plan!"

The acclamations drowned out Mademoiselle Lauriot's final phrase, proposing a certain stage-setting, of which she took charge in company with her comrade Fortier.

That stage-setting was simple and paschal.

On the eve of the great Sunday, the two students presented themselves at the establishment of a renowned confectioner, whose shop-window was overflowing with visibly comestible bells and eggs. They asked to speak to the proprietor in person, and in the presence of that merchant, they took the dinornis egg out of its box.

"Well," said Fortier, "have you ever seen one as big?"

But the confectioner was not astonished. He opened a cupboard in which eggs of all sizes were to be seen, several of which surpassed the dinornis egg.

"Yes," said Mademoiselle Lauriot, with a mocking smile, "but this one has been laid by a kind of ostrich whose species no longer exists. It's a real egg.

"Possibly!" retorted the strangely limited man. "But if you knew all the surprises that my articles contain! Some of them are mechanical; you can't imagine how ingenious they are. Believe me, if you want to have an effect, buy one of my eggs instead."

They had difficulty making him understand that they simply wanted him to ornament the dinornis egg with a fine ribbon, in order to give it a circumstantial air. He resigned himself to it with an ill grace, asking that the "article" be left with him and promising to deliver it at the appointed hour, fully beribboned.

"Above all," Fortier recommended, "Don't break it. Four thousand francs eh?"

"Have no fear."

"God, it's hot!" moaned Mademoiselle Lauriot.

"Damnably," replied Fortier, preoccupied. "But I repeat, one can't open anything; the master has a cold."

And he looked at old Monsieur Dubois-Dontonfet, who was sitting opposite him presiding over the table of honor and not taking his eyes off the formidable egg that rose up between them in the quadruple strap of a periwinkle blue ribbon knotted at the summit in multiple bows. The paleontologist already knew that it was a dinornis egg and he was feasting on the spectacle even more than the dishes of the banquet.

That was taking place in a torrid heat.

"But what's the matter with you, Fortier?" asked Mademoiselle Lauriot. "Is it the heat that…?"

"Yes," murmured Fortier, in a faint tone. "I believe it's the heat that…incline an ear a little, toward the egg. Can you hear that noise? One might take it for the beak of a chicken tapping the interior of its shell. Don't you think, in fact, that the heat has brooded the egg and that we're about to see it hatch?"

"That would be marvelous but it scares me!"

The second that she pronounced those troubling words, the event occurred. The egg exploded, projecting a quantity of other eggs in all direction, all tiny and made of chocolate, as crackers contain paper hats.

Having jumped at first, Monsieur Dubois-Dontonfet scented a practical joke.

"Curses!" proffered Fortier. "The confectioner has switched the egg. This one is sugar, naturally. Where's the other one, ours, the veritable one?"

The other, theirs, was also decked out in blue satin on a well-served table, and as it decided not to explode, even though they were on the dessert, the impatient youths set about hacking it into pieces, in order to discover the surprises, which were reduced to one alone: it was empty.

Originally published in Le Matin, *8 avril 1933.*

Maurice Renard: *Sirens*

That morning, Captain Jolliet, the captain of the yacht *Anemone*, took a bearing and noted: 78° east longitude, 41° south latitude.

"Where the devil are we?" he said. "Steer to the southeast, that doesn't lead anywhere. Bah! We'll see. With Cyrus Villars, it's all well and good."

His jovial face did not express any anxiety.

A sailor came to him. "Commandant, the boss is asking for you in his cabin."

The captain went down the narrow stairway rapidly. Cyrus Villars was beside a porthole wide open over the opaque waves of the Indian Ocean. He was looking out of the porthole. There was an open book on his knees: *Miss Waters.*[55] He turned his head and fixed Jolliet with a gaze shiny with sudden enthusiasm.

"Do you know what I'm doing, Commandant?"

Jolliet adopted his most jovial manner. "You're looking at the waves and the sky, Monsieur," he said.

"I'm not looking, old chap, I'm listening. Tell me, didn't you hear anything a little while ago? About five minutes? In the distance, over the sea...anything?"

"No, Monsieur."

"Sit down. Cigarette? Do you know what a siren is, Commandant?"

"It's a steamer's whistle. And I'm not unaware that the question interests you, since, when you bought the *Anemone* six months ago, you had her sonorous apparatus reinforced. At

---

[55] *Miss Waters* was the title under which H. G. Wells' novel *The Sea Lady* (1901) was translated into French,

present, no ship can compete with your yacht in making a din."

"I'm not talking about those sirens," said Cyrus. "I'm talking about…the others, those of mythology—of mythology, until further notice. Do you know what that is?"

"When I was young a professor asked me the same question. I replied: *a siren is a woman who has the legs of a fish.*"

And while laughing, Jolliet made a tour of the luxurious cabin with his eyes. A profusion of paintings and statuettes representing the fabulous enchantresses were seen there.

"Do you recall Ulysses?" Cyrus continued. "The ancient Ulysses ordered his sailors to block their ears with wax and had himself tied to the mast of his ship, in order to be able to hear the sirens without running the risk of being attracted by their songs."

"Of course! You're insulting me, Monsieur. I translated Homer at school."

"Pick up that box."

"What does it contain?"

"Malleable wax for your sailors, for you and for me. And, by excess of precaution, when the time comes, you'll activate the *Anemone*'s steam siren."

"In order to cover any other sound?"

"Exactly, Jolliet. Don't look at me like that—no, I'm not mad. Last year, I was returning to France from Melbourne. Not very far from here the steamer on which I'd booked passage picked up a shipwreck victim, who died a few days later. I was present during his last moments, as a privilege of the renown as a poet by which I'm favored. All doors open before Cyrus Villars…who isn't unworthy of it."

"Oh, Monsieur!" Captain Jolliet protested.

"In brief, my friend, that shipwreck victim, in his delirium, pronounced incredible words. He made allusion, with terror, to marine creatures whose song had drawn into the sea the entire crew of his ship, which was now sailing alone, adrift. He didn't know how he had managed to escape the 'charmers' as he put it.

"Well, Commandant Jolliet, I'm convinced that it's a matter of sirens. They're no longer encountered in the Mediterranean. For me, they took refuge in these lost regions in the depths of the Indian Ocean, far from modern perils. Note, in passing, that their survival would explain marvelously a bizarre phenomenon with which you're familiar, as an old sea-dog. I mean those deserted boats which don't show any damage and whose crews have quite simply disappeared without anyone being able to divine the cause."

"So, Monsieur, it's toward the zone of the sirens that we're steering? And those nets and the trawl we embarked are…in sum, if I'm not mistaken, you've had the *Anemone* fitted out for siren-fishing?"

"Can you imagine the effect produced?" Cyrus said to him. "What a sensation in society! To be the man who has broken through the mystery and mingled legend with reality! They have lived. They're still alive. Someone can bring them out of the shadow, bring them among human beings—and I shall be that man!"

They fell silent. Around them, the panted and sculpted sirens evoked dreams of beauty and grace; those works of art exhaled silently the music of unimaginable voices.

At that moment, far in the distance, a cry, an extraordinary appeal, made itself heard. The two men shivered. Cyrus seized a marine telescope and scrutinized the horizon.

"I can't see anything," he said, in a troubled voice.

"Shut the porthole!" cried the captain, suddenly. And precipitately, he slammed the heavy glazed circle which he bolted.

"Didn't you feel it, Monsieur? A numbness…a kind of vertigo. An attraction, in sum…"

"Yes!" said Cyrus, very excited. "Quickly! To the nets! Take your precautions, Commandant, like Ulysses. I'll follow you on deck."

They perceived, a few cables away, several living beings, which resembled dolphins but which, sometimes assuming an upright stance, allowed the sight of a torso and floating hair.

They were singing…but can one say "singing"? An unusual howl traversed the air, a long plaint charged with hypnosis. Melodious? Hmm! It was, above all, fascinating. Reptiles gaze as those creatures "sang."

With the aid of powerful binoculars, Cyrus watched them, fearful of frightening them by provoking the deafening clamor of the *Anemone*.

They came closer. He distinguished them more clearly…

Horror! They were monsters, frightful amphibians endowed with a frightful power. They revealed their ferocious mouths, armed with fangs, their hirsute tresses. At a distance, the shiny necks figured vague human bodies; strangely placed fins simulated excessively short arms. Nothing was more hideous, more bestial.

The poet made a sign to the captain. The beautiful millenarian legend was haunting his sad heart,

"Come about!" he shouted. "And full speed ahead!"

The *Anemone* described a curve and drew away.

When the maneuver had been executed, the captain said: "Why?"

Cyrus put a finger over his mouth. "No one must know," he said. "Ever. We've seen nothing, and heard nothing."

"But…the sirens?"

"Beauty, poetry, amour…and mystery."

"However Monsieur, those animals…"

"We haven't seen anything, I tell you. The sirens are incomparable young women; their faces are charming, their breasts virginal; multicolored scales make their bodies iridescent. They know the cradle-songs of sensuality and exquisite death. So, silence."

"Understood, Monsieur. But then, our campaign is finished?"

"Oh yes," said Cyrus, playing his part gallantly. "Finished…in a fish's tail. I don't regret it. I've continued Homer!"

Originally published in Le Matin, *5 décembre 1933.*

Maurice Renard: *The Aerolith*

I saw the aerolith fall quite distinctly, and set fire to the little house on the mountain.

Doctor and Madame Tourneil had invited me, for the first time, to spend a few days with them in their Savoyard villa. I had arrived from Paris at dinner time, and, night having fallen, we were still chatting on the terrace, savoring the charm of an admirable evening.

I had never seen the firmament living a more marvelous life. The month of August was beginning. In front of us, in the blue and brown shadows, the valley fled toward the heights; very close, on the left, the enormous mass of a mountain rose up, as if to touch the stars, and the sky, swarming feverishly with confused sparks, was furrowed by shooting stars, which traced incessantly here and there, the curves of their fulgurant streaks. Sometimes one of them, slower, made a light of which the panorama received the glow and lit up in a troubling fashion.

A few seconds before the fall of the bolide, I had been unable to retain an exclamation, while following with my eyes a particularly resplendent streak.

"Quickly, make a wish!" Madame Tourneil said to me, laughing. "You know the belief: a wish formulated during the appearance of a shooting star is always granted."

"One could make wishes constantly this evening," I remarked.

It was then that the event happened, suddenly.

A jet of fire, accompanied by the whistle of a shell, traversed space from top to bottom, like a flash of lightning, a little like a rocket that, instead of going up, was coming down. It came to land in the middle of the mountain, at the summit of a ridge, and at the very moment that the sound of the explosion reached us, delayed by the distance, a flamboyance informed us that the explosion had just ignited a conflagration. Doubtless the woods had caught fire.

Madame Tourneil was frightened. Her husband soothed her, certifying to her that the phenomenon was exceptional and that there was no need to fear a repetition; it was very rare that a shooting star penetrated the terrestrial atmosphere steeply enough to fall to earth; it was rarer still to observe it in this region.

Calmed, Madame Tourneil asked him: "Isn't that Couteau's house burning?"

"One might think so. That would really be a freak of chance—the aerolith hitting that isolated hovel."

A minute later he aimed his binoculars at the distant blaze.

"No doubt about it," he said. "It's Couteau's house. I can see the framework silhouetted against the flames. That Couteau is scarcely sympathetic; however, it's necessary to go to his aid."

"I'll go with you," I said.

"You realize that it's a matter of walking all night? We won't get up there until dawn. So there can't be any question of reducing the disaster; when we arrive, nothing will be left of the building. But Couteau might be injured."

"A small loss, if he's dead," said Madame Tourneil.

"I agree. It doesn't alter the fact that I have to leave without delay."

"I'll go with you," I said, again.

Toward midnight, Tourneil's automobile deposited the two of us on the mountain, at the place where the negotiable road ended. Solidly shod, we started to climb the slope via the zigzag paths.

A few mountain men had joined us. On the way they talked about Couteau, whose habitation was on fire. Their conversation conformed what my host had said. Couteau was a rather undesirable solitary, whose pride, cruelty and vices had caused his ruination. He lived apart now, hateful and sordid, in a former barn in the middle of a meadow, the last vestiges of his lost property.

Tourneil said to me in jest: "If I were superstitious, I'd think that the shooting stars were exacting vengeance."

"Why is that?"

"Because Couteau is superstitious. Can you imagine that that sad fellow interests me? Every time I pass near his retreat, I never fail to go and see him. He's a somber figure, blasphemy incarnate, evil made man, in truth. But he's superstitious, yes. And the other evening, having been delayed nearby, and reposing under his wretched roof, at a time similar to this, I heard him, standing on the threshold, saluting every shooting star with a wish, always the same, proffered wrathfully: "Wealth! Wealth!" Wouldn't one think that Heaven has taken exception to it? "Wealth! Wealth!"

The doctor had started to laugh, which awoke a fantastic echo in the obscurity of the gorge that we were skirting: "Wealth! Wealth!"

As the doctor had foreseen, it was at dawn that we arrived at the summit of the ridge. First light illuminated the smoking debris of the small house; a heap of blackened beams, mingled with rubble. Around the debris, the soil of the meadow was strewn with pieces of the aerolith, which had exploded.

In the meantime, groans were heard, and Couteau appeared to us, covered in blood, haggard, his clothes in tatters, his face frightfully ravaged by the explosion.

"Help!" he begged, weeping. "I'm blind! My eyes...! Oh, my eyes...! This way! Help! I can't see any more...!"

The doctor went to him. His wounds were so horrible that I turned my gaze away.

Then the sun rose in its glory; the shards of the bolide gleamed strangely red. I took a few paces and picked one up, scarcely cooled.

"Doctor!" I said, marveling. "Gold! It's gold!"

"Do you hear?" said Tourneil, in Couteau's ear. "Good news! This will give you courage. Do you understand? The aerolith was gold. Your field is full of gold now. You're rich."

"I tell you that I'm blind!" howled the bloodied man. "My eyes! Oh, to see! To see! That's what I want."

We looked at one another, Tourneil and I, while the peasants, stupefied but incredulous, slowly wandered around the field of gold. And I thought I heard sarcastic laughter from the ravine, and the words that the darkness had thrown back with so much irony:

"Wealth! Wealth!"

Originally published in Le Matin, *28 septembre 1935.*

Maurice Renard: *The Enchanted Mirror*

On arriving at the Château de Saint-Viry, where Alexis de la Baille had invited me to spend a few days, I found in my old childhood friend an air of contentment—of jubilation, to put it better—which the pleasure of our reunion seemed to me insufficient to explain. That kind of slightly mysterious gaiety was accompanied by a slight but undeniable agitation. While talking to me about one thing and another, Alexis made a quantity of small gestures that were not habitual. Furthermore, he continually lost the thread of the conversation and suddenly fell silent, in order to follow I know not what absorbing idea.

He was alone at the château. We dined together very cheerfully. Several times, however, I considered him in silence, with an intrigued eye, so surprising was his behavior; and it happened, at those moments, that he also stared at me, putting into his gaze all the amusement of a man diverting himself by keeping a secret, of which he is enjoying the delay in giving you the surprise.

In the smoking room after dinner, when his attitude had piqued my curiosity acutely, Alexis planted himself in front of me and, with his eyes gleaming, said: "Guess what I've discovered in the attics of the château. The thing most appropriate to impassion you and me—which is to say, if I'm not mistaken, two famous lovers of the marvelous.

"Really?" I said, powerfully interested.

"Pay attention! Don't get too carried away. It's only a story recounted in a letter; but the story is strange and the man who wrote the letter can't be suspected of either candor or lying. It's Maréchal des Essarts himself.[56]

---

[56] Jean-Baptiste Bouquerot des Essarts (1771-1833) was made a baron by Napoléon I as well as a maréchal de camp, but his

"Last week, masons who were repairing the eaves perceived that a wall, thick in appearance, rendered a hollow sound. They attacked the stone and exposed a sort of redoubt where there was a box stuffed with papers. Seventeenth and eighteenth century—all, as you can imagine, very precious. Several letters from important people, and some of the maréchal's correspondence, including…this."

Alexis de la Baille had gone to his writing desk and taken out a well-conserved parchment.

I read it.

On the Wednesday after Corpus Christi, the Marquis d'Espanges searched for his wife and could not find her. Men of good intention told him then that he might find that Monsieur de Soubrécourt had also disappeared; at which Monsieur d'Espanges remained open-mouthed and enquired for what devil of a reason that gentleman was also undiscoverable. Some of them told him to go and see. The others did not beat around the bush and started sniggering, asking him whether he did not find it humorous, and whether, in truth, he did not know that Madame d'Espanges and Monsieur de Soubrécourt had coiffed him in the manner of the minotaur.

With that, behold a man who bounded, foaming, and fled in a fashion to rouse the court and the city, swearing to the great gods that he knew nothing at all, that it was an abominable thing, and that he would take an exemplary revenge on the criminals, that he did not know yet to what treatment he would subject Madame d'Espanges, but that, as for the other, he knew in what fashion to chastise him, for Monsieur de Soubrécourt was a sorcerer and, as such, must end up on the Place de Grève.

"Yes," he cried, "a sorcerer, and no doubt about it. He has an alchemist's lair in his house; I've been assured of it

dates are not consonant with the chronology of the story so he cannot be the author of the rediscovered letter.

many times. It's high time Monsieur de la Reynie[57] asked him the question of whether he's a commoner and not a nobleman, who, moreover, enjoys a good reputation. But now there are no titles or renown that will hold! Now he has accoutered me, we shall see with what kind of wood I warm myself, damn it, and what I do to a henchman of the Evil One."

Everyone laughed surreptitiously. Monsieur de Soubrécourt, as some had scented, had quit Versailles. It could be taken for granted that the lovers were already far away, galloping toward the Low Countries, England or Spain, and that catching up with them would not be easy. Monsieur d'Espanges did not care. He launched horsemen in all directions with a mission to bring the marquise back, dead or alive. The king had not been able to refuse him a *lettre de cachet* in the name of the adulteress. Furthermore, His Majesty, rather annoyed by the affair, permitted the Hôtel de Soubrécourt to be visited and gave orders to the lieutenant of police to proceed there immediately in the presence of such persons as he judged it good to take with him.

Monsieur d'Espanges wanted, at all costs, to be there. As Monsieur de la Reynie saw that he was furious and in a humor to break everything, he asked a few men to come whose rank and character ought to impose upon that boor. It was thus that I took part in the operation, in the company of Messieurs de Solce and d'Aigreville, and with fellows that I had never seen before but whom I was told were well-versed in the chemical and alchemical sciences.

The Hôtel de Soubrécourt was closed and appeared to be deserted. The door was opened by mans of false keys. I will tell you without further delay that, having gone swiftly through the rooms and halls, which were beautifully decorated, and having found them totally abandoned of any human being, we went down into the cellars and we discovered in fact, an apparatus formed of pots, vats, retorts, bizarre con-

---

[57] Gabriel Nicolas de la Reynie (1625-1709), Lieutenant-General of Police under Louis XIV.

tainers and a quantity of vials containing liquids of all appearances.

"I told you so! I told you so!" repeated Monsieur d'Espanges, relentlessly, stamping his feet with joy. "He'll be broken and burned, the bandit!"

Then we went back upstairs, and, pensive as we were for the most part, we saw the rooms again. There was a small one into which none of us had passed before. A curtain had dissimulated it from our eyes. It was that madman d'Espanges who stuck his nose into it. He went in, and we heard him exclaim in surprise. Immediately, we were ten in the cabinet. And we saw our man stupefied before the most astonishing object that it had ever been given to me to contemplate until then.

A mirror, of small dimensions, was hanging on the wall. It was inclined, in order that it would be comfortable to look into it. But to mirror oneself therein was quite impossible, for—this is the prodigy—an image already occupied it: that of the pretty face of Madame d'Espanges. By a magical effect, you saw her smiling in that mirror as if she were there, in front of it, and the glass were reflecting her. However, she was not there, and the sole explanation of that marvel was that Monsieur de Soubrécourt had constrained the mirror diabolically to keep forever the charming image of his beloved.

Unfortunately, Monsieur d'Espanges, irritated by the sight of the inconstant beauty, lifted his cane and broke the enchanted object into a thousand pieces before anyone was able to do anything to retain him...

"Magnificent, isn't it?" Alexis asked me. "It's a great pity that I haven't found the rest of the letter. What do you think of it?"

"I think," I said, "that our scientists had precursors in the times of obscurantism, when the most terrified and stupid superstition obliged them to hide their endeavors and their inventions, under pain of being torn apart by four horses and roasted more or less alive. Monsieur de Soubrécourt seems to me to have realized color photography in the seventeenth century, and to have savored in peace all the recompenses that amour could lavish on the skies of Flanders, England or Spain."

Originally published in Le Matin, *28 novembre 1936.*

Maurice Renard: *The Oysters and the Sleeper*

To tell the truth, I was falling asleep, and several times I had proposed timorously to Estèphe Iliaz that we go to bed.

Now I was informed as to his intentions I was no longer persisting. Estèphe Iliaz did not want to go. He had not even responded to my feeble invitations. With one elbow on the table sustaining a hand clenching a chin, which I dared to qualify as aggressive, he was very red and he did not take his eyes off the beautiful little Tonine, who was dancing recklessly with the big Gabirus.

From time to time Estèphe poured himself a glass of white wine—that joyous little swilling wine that bites your tongue as it passes by—and apart from those Bacchic moments, he only opened his mouth to bark in a hoarse voice: "Hey, Omer, another bottle!" or to reproach me angrily: "But you aren't drinking, Léonard! Drink, then, damn it!"

I stammered vague excuses and strove to drink, for the sake of condescension, but I was struggling less and less victoriously against sleep; my head nodded and I straightened up, sometimes with a start, squinting, surprised to find myself in that noisy room..

The mechanical piano was making its harsh racket amid the loud hubbub of rustic voices and coarse laughter.

It was a sort of little casino in planks and tent canvas, illuminated by oil lamps suspended from the roof-beams. The sea was there, close by, behind a hedge of young pines growing in the sand. The young women of the coast and the fishermen were giving themselves with a joyful heart to the violent rhythm of the music machine. Round the floor, which they were hammering to the measure, a crowd was heaped up at long tables in raw wood, on narrow benches, with their feet in the soft, fluid sand, which was chilled by the night.

At our table we were packed like herrings. I ask you: was that the place for an Estèphe Iliaz? A scientist? A renowned biologist?

It was perfectly absurd that Estèphe was infatuated with Tonine. The syndicate of oyster-cultivators had asked him to come from Paris in order to study on location the best means of ameliorating the region's oysters. The activity of the dear man should have stopped there. But Tonine had appeared before him one morning in her father's parks, wearing the tight trousers of oyster-fishers with grace, sheltering her pretty face in the shadow of a pretty whimsical "quichenotte." And on that day, Esther had become another man, a lunatic.

Absurd, I tell you. For not only had the child just reached her seventeenth year-and Estèphe was a good forty—but no one could deny that she had a marked preference for that great rogue Gabirus. She had as much concern for the scientist's science as a fish for an apple, and it was perfectly fine by her to see him unhappy, provided that big Gabirus looked at her with a complicit eye.

Furthermore, don't think that Gabirus was some good-for-nothing mariner. No, no, he too was his father's son, and his father was one of the principal cultivators in the locale, who, believe me, wasn't to be disdained. That is to tell you that our Estèphe Iliaz, with all his knowledge and the armchair that as waiting for him in the Académie des Sciences, had no chance of pleasing Tonine.

I admit that his misfortune had completely disappeared from my mind and that I was savoring the pleasure of slumber—precarious, alas!—when I felt a rather brutal nudge bruise my ribs.

Sudden awakening. "Eh! What! What is it?"

Estèphe had struck me cordially. And why? To tell me, growling in a low voice: "Léonard, I'll have my revenge."

He continued staring, from behind his spectacles, at the happy couple, who were whirling and whirling, looking into one another's eyes.

"Yes, Léonard, I'll have my revenge, I tell you."

"Let's go to bed," I replied, mildly and without conviction.

Estèphe growled again. I hastened to regain the darkness, the beneficent abode of unconsciousness and dreams.

This time, I was extracted from it more gently. A hand squeezed my wrist, and I heard the Mephistophelean voice of Estèphe hissing in my ear: "I'll ruin them, Léonard, do you hear? I'll ruin the father of that little idiot I'll ruin the father of that fop. I'll ruin them all all! Aha, Messieurs! You've summoned me, Estèphe Iliaz! You're expecting me to enrich you, and you suffer that I'm disdained, mocked! Enrich you? Certainly, I can. It only depends on my will whether, three years from now, perhaps four, your ponds are overflowing with fat and flavorsome oysters. Patience! Fat and flavorsome they will be, I swear it. But I have a surprise in store for you, of which you'll give me news!"

"Estèphe, Estèphe!" I protested. Reflect, my good friend. Tonight you're excited..."

"It's all reflected," he affirmed, dully, with a somber irony. "I've promised to ameliorate the species. Well, I'll keep my promise!"

Was it three years later, or was it four?

Estèphe Iliaz had quit that oyster-farming region a long time ago, leaving behind the instructions of his science. Gradually, the oysters, as many Portuguese as flat, had become magnificent, thanks to all sorts of procedures, the secret of which he had sold very dear. Tonine and Gabirus were married and loved one another at present with tranquility. I continued to spend the summer season in the little villa where I had once accommodated my friend the scientist.

And it happened that I received some Parisians there, delighted to spend a few days by the seaside.

Those charming ignorant individuals only knew that, in the area, the summer oysters are as succulent as one could wish, because they are milky. I rejoiced in having them swallow a few dozen at lunch when they arrived, and I ordered my hundred number three oysters from the father of Gabirus.

In my drawing room there was a delightful young woman, her husband and her brother, all three of them the most agreeable conversationalists; and we were, in fact, conversing, waiting for the meal to be ready, when Dominique, my old manservant, opened the door by a crack and made me desperate signals. I saw that his face was strangely distressed.

"What is it?" I asked, approaching him.

Then I saw that his wife, the cook, was behind him, just as troubled, pale and incomprehensibly livid.

"Pardon me," I said to my guests. Then I went out and closed the door behind me. "What is it, Dominique?"

"It's the oysters, Monsieur."

"Well, what's wrong with the oysters? Not fresh? That would astonish me considerably."

"Come Monsieur, come…," begged the cook, tremulously.

"Well!" I grumbled, heading for the kitchen. "I'd like to know what it is about these oysters that frightens you so much."

I went in. It was obvious that Dominique has begun to open the shellfish and that he had interrupted himself in his task, only having opened three."

On a large platter of my beautiful service, three oysters of great splendor were showing their fat folds, the color of emerald.

"So what?" I said. "Superb! Those are exhibition oysters!"

Without saying a word, Dominique put in my hand the knife for opening the oysters, and, taken by him from the tank, one oyster from a hundred.

"You want me to do it myself? What's got into you, my friend."

Dexterously, I dug the knife in between the two valves…and, shivering from top to toe, I threw it away in horror.

The oyster—listen to this!—the oyster had screamed!

A poor scream of pain; faint, to be sure, but frightful, for it was recognizable as the cry of a beast having its throat cut.

"There!" said Dominique simply.

For a moment I remained stupefied, quivering with a sort of abomination. Finally, bravely, in order to make the experiment, I seized one of the open oysters and, with an *ad hoc* fork, I detached it...or rather, I was trying to, when the unfortunate mollusk began to emit minuscule but atrocious howls. The mere thought of eating that martyr made my hair stand on end.

"There's no error," Dominique concluded. "The oysters are no longer mute. To eat them, Monsieur, no way. There's nothing more to be done. And yet, tell me, when they didn't cry out, were they perhaps suffering just the same? The oyster-farmers will pull long faces! They'll be ruined!"

"Ruined...," I repeated, mechanically.

Then I remembered Estèphe Iliaz's threats, and I slapped my forehead violently...

It was the wooden table that had struck my head, not my hand. While asleep, I had ended up falling nose down. The couples were still whirling. Estèphe Iliaz was continuing to follow the beautiful Tonine with his eyes. I had dreamed it all: his threats and their fantastic realization.

"There!" he said. "You've bumped your head. Are you going to sleep again now?"

"Not for anything in the world!" I cried.

Originally published in Le Matin, *7 août 1937.*

Maurice Renard: *The Scientific Adventure of Ambroise Peupiot*

Professor Ambroise Peupiot's course at the Collège de France had only attracted a limited and undistinguished audience when that philosopher, who was also a physicist, undertook a series of lectures on the subject of space and its dimensions. The first of those lectures caused so much noise that the scientist, mounting the lectern to begin the second, found himself facing a packed amphitheater.

Such an influx was not ephemeral. It was reproduced for session after session. The administration was forced to allocate Ambroise Peupiot's course a hall of triple capacity, which soon proved insufficient.

There was the wherewithal to excite to paroxysm the interest of cultivated society, and even the other, for not only did Ambroise say remarkably original things about the fourth dimension of space, but also, representing for the count of science a theme that had previously only been the object of brilliant fantasies due to the imagination of pseudoscientific novelists, he went so far as to claim that humans ought not to renounce making the acquaintance of the fourth dimension by means of their own senses, and not merely by the play of reasoning. That came down to affirming the possibility, for a human creature, of going beyond the space of three dimensions—height, width and depth—in which we have the impression of living our petty and short lives, and perceiving, more or less, the mysterious fourth dimension which had thus far only been anticipated.

Professor Ambroise Peupiot was a middle-aged man of below average height, who bore an indisputable resemblance to Socrates, if one could rely on the effigies of the celebrated philosopher that have reached us. Like Plato's master, he was seen to have a debonair nose, a sagacious eye, hair covering the seat of thought, and, to top it all, a good beard, with the moustache rolled round the mouth, in order that the words could emerge more freely.

What perhaps impassioned all the people who were fortunate enough to see and fear Ambroise Peupiot—not counting the multitudes who listened to him over the wireless—was, we believe, what he did not say but which one sensed, that which, assuredly involuntarily, was suggested by something vibrant in his voice and blazing in his eyes. And what he did not say, it seemed, was that he was toiling with all his might to penetrate, so to speak, yes, to penetrate himself, with his physical person, into the fourth dimension.

One reporter got in ahead of the others and interviewed him resolutely on the matter: "Has the master any intention to put into practice…?"

The professor was not discomfited by that, without, however, delivering himself totally. He had received the journalist in a work-room of sorts, which was something of a laboratory. There, an admirable disorder was accumulated, over which the visitor paraded curious and interrogative gazes. But Ambroise Peupiot, smiling, confided to him: "Don't search for a machine to explore the fourth dimension. It will, I think, only require a drug, and, above all, a great effort of will for a few minutes…"

The other did not find out any more, not because Ambroise Peupiot manifested the desire to break off the conversation, but by reason of the sudden and stormy appearance of Madame Peupiot. That lady, very beautiful, in truth—and young, believe me!—was animated by an anger that fell upon her husband in generous abuse. The journalist, in spite of the power of indiscretion of which he made a professional duty, wanted to spare the scientist the embarrassment of his presence and retired, murmuring: "Xanthippe!"

Thus was named, as everyone knows, the shrewish wife of Socrates.

The next day the article appeared; it was sensational. One read therein that Professor Ambroise Peupiot was preparing to travel, for a few moments, into the enigmatic land of the fourth dimension, by means of a drug, and above all by means of his will.

The consequence was that people literally rushed on that day to the professor's lecture—which did not take place.

He had, in fact, disappeared. Madame Ambroise Peupiot affirmed, with stupor, that he had gone into his study immediately after lunch in order to work there, as he did every day, but that no one was there when she opened the door in order to remind him that it was time for his lecture

Hastily penciled notes were found on his desk:

I'm drinking the drug...ten minutes to wait...stomach cramps, but no other sensation...to pass the time I've rinsed the glass and put everything back in order...the ten minutes have elapsed; now let's concentrate our will...

That was all. There was no doubt that the professor, having departed for the land of the fourth dimension, had lingered there. He stayed there for much longer than he had let it be understood, and longer, no doubt, than he had anticipated.

The journalist, inspired by fantastic literature, had foreseen the circumstance accurately, putting into his account, of course, all the humor that was appropriate to it. That evening, enjoying his good luck, he published boldly:

Professor Ambroise Peupiot will not come back; he might have been able to emerge from our good old dimensions, but he is now a prisoner in the fourth, in a world that he does not have the power to quit.

Events proved him right. Those who remained for days and weeks on sentry duty in the work-room saw nothing and heard nothing of a nature to make them believe that the professor was there while being elsewhere. Nothing! Not the most diaphanous of shadows! The unknown had completely and definitively absorbed the reckless and prodigious pioneer of the mystery.

After the weeks there were the months, and then the years...

People were no longer thinking about the glorious and frightening end of the professor. Floods of ink had flowed on the subject. Works of every kind had tried to reconstitute the extraordinary drama. Several films had been made, with renowned stars who had played Ambroise Peupiot, and one saw on the screen, thanks to the inexhaustible resources of cinematographic technique, all the phenomena of gradual effacement that had been Ambroise Peupiot's departure for God knows what country.

Madame Ambroise Peupiot, rid of her mourning crepe—which she had, moreover, worn with coquetry—began to put everything to work to be able to marry again as soon as possible, and in that design, she strove to appear the most amiable of women. Monuments had been erected to the martyr of science. The *Dictionnaire encyclopédique* contained the name *Peupiot* between *Peuls* and *Peutinger*.[58]

Years, then.

And then, one fine morning, as a consequence of an unfortunate lack of fuel, having gone astray in mists, an airplane came down in mid-Pacific, fortunately very close to an island no less lost.

The indigenes, with their pirogues, saved the shipwreck victims: a pilot, a navigator and the philologist Ernest Sémanty, of the Institut, on a mission to Hawaii.

How did a European come to be sharing the primitive existence of those peaceful savages, on that island where no one ever went? Ernest Sémanty asked himself that on finding him-

---

[58] *Peuls* is the French name for an African tribe nowadays known in English as the Fulani. The *Tabula Peutingeriana*, or Peutinger Map, is a thirteenth-century map of the roads of the Roman Empire.

self face to face with the individual in question, who, certainly emerging from a siesta, knew nothing about the adventure of the airplane, for he opened wide the very mouth and eyes of Socrates.

"Peupiot!" cried Sémanty. "What a story! Scarcely aged! In excellent health! Prosperous and ruddy! And how pretty those garlands of flowers are with which you're ornamented! But how the Devil do you come to be here, alive?"

"Shh!" said Ambroise, a finger barring his lips. "Shh! It's quite simple. My wife had made my life a torture, and the infernal Megaera would have followed me everywhere. So, my dear friend, mercy. Silence! Silence!"

"Don't count on me, Peupiot!" said Sémanty. "As soon as I return I shall publish the truth. Very glad to know it!"

"You won't do that!" exclaimed Ambroise Peupiot, who turned white, dismayed. "Why refuse me secrecy? I'm so happy!"

"I don't doubt it! But I'm not, and I won't miss such a fine opportunity to become so again!"

"How is that?" stammered the unfortunate.

"My marriage is void, since you're alive. It's me, old man, who married your execrable widow!"

Originally published in Le Matin, *8 janvier 1938.*

Maurice Renard: *The Fantastic Eye*

For several years I lived with my brother. We occupied an apartment of two rooms and a storage space in an old house, demolished today, in the heart of the Latin quarter, at the top of a narrow, short and rising street. Alfred was an employee in a bank, and I made my daily journey to the ministry.

Alfred didn't like the bank but he said: "As well that as something else." I can't think, in any case, of any profession that would have contented him. He was made to possess a laboratory and a library, and to work all on his own without having to account to anyone else. My own room was always tidy, but if you had seen his, cluttered with piles of books and all sorts of instruments!

Alfred was always in the process of planning some apparatus. It's necessary to tell you that if an idea can obsess a man, it's the one that obsessed him. My brother had got it into his head that nature is populated by a quantity of beings that we can't perceive, because we only have five senses, and many others would be required to take cognizance of those creatures. That was Alfred's idea. The existence of that world was no longer in doubt for him, but he strove doggedly to obtain proof—which is to say, to arrive at seeing, touching or hearing what had thus far remained invisible, impalpable and silent.

So, whenever he had a few minutes to spare, Alfred plunged into his studies and his experiments. We had rented those lodgings because they were close to the bank. At midday you would have see him coming back up the boulevard at a run. He ate one or two croissants dipped in coffee, in the midst of his clutter, while pottering around. In the evening we dined together at the restaurant; when I talked, he almost always paid little attention, lost in his ideas, impatient to get home in

266

order to work there by night until impossible hours; or he brought me up to date with his endeavors, his experiments, his disappointments—and with what passion!

For a long time he had been attempting to make the invisible world appear. I mean that for a long time he had been trying to discover by what means, chemical or otherwise, he could treat space in order that the invisible that it contains would become visible. But at that time I had already expressed certain fears that had come to me on reading a newspaper article.

"Do you know that you're not the first, Alfred?"

"I know that very well," he said, "but what does it matter?"

"And I know very well why you've never talked to me about your predecessors, a man named Gardner and one named Chambrun.[59] That's because they died in an odd fashion. Look at me Alfred, don't turn your head away. It's said that the invisibles killed them both when they were on the brink of violating their mystery."

"No," said Alfred, tranquilly, "it's a matter of simple coincidences. There's no proof. Gardner and Chambrun died quite naturally. In any case, if we admit the contrary, so what?"

All I said was: "Be careful. Until today, I hadn't understood sufficiently that the invisibles—if there are any invisibles—might be able to distinguish us, and might control us."

I had to be content, for all response, with an enigmatic smile.

Sometimes I estimated that my brother was prey to an innocent mania, as perhaps Gardner and Chambrun had been—who, after all, might have died normally. And sometimes I took it completely seriously, struck as I was by the rigor of his reasoning and the logic of his conjectures.

---

[59] Chambrun is the protagonist of a story entitled "*Eux*", which appeared in *La Revue des vivants*, août 1934 and is translated as "*Them*" in *The Doctored Man* (q.v.).

One day, therefore, Alfred said to me that he was changing tack, that he was renouncing making the visible appear, as Gardner and Chambrun had tried to do.

"I'm turning the matter round," he said. "Do you understand? It's sight that I'm going to try to modify appropriately."

"Get way! You can't modify the human eye, nor, I presume, add to it spectacles that..."

"No—although you're forgetting at present that the microscope and the telescope have enabled us to see the invisible in their fashion—no, but I can manufacture a scientific eye...you'll see."

A few weeks later, I fact, he showed me a photographic apparatus of the latest model, but the objective lens of which he had replaced by a system of his own invention, more voluminous that the apparatus itself, and which a flexible wore linked to a supply of electric current.

It was a fine Sunday in May. I was free. I witnessed his experiment. But I've forgotten to tell you that Alfred had made our storage cupboard into a darkroom in order to develop his pictures there conveniently.

You will have grasped without difficulty that the "scientific eye" was nothing other than the mysterious objective lens, capable of fixing on the plate the image of forms that the human eye cannot perceive.

"Well," said Alfred, certainly excited, "the moment has come! Let's try it!"

At that moment I recalled the suspicious deaths of Gardner and Chambrun. I didn't breathe a word. What was the point? No consideration would have retained my brother. I confess, however, that I sounded the void with a strange anxiety, wondering what was happening there unknown to us. Doubtless nothing, of course! But, involuntarily, I imagined a host of invisibles pressing around the apparatus, an avidly curious, irritated, ferocious crowd. And I lent those beings the most bizarre appearance...

Alfred took a picture. I heard a mechanism purr in the objective, and I saw a tremulous violet glow light up within it.

Then my brother took the frame containing the 13 x 18 plate into the storage cupboard. He shut himself in. He was calm. And I rejoiced, since nothing tragic had occurred.

One could draw various conclusions from that, of course, but I only retained one thing, which was that Alfred was alive, and I asked no more than that.

Suddenly, the door of the storage cupboard opened violently and Alfred launched himself outside. He was paler than one can imagine, and an inconceivable terror, an atrocious amazement, caused him to dart crazed glances around him.

I howled: "What's the matter? Alfred! Alfred!"

Was it presence of mind? I hurled myself into the storage cupboard, closing the door behind me. But as I had foreseen, the sensitive plate, at the bottom of the developing bath, was completely veiled, having been exposed to the light by the wide open door. It was no longer anything but an obscure pane of glass.

I returned to Alfred. He was stammering incessantly: "What horror! What horror!" and covering his eyes with his hands.

And since then, for years, he has never said anything else or made any other gesture, until the evening when his haggard eyes, which had seen something terrifying on the plate, ceased scrutinizing the void, which now maddened them.

The photographic apparatus remained in my possession. I didn't want to destroy it; nor did I dare—no, never—to repeat the experiment. One can see enough vile things with the eyes that nature has given us.

I'm married. I have children. One day, the little ones unearthed the famous apparatus and started playing with it—which is to tell you that very rapidly, nothing remained of it but debris.

Originally published in Le Matin, 19 mars 1938.

Maurice Renard: *The Year 2000*

In the month of March 1938 the celebrated physiologist Clément Choysel, having discovered the means of realizing what had previously only been imagined by a few novelists smitten with fantasy, went to sleep voluntarily for a period of sixty-two years. He was forty-five.

The rather complicated operation of putting him to sleep was carried out in the presence of his numerous family and several scientists, his friends and collaborators. The latter of course, were not unaware of what it was necessary to do in the year 2000, in a similar season, to reawaken Clément Choysel, if the thing were possible. The elder son of the sleeper, Stéphane Choysel, had taken the direction of the whole affair and intended to follow with a meticulous fidelity the instructions of his audacious father; but it goes without saying that those messieurs were counting on their successors and not on themselves to proceed, sixty-two years later, with the revival of the distinguished subject.

Clément Choysel, firmly convinced that his method would permit him to be woken up on the threshold of the twenty-first century, without age having left any trace on his sleeping body, closed his eyes on the vision of the laboratory where the emotional audience watched him become drowsy...

He reopened them, those eyes, on the spectacle of an immense hall, a sort of circular amphitheater whose heights rounded out in a cupola. An innumerable crowd filed he steps. He was in the center. Individuals clad in white and black clinging leotards surrounded him. One of them, who was watching carefully for the eyelids to life, whispered in his ear:

"Bonjour, Grandfather; don't try to talk yet. I'm your grandson, Arthur. Today is the thirtieth of March 2000, the day that you fixed yourself. I hope that you've slept well.

270

We'll transport you into a nice tranquil room as soon as you've been able to demonstrate manifestly your return to life. It's because of the public. I wasn't able to neglect such a magnificent opportunity to make money. You'll approve, I'm sure..."

"A drink!" murmured Clément; and he sneezed, which is classic.

Immediately, an ovation rang out. Having drunk a little sugared water, Clément Choysel was taken away on a stretcher. He remarked, at that moment, that the gigantic hall was illuminated by electricity. The crowd clustered around his passage; the faces of all those people seemed wan, but he was still in a state of weakness that left him indifferent to the details of the ambience.

A few hours later he felt quite different. Clément Choysel, reinvigorated by the ingestion of the appropriate drugs, was chatting at reduced speed with his grandson.

Dr. Arthur Choysel was sixty-five years old and appeared to be twenty years older than his ancestor, who truly had a fine face, in spite of its thinness and in spite of his beard, which had grown bushy and very black, emphasizing the hollowness of his cheeks.

Clément Choysel enquired after various people, dead and alive. But, a scientist before anything else, he was interested principally in the observations that had been made of his case during his long sleep, and the state of the world in the year of grace 2000 A.D. He did not doubt that science had made extraordinary progress; that civilization would be admirably refined; and, recalling the anticipations that he had once made in order to attempt to foresee what the year 2000 would be like, he was impatient to see whether reality had confirmed any of them.

"By the way," he said, "I suppose that we're in Paris?"

"Certainly!"

"Couldn't I be transported into a room with windows? This artificial light...is this a clinic?" Then, leaping on to other ideas: "And what is happening in Europe? And Asia? Peace? In sum, what of humanity?"

"Grandfather," said his aged grandson, "You're resuming contact with your fellows on a date that will remain famous in the history of peoples and their happiness..."

"Truly?" said Clément Choysel, his eyes shining.

"The earth is joyful, humankind reborn in the last few days. News has just been announced that fills us with delight."

"What's that?"

"A discovery," said Arthur, looking at his interlocutor with a strange attention. "A scientific discovery..."

"Let me think. Is it a matter of an entirely unexpected discovery? Or was it already 'in the air' in my time? Were people already seeking it when I went to sleep? A discovery. It's so beautiful, a discovery! I remember! Pasteur's serums! Radio! The conquest of the air by aircraft! Let's see, what were we still seeking? No, don't tell me, I want to guess it by myself. But Arthur, I beg you, have me given another room. I'm in haste to see the light of day!"

"There is no other room," said Arthur, slowly. "We've been living underground for a long time. All cities have emigrated into the depths of the earth. The Paris that you knew is above us, and nothing remains of it but a deserted city, empty houses, silent streets. And there isn't a capital or a village on the entire surface of the globe that isn't similar: dead, duplicated by a subterranean capital or village. Dead, I tell you, and populated by pale beings who go up in the daylight as often as they can, to roam the country and breathe the open air. But living on the surface, especially in agglomerations, has been forbidden for a long time."

"Is that possible?" Clément exclaimed. "What! The world hasn't disarmed and that's where we are?"

"That's where we were, Grandfather. But everything has changed, thank God. Now people will be able to live under the sky again. I told you: the most beneficial discovery of all the centuries has just been made. Several times, we believed that it had been accomplished, but they were false joys. Today, it's certain. And it's superb!"

"So," said the scientist in a low voice, "A method has been found that paralyzes aircraft, which forbids them to fly? That's really it?"

"That's it."

The sleeper, awakened, lifted his diaphanous hands, and only said: "Poor humans!"

OTHER ANTHOLOGIES OF
FRENCH SCIENCE FICTION & FANTASY
by Brian STABLEFORD

The Aerial Valley: Five utopian fantasies by Jacques Fabien, Victor Hugo, Gustave Marx, Jean-Baptiste Mosneron de Launay and Turrault de Rochecorbon.

Automata: The Imaginative Legacy of Jacques de Vaucanson; Fourteen scientific romances by Charles Barbara, Jacques Boucher de Perthes, Frédéric Boutet, Didier de Chousy, Léon Daudet, Emile Goudeau, Arnold Mortier, Henri Ner, François-Félix Nogaret, Jean Rameau, Romain Rolland, Ralph Schropp, Marcel Schwob and Edmond Thiaudière.

The Bald Giants: Thirty-Nine scientific romances by Alfred Capus, Louis Champeaux, Gustave Geffroy, Edmond Haraucourt, Albert Keim, Pierre Mille, André Monselet, Maurice Montegut, Joseph Montet, René Morot, Maurice Renard, Gabriel Tarde, Louis Ulbach and Adrien Vély.

The Conqueror of Death: Eight scientific romances by Alphonse Brown, Paul Combes, Camille Debans, Emile Gautier and Georges Price.

Funestine : Five *contes de fées* by Guillaume-Hyacinthe Bougéant, Pierre-François Godard de Beauchamps and Catherine de Lintot.

The Germans on Venus: Thirteen scientific romances by Alphonse Allais, Rémy de Gourmont, Jules Lermina, André Mas, Eugène Mouton, Louis Mullem, Charles Nodier, Nicolas-Esmé Restif de la Bretonne, Adrien Robert, X.B. Saintine, Marcel Schwob, Louis Ulbach and Théo Varlet.

The Humanisphere: Four utopian fantasies by Paul Adam, Victor Considérant, Joseph Déjacque and Fernand Giraudeau.

The Incredible Adventure: Three interstellar excursions by Louis Forest, Paul Gsell and François Léonard.

Investigations of the Future: Seven scientific romances by Pierre-Simon Ballanche, Victor Fournel, Alfred Franklin, Théophile Gautier, Arsène Houssaye, Jean Jullien and Maurice Spronck.

Journey to the Isles of Atlantis: Seven scientific romances by Pierre Billaume, Félix Bodin, Gaston Derys, Pierre Grasset, Gustave Guitton, Pierre Hégine, Julie Lavergne and Louis Lemercier de Neuville.

The Man With the Blue Face: Eight scientific romances by Alfred Assolant, Camille Debans, Arnould Galopin, Charles Guyon, Ernest d'Hervilly, E.M. Laumann, Bernard Lazare and Gaston de Pawlowski.

The Mirror of Present Events: Ten scientific romances by Georges de La Fouchardière, Henri Lanos, E.M. Laumann, François-Félix Nogaret, Jean Rameau and Régis Vombal.

Nemoville: Twelve scientific romances by G. Bethuys, Alfred Bonnardot, Alphonse Brown, Emma-Adele Lacerte, Claude Manceau, René du Mesnil de Maricourt, Pierre Mille,José Mosellli, C. Paulon and Emerich de Vattel.

The New Moon: Four fantastic voyages by Henri Delmotte, Alexis-Jean Le Bret and Edmé Rousseau.

News from the Moon: Nine scientific romances by Georges Eekhoud, Stéphane Mallarmé, Guy de Maupassant, Louis-Sébastien Mercier, Eugène Mouton, Fernand Noat, Jean Richepin, Adrien Robert and Albert Robida.

The Nickel Man: Eleven scientific romances by Jacques Boucher de Perthes, Pierre Bremond, Léon Daudet, Georges Espitallier, Louis Gallet, Pierre de Nolhac and Ralph Schropp.

On the Brink of the World's End: Seven scientific romances by Raoul Bigot, Jacques-Antoine Dulaure, Charles Epheyre, Jules Hoche, Joseph Méry and Colonel Royet.

The Origin of the Fays: Thirteen *contes de fées* by Louise Cavelier, Charles-Antoine Coypel, Catherine Durand, Marianne-Agnès Falques, Marie-Madeleine de Lubert, François-Augustin de Paradis de Moncrif, Charles Pinot Duclos, Jean-Jacques Rousseau and Carl Gustaf Tessin.

The Queen of the Fays: Twenty-seven *contes de fées* by Catherine Bernard, François Fénelon, Louis de Mailly and Jean de Préchac.

The Revolt of the Machines: Eight scientific romances by Michel Epuy, Emile Goudeau, X. Nagrien, Gaston de Pawlowski, Jules Perrin, Edouard Rod, Jules Sageret and Louis Valona.

The Supreme Progress: Eighteen scientific romances by Paul Adam, Charles Cros, Charles Epheyre, Eugène Mouton, Louis Mullem, X.B. Saintine and Victorien Sardou.

Tales of Enchantment and Disenchantment: A History of Faerie, with an Exemplary Anthology of Forty Tales by Marie-Catherine d'Aulnoy, Charles Baudelaire, Catherine Bernard, Frédéric Boutet, Nicolas Bricaire de Dixmerie, Charlotte-Rose Caumont de La Force, Louise Cavelier, Philippe de Caylus,

Charles Duclos, Catherine Durand, Marie-Antoinette Fagnan, Marianne-Agnès Falques, François Fénelon, Anatole France, Marie-Jeanne L'Héritier, Édouard Laboulaye, Jeanne-Marie Leprince de Beaumont, Catherine de Lintot, Jean Lorrain, Marie-Madeleine de Lubert, Louis de Mailly, Catulle Mendès, Henriette-Julie de Murat, Charles Perrault, Pierre-Alexis Ponson du Terrail, Jean de Préchac, Nicolas Edme Restif de la Bretonne, Marie-Jeanne Riccoboni, Sophie Rostopchine de Ségur, Jean-Jacques Rousseau and Carl Gustaf Tessin.

The World Above the World: Nine scientific romances by S. Henry Berthoud, Michel Corday, Alphonse Daudet, Camille Flammarion, Henri Lanos, André Mas, Jules Perrin, René de Pont-Jest and Charles Recolin.

Weird Fiction in France: A Showcase Anthology of its Origins and Development. Stories by Alphonse Allais, S. Henry Berthoud, May Armand Blanc, Frédéric Boutet, Gaston Danville, Lucie Delarue-Mardrus, Erckmann-Chatrian, Paul Féval, Xavier Forneret, Anatole France, Judith Gautier, Théophile Gautier, Remy de Gourmont, Jules Hoche, Jules Janin, Gabriel de Lautrec, Jules Lermina, Jean Lorrain, Guy de Maupassant, Catulle Mendès, Gérard de Nerval, Charles Nodier, Jean Richepin, X. B. Saintine, Marcel Schwob, Auguste Villiers de l'Isle-Adam, Renée Vivien.